"Gabriel? I'm afraid."

"I know. Sometimes so am I."

Something occurred to him, something she'd said before, something bad—something ugly.

"Laura? I know you're afraid...but please God, tell me you're not afraid of me?"

Her hesitation was brief, but it was enough to make him sick. He had turned her loose and started to roll out of bed when she caught him by the arm.

"Don't go! For God's sake, don't leave me now."

"Why, Laura? Why me?"

"Because I can't help it. I love you, Gabriel."

Sharon Sala "knows just how to steep the fires of romance to the gratification of her readers."
—*Romantic Times*

REUNION
SHARON SALA

ISBN 1-55166-487-9

REUNION

Copyright © 1999 by Sharon Sala.

Printed in U.S.A.

It doesn't matter how fast you run to win a race, or how many sacrifices you make to achieve a certain goal. Winning isn't everything. It's finishing what you start that really counts.

This book is dedicated to the tough ones... to the people who don't know when to quit.

Prologue

Gabriel Donner's chest rose and fell with each slow breath he took. The woman beside him paused in her duties to stare in mute fascination as a tiny rivulet of water ran between the bands of muscles across his belly. Just before it fell onto the covers, she leaned across the bed and caught it with the cloth in her hand.

"Sorry about that," she said softly, and then dipped her washcloth into the basin at the side of the bed and sloshed it around.

She was a nurse—a professional health care worker who was pulling a double shift this day. She'd spent many long hours on the floor and it would seem that they weren't over yet.

With a deft twist, she wrung the excess water from the cloth and then laid it on the side of his cheek, following the contours of his face as she continued to wash him clean.

At the moment of contact, his eyebrows knitted

and a muscle twitched along the side of his jaw, but he didn't move or speak. Sometimes she wondered if he ever would again. Her eyes darkened with compassion. Such a magnificent man, and he was so hurt. She'd seen his chart. She'd heard the doctors talking in the halls. They were hedging their bets with this one's recovery, and she understood why.

She knew the story, and in her occupation, it was all too common. A family...his family...had been decimated because someone else had chosen to drink and drive.

A frown ran across her forehead as she scrubbed at the length of one leg and then back up the other. The poor man. It was so sad. Lost in a subconscious world somewhere between life and death, unaware that there had even been an accident, or that he'd survived when his parents had not.

More than two weeks had passed since he'd been admitted to the hospital, and he had yet to come out of this coma. And even though he was virtually motionless, there was something remarkably alive about him.

Part of it was his size. In a way, it was an odd sort of proof that he still existed, if by nothing more than power alone. The hospital bed in which he was lying was one of their largest, and they'd still had to angle him slightly so that his feet would not be pressing against the footboard. His shoulders were wide, the muscles in his arms and chest impressive. His legs were long and strong, and it took her twenty-five minutes each day to wash and dry all there was of Gabriel Donner.

Her gaze returned to his face—to the short black strands of his hair lying across his forehead. Having already shaved him, she took the washcloth and swiped the hair to one side, doing her best to keep his appearance neat, as well as clean. His eyelashes were thick, and there was a slight cast to the shape of his nose, as if it had once been broken and healed slightly off keel. The cut of his jaw looked as stubborn as the thrust of his chin. His lips were slack, but full and shapely. She could only imagine the life he exuded when awake.

Even after she had finished with his bath, she stood beside his bed, gazing down upon his face. Every now and then his nostrils would flare slightly, reacting to a stimulus only he could sense. Then, with the help of two other nurses, she made up his bed, turning his near-lifeless body to accommodate the fresh linens.

Adjusting her glasses on the bridge of her nose, she glanced at the IV, reading the flow and adjusting the drip before gathering up her things to move on. At the door, she paused and looked back, as if by mere will alone she could wish him awake. But he was as quiet as he'd been when she entered. She left, knowing she'd done all she could do to make him comfortable. The rest was up to God.

Before cognizance came the voices. Bits and pieces of the life that he had refused to give up. Some of them were indistinct and faint, like a conversation that had come unraveled, leaving nothing but unconnected syllables behind. Some of the voices were close and taunting, reminding him of where he'd been and how far it was back to the land of the living.

One particular sound kept replaying in his mind like a video stuck in rewind. It was always the same: one loud shout and then two sharp screams. Sometimes he thought to wonder if he'd been the one shouting or screaming. The rest of the sounds were in a jumble, as if someone had tossed a conversation into a blender and then mixed it all up. The words were still there, but they were all out of context.

Shame...blood...buried.
Lift her...dead...move him...won't live.
Head injury.
Help me...lost.

None of it made any sense, but when it was time, he would sort it all out. He had to. It was what kept him alive.

Time passed, and the voices were still with him, never leaving him alone, never giving him peace. One in particular would wake him as he slept, invariably with the same, persistent request for help. His struggles to come back to reality also persisted, if for no other reason than to tell whoever it was that kept talking to do it out of his presence. And now there was enough cognizance within Gabriel's mind to resent the request.

Why did they keep asking him to help? Didn't they know, couldn't they see, that he was in no shape to help anyone? In fact, he was the one who needed help. It was taking everything he had just to come back from where he'd been. And God knows it would have been easier for him to quit— to give up on life and let himself go. More than once, he'd felt his parents' presence nearby. Each time he'd tried to talk to them, to ask them what was wrong, but they kept leaving before he could speak.

He didn't understand. It was almost as if they didn't want him along. And each time he'd been at his weakest, that same persistent voice would intrude, begging to be found, pleading for help, refusing to let him go.

And so he waited for a sign, listening for the voice that would be strong enough to bring him home.

Roses. He smelled roses. Mother must be here. He struggled to open his eyes, but there was a thick shroud of darkness he couldn't get past. *What's wrong with me? Why can't I wake myself up?*

He lay without moving, trying to focus on what he could hear—what he could feel. Someone was laughing, but the shrill cackle seemed distant, as if the sound had been bottled and the bottle had just been uncorked. His arms and legs felt more than lethargic, almost immovable, like he'd been tied down. But that made no sense. Restraints were not a part of Gabriel Donner's world.

The awareness of pain came slowly, and as it did, he realized its presence was old and familiar. *That explains it,* he thought. *I've been hurt!*

He tried moving his arms and legs, then tried opening his eyes, and although he went through the motions in his mind, nothing worked—nothing moved. A small spurt of panic came quickly, and he wondered if this was what death was like. Was there an awareness of self without any control? *Am*

I dead? he wondered. And then a door banged, and someone called out a name. Wherever he was, it was noisy.

His eyelids began to flutter. The stimulus of noise was keeping him focused. He struggled within himself, beginning to realize that all the while he'd been thinking, he'd also been moving toward a pinpoint of light.

Help me.

The voice was intrusive, but Gabriel recognized it. He'd been hearing it for days. He frowned, trying to find the impetus to speak—to tell whoever it was who kept talking that he would help if he could—if for no other reason than to shut them up.

Another scent suddenly overpowered the smell of roses and he wrinkled his nose at the strong, acrid odor of industrial-strength disinfectant.

Help...afraid.

Gabriel swallowed. Afraid? What did they have to be afraid of? He was the one who couldn't move.

Too loud...too loud. Help me hide.

Gabriel's fingers clutched the sheet, physically pulling himself closer and closer to the light. A faint sheen of perspiration broke out upon his body, and his heart rate began to increase. Muscles began to twitch, and his eyelids began to flutter as he moved through the tunnel in his mind. Ah, God, he was almost there!

After weeks of darkness, he opened his eyes. The sudden burst of illumination was blinding. He closed his eyes against the glare and then, moments later, opened them more slowly, letting himself adjust.

He saw pale blue walls and a window with blinds. There was a door to his left, and a television that had been mounted on the wall above his bed. Shock hit, coupled with a sudden understanding. Hospital! He was in a hospital! He wanted to move and, instead, found himself struggling for breath.

There were needles in his arms and tubes down his nose, as well as one down his throat. A dull but persistent pain pulsed between his eyebrows, moving from one temple to the other like the pendulum of a clock. Why? How? His hand curled into a fist, and he closed his eyes, trying to concentrate.

Angela, look out!

He jerked, then groaned, remembering the series of shrill screams that had come after his father's warning shout, followed by the sound of crunching metal and the scent of burning rubber.

No...oh, no. When he opened his eyes, they

were filled with tears, and in that moment, he didn't have to be told, he knew they were dead. There was an emptiness inside him that he wouldn't have been able to explain, but he sensed that the energy that had been Brent and Angela Donner was far beyond the realm of this earth.

Ah, God, make me understand why I'm still alive.

But God wasn't the one who answered. Instead, it was that same whiny voice that had kept plaguing his rest.

Help me. Help me.

He turned his head, expecting to see someone standing in the doorway; then he frowned. There was no one there. He looked to the right, and his heart skipped a beat.

Lost. Help me.

The room held nothing but shadows. His eyes widened, and his pulse began to hammer as the voice came closer, more persistent—even more intense.

Lost. Help me. Lost.

A sickly sweat broke out on his body as he closed his eyes against the truth. Except for him, the room was empty. All these days...all this time...and the voice he'd been hearing was inside his head.

One

There were no clocks in Laura Dane's house. There was no need. For her, time was relative. She ate when she was hungry and slept when she was tired. She was the heir to Texas oilman Wallace Dane, her grandfather, and the fortune he'd left her was vast. She didn't have to lift a finger to help herself.

But she hadn't always been this way. Once she had tried, and tried very hard, to be part of the real world—to ignore that thing within herself that others couldn't understand.

She'd taken herself and her education, leaving the coddled comfort of the family estate outside Santa Fe, and tried in every way she knew how to be normal. She'd gotten a job in a bank in Albuquerque, rented an apartment nearby and pretended she was just like everyone else. She'd shopped at the advertised sales and rushed through life like the people with whom she worked—living on borrowed time and ruled by schedules of someone else's making. And then a common thief had upset her carefully balanced world and sent it into a spin she couldn't right.

It had happened at work—in broad daylight—on a beautiful, sunny Saturday morning. A man walked into the bank wearing an elaborate disguise and went straight to the teller window where Laura was working. He handed her a note, pushed a large bag across the counter and then stuck his hand in his pocket.

She touched the note and then gasped, looking up without having read a word. Even after she read the message, she couldn't believe it was happening. He wanted money. He had a gun. She remembered looking up in stunned confusion and staring into an unfamiliar face.

His hair was long, red and pulled back into a ponytail beneath a black cap. His beard was sandy, his eyes hidden behind a pair of dark glasses. His clothes were denim and dirty and when he leaned toward her and whispered, she froze.

"Hurry up, and don't play the heroine."

She did as she was told, opening her cash drawer and, with calm, methodical movements, putting the cash into the bag. Moments later, she pushed the bag back across the counter. His lips curled into a smile as his fingers closed around the fabric. Then he took his other hand out of his pocket and sprayed something into her face. She gasped and slumped, unconscious before she hit the floor.

His cry of alarm was all that was needed to cover the robbery. As people rushed to her aid, he turned and walked out of the bank. It was several minutes before anyone knew what had transpired. The police were at her side when she came to, asking her for a description. Unfortunately for Laura, the description she gave them was of the face she'd seen *beneath* his disguise, not the man that the security camera, and everyone else, had seen.

Her beautiful Saturday turned in to a miserable day. Marked by suspicion as a possible accomplice, she was forced to admit her secret—that she sometimes *saw* things that weren't really there, and that, at other times, *knew* things before they could happen. It had taken her more than five minutes of explanation before she'd had the guts to utter the word.

Psychic.

At that point the police had debated about whether to lock her up because she was a possible criminal or because she was possibly insane.

And even though the thief was eventually

caught, and entirely from her description, it was too late to undo the damage done by her revelation. The truth about her "power" had cost her a job and several so-called friends. Hounded by the press and shunned by others, she moved out of her Albuquerque apartment and back into the family home on the outskirts of Santa Fe to lick her proverbial wounds.

Getting fired and moving home had accomplished two things. Boredom became the incentive she needed to take an active role at the corporate level of her late grandfather's holdings, and the New Mexico authorities were forced to accept the fact that she wasn't a fake after all. Over the next seven years, those same authorities accepted her help in solving several other cases, gaining her a solid reputation as a true psychic.

But that was then and this was now, and Laura had long since accepted the solitude of her existence. She no longer apologized for the fact that she didn't operate on the same set of principles as everyone else. Her realities were in the images that flowed through her mind. Sometimes they came quietly, like leaves falling onto the still surface of a pond, and sometimes they poured through her senses like rain through a downspout. And there were the times, not often, but they were there, when the images crashed in upon her like breakers onto an eroding shoreline. When that happened, it took all Laura had to retain her sense of self.

If she had lived in an earlier time, she would have been burned at the stake for being a witch. Instead, she suffered a different sort of ostracism from society. One that isolated her from any sort of normal relationship. She accepted her fate as her due, and only now and then did the truth of her situation surface. When it did, she battled her own demons and accepted the isolation, knowing there would never be a man who would love her enough to get past what she was.

Gabriel Donner slipped his belt through the last loop in his pants and then buckled it. It felt good to be wearing real clothes. Hospital garb left little to the imagination, and for Gabriel, who was four inches above six feet, even less than that.

He stood before the mirror, adjusting the collar of his blue knit shirt and tucking the shirttail into his slacks before turning away. Ever since the accident, he'd become uncomfortable with his own reflection. There was a sense of loss that had nothing to do with the deaths of his parents and came more from a loss of his own identity. He couldn't remember a time in his life when he'd been afraid.

At least not like this. But now there were times when he caught himself hesitating before turning a corner in the hospital hall. And when the nurses were making their nighttime rounds, the urge to sleep with a light on was almost overwhelming. If Gabriel Donner had been a lesser man, the fear inside him might have won, but he was strong, both in body and in mind, and he refused to let it take hold.

He strode to the window overlooking the hospital parking lot, trying to pick out the familiar color of his uncle Mike's car. If it was down there, it wouldn't be hard to find. Canary yellow was impossible to miss. When he saw it parked at the end of a row, a bit of his anxiety lifted. Good! That meant Mike was already here. Within the hour Gabriel would be home.

Then his expression stilled. Home would never be the same. Pain dug a little deeper as he turned away from the window. It seemed impossible to believe that his mother and father were no longer of this earth. That they'd died without his knowledge, been buried without his presence, seemed obscene. His only comfort had come from knowing that Mike Travers, Brent and Angela's best friend and the man Gabriel called uncle, had stood in his stead at the graves.

He took a deep, shuddering breath, raking his fingers through his hair and telling himself to focus on the future and not the past. But it was hard. His last memories of his parents were of his father's sudden shout of warning and his mother's screams. After that, everything was a blessed blur that had faded to unconsciousness.

Guilt ate at him constantly. He'd replayed the moment over and over in his mind a thousand times, watching his father sliding behind the wheel of Gabriel's new car and insisting on driving to the restaurant where they were going to eat. Now he wished to God they'd stayed at home. If they had, they wouldn't have been driving on the Northwest Expressway, and the drunk who'd crossed the center median would have crashed into someone else.

He pivoted angrily, slapping the flat of his hand against the wall, unaware that he was no longer alone.

Mike Travers paused in the doorway. When he saw Gabriel's mood, his smile disappeared. This man was like the son he'd never had. He'd adored him as a child and loved and respected him as an adult. He was well aware that he could never take Brent and Angela's place in Gabriel's life, nor did he want to. But something had to be done about

Gabriel's growing anger. This wasn't the first time he'd witnessed such an outburst, and, as a psychiatrist, Mike knew only too well the long-term effects that guilt could have on a man.

"Gabriel."

Surprised to find he was no longer alone, Gabriel looked up, and when he saw Mike's face, the anger within him began to subside. He managed a smile, shamed that he'd been caught acting out on these moods that had taken over his life.

Michael Morris Travers was a small, frail man pushing his way toward his sixty-eighth birthday. His hair was thin and graying, and his clothes were always rumpled. Considering his skill and reputation as a top-notch psychiatrist, his appearance was often deceiving.

It had been a source of constant amusement between Brent and Angela that their best friend looked more like an absentminded professor than the consummate professional he actually was.

Gabriel frowned. "Look, Uncle Mike, I, uh…"

Mike put his hand on Gabriel's arm and felt the muscles knotting beneath his touch.

"It's all right, boy. I've had a few days like that lately myself."

Gabriel relaxed. He never had to explain himself with his uncle Mike.

"Ready to go home, boy?" Mike asked.

Wariness crept into Gabriel's expression, and he shrugged.

"As ready as I'll ever be." He picked up the phone and called to notify the nurses' station that he was ready to leave. Then he turned to Mike. "Did you bring them?"

Mike thought of the roses lying in the back seat of his car and nodded. "Yes, all twelve dozen."

Gabriel seemed to relax, but Mike was still bothered by Gabriel's earlier request.

"I'm not certain this is the right moment to make a visit to the cemetery. This is your first day out. The flowers will certainly keep a couple of days if you'd rather wait."

"I've already waited too long," Gabriel said.

There was a stillness about Gabriel's expression that made the old man nervous. As a child, Gabriel had been exuberant to the point of aggravation. As an adult, the wild streak in him had matured to a strong, dependable man who had a tendency toward playing practical jokes. This quiet rage was unlike the real Gabriel. More than once during the past few days, Mike had felt as if the Gabriel of old had died along with his parents in that wreck, and that this man was little more than a skilled imposter.

A few minutes later, they were on their way out of the hospital. Within the hour, Mike was pulling off the highway and through the main gates of Rosemound Cemetery. It was the first week in June, and already the Oklahoma days were miserably hot, although the grass around the headstones was still green and well-clipped.

"We're here," Mike said, parking beneath a spreading oak to avail himself of the shade.

Gabriel's mind blanked as he gazed out across the rows and rows of tombstones. It seemed impossible to think he would never see his parents again. The fact that they were buried beneath six feet of Oklahoma soil was more than he could take.

His voice was shaking as he wiped a hand across his eyes. "This is so damned obscene."

Mike reached across the seat, gripping Gabriel's arm and giving him an understanding squeeze.

"I know, boy, I know. Sometimes life is just plain unfair."

Gabriel reached for the flowers in the back seat and got out without answering, intent on what he'd come to do.

"Let me help," Mike said, handing Gabriel three of the wrapped bundles, before gathering the remaining three up for himself.

He started across the grounds, leading the way

for Gabriel to follow. "When I called in this order, I cleaned out the florist," Mike said. "They put these in bunches of two dozen each. I assume that's all right with you?"

The sweet scent of the bloodred roses was rich beneath Gabriel's nostrils as he followed Mike across the grounds. He lowered his head, slowly inhaling their essence and remembering his mother's love for the blooms. Tears were thick in his throat, but they stayed, refusing to fall.

"It's fine," he said.

Moments later, Mike paused.

Only then did Gabriel think to look down. When he did, reality hit. The physical evidence of his parents' deaths was staring him in the face. The tall marble edifice bearing both their names was right before him, and it was all he could do to keep breathing.

"Can I help?" Mike asked.

"No."

Gabriel's answer was stark and filled with pain. Mike's heart went out to him, but this was something Gabriel needed to do all on his own.

"I'll wait for you at the car. If you feel weak, or need help in any way, just call. I'll be watching," Mike said.

Then he laid down his flowers and walked away, leaving Gabriel alone with his sorrow.

The sun was warm on Gabriel's face as he dropped to his knees. A robin swooped from a nearby tree, landing a few feet away before hopping across the ground. He rocked back on his knees to watch and, just for a moment, could almost believe he was at home helping his mother tend her garden of roses and not kneeling at her grave. But then a pushy little breeze rattled the papers in which the roses were wrapped, and he was reminded of why he'd come.

With a heavy heart, he unwrapped the first three bundles of roses and laid them on his father's side of the grave, spreading them as he went, until the fresh mound of earth was completely covered by the long-stemmed beauties.

But when it came time to decorate Angela Donner's side of the grave, he unwrapped the first bundle of roses, then hesitated. There was something he'd left undone. He dropped back to his knees and picked up a single, long-stemmed rose. Then, one by one, he began breaking the thorns off the stem. Only after it was completely smooth and unable to harm did he lay it upon the ground. He picked up another and began to repeat the same process all

over again, echoing a habit his mother had practiced for all her life.

The rose had been her favorite flower, but she
had frequently commented upon the irony of such
beauty being capable of causing such pain and had
done what she thought was fitting by removing the
thorns from her glorious bouquets.

The process was tedious, and more than once he
pricked his own finger. But the pain was nothing
to what he was feeling inside. His grief gave way
as he dropped the last rose to the ground. Tears
ran hot and angry, and rage filled him.

"Ah, God, why them and not me?"

But there were no answers. In spite of the heat
of the day, a chill settled inside him. Weary beyond
belief, he started back to the car. A few yards
away, he heard someone sobbing. Startled, he
turned to look. There was no one there. He touched
his cheeks, but his own tears had already dried.

The voice. It was back. Foreboding swept over
him in waves of defeat. He thrust his hand through
his hair, feeling the place where they'd shaved it
to stitch up the wounds.

"Leave me alone," he muttered. "I've got troubles of my own."

After that, the voice was strangely silent.

Two

Brent Donner had founded Straight Arrow Security when Gabriel was ten. Gabriel had joined the company straight out of college. Now it was all his, and he didn't want it.

It wasn't that he didn't know the job. It was the being in control that bothered him. He kept asking himself how the hell could he operate a million-dollar business when he couldn't control his own thoughts?

Twice in the past few days he'd come close to telling his uncle Mike about the voice. The man was a psychiatrist. Surely he'd heard wilder stories from other patients. But an instinct for self-preservation kept him quiet. He'd convinced himself that this was nothing more than an anomaly, and that it would eventually go away. Therefore, the less people who knew what was happening to him, the better off he would be. That was what he'd told himself. That was what he believed.

And yet, when they turned into the winding drive leading to the Donner estate, Gabriel found himself beginning to panic. Could he live among the memories without losing his mind? He shuddered. Maybe it was too late. Maybe his sanity was already coming undone.

He shoved aside the negative thoughts and made himself focus on the three-story mansion with its gleaming white walls and elegant Corinthian columns. Like four guards on duty, they stood two stories tall, bracing a third-story balcony that ran the length of the home.

His gaze moved from the house to the grounds, and even though he couldn't see it, he knew the most beautiful spot was his mother's rose garden at the back of the estate. His belly knotted, and he wondered if this would ever feel like home again.

Mike parked and then pointed toward the house. "Matty must have been watching for us. Here she comes."

Gabriel tensed. Facing her wouldn't be easy.

Matty Sosa was more like a grandparent to Gabriel than the family housekeeper. When she saw him, her face crumpled, and she began to hug him fiercely.

"*Madre de Dios.* You are too thin."

Gabriel managed a smile as he returned her embrace. "Hospital food isn't as good as your cooking."

Matty dabbed at her eyes with the hem of her apron. Desperate for something to do, she reached for Gabriel's bag.

"Enter, enter," she commanded, and led the way inside the house. "I will put the bag in your room. You...boy...take your uncle Mike out to the patio and sit. I will bring cold drinks."

Gabriel watched her bustling away and wondered how old he would have to be before she quit calling him boy. He glanced at Mike.

"Hope you didn't have other plans. Sounds like you're expected to stay for dinner." Realizing how offhand the invitation sounded, he added, "And I would appreciate the company."

Mike pretended not to notice Gabriel's despondency. "It's a good thing she offered. It saved me from having to beg later."

They started through the house, talking amiably about nothing in general and moving at a pace that would accommodate Gabriel's healing injuries. But he was having a difficult time focusing on Mike's conversation. Everything reminded him of his parents and the happy life they had shared. He wondered if coming back here had been wise after all.

And then they turned a corner in the hallway, and it felt to Gabriel as if the air was suddenly devoid of oxygen. His chest felt heavy with each indrawn breath, and the skin on his face began to tighten. Even though he knew it was impossible, something was invading his mind.

Help me.

Gabriel cursed beneath his breath as he staggered toward a nearby wall, desperate for the touch of something solid—something he knew was really there. When his hand connected with the cool, flat surface, he closed his eyes and groaned.

Startled, Mike reached for his arm.

"Gabriel? Are you okay?"

Gabriel braced himself with both hands against the wall, shuddering as a cold sweat covered his body.

Can't find you.

Struggling against the unwanted invasion of his mind, he made himself stand when he wanted to fall. He hated this. He wasn't a weakling, but it seemed that his mind didn't know it. This constant cry for help was making him crazy. He hit the wall with his fist.

"Son of a bitch."

Mike spun away. "I'm calling a doctor."

Gabriel stopped Mike's intent with a fierce glare and a firm grip.

"Let it go. I'm all right."

Mike took one look at the pallor of Gabriel's face and shook his head. "No, damn it, you're not."

"A doctor can't fix what's wrong with me," Gabriel muttered, then walked away.

The house was silent. The evening meal had been strained, but somehow they'd gotten through it, as well as Mike's reluctant exit to his own home. Now Gabriel walked through the empty rooms, listening for the echoes of happier times. He paused in the hallway just off the kitchen and closed his eyes, remembering the sounds of his mother's voice and his father's exuberant shouts of laughter. But when he walked away, all he heard were the distinct sounds of his own footsteps upon the gleaming floors.

Without conscious thought, he was following in the footsteps his father had taken each night before retiring. He paused in the foyer, glancing at a panel of numbers in a small, recessed area of the wall near the front door. A red light glowed. The security system was on and locked. Having seen to that much of the business of living, Gabriel turned and walked to the foot of the stairs, then paused and looked up.

The upper two stories of the house seemed to mock him. He shook off the feeling and took the first step. It was the hardest. After that, it was simply a matter of putting one foot in front of the other.

Within the hour he'd fallen asleep.

The man lifted his head and sniffed—like an animal testing the air for things that didn't belong. It was dark beneath the trees, and he moved quickly toward the clearing beyond, anxious to get away from things unseen.

Gravel crunched beneath his feet as his steps hastened. The bag he was carrying bumped against his leg. Moments later, he dropped to his knees before the marble edifice and then down on all fours, stretching out upon the blanket of roses as if it were the softest of beds. His cheeks were wet with tears as he turned his face to the earth. The leaves felt like feathers against his skin and the wilted petals of the roses like kisses.

A car, minus a muffler, sped by on the road beyond, rattling its way through the night. At the sound, his fingers curled into mighty fists; then he raised his head, searching the night. There was no one in sight. Tension slid away as weariness hit him. He was tired. So tired. And his head was aching.

"Mother...Mother, can't find you."

He curled in upon himself, wishing himself back into familiar surroundings. But somehow he'd gotten himself lost and forgotten how to get back.

"Help me."

No one answered. No one came. He sat like that for hours, until the moon was high in the midnight sky. Suddenly a light appeared at the far end of the locked gates at the end of the road. Panic came upon him, and for a moment, he froze, uncertain of what he should do.

Then he remembered a day long ago and his mother telling him that when he was afraid, he was to run to her, that she would take care of him always.

He looked down at the roses upon which he was sitting. Mother liked roses. He began gathering a bouquet, careful to get only the ones with no thorns.

A night bird swooped just beyond his line of vision as he knelt among the tombstones, but he knew it was there. He felt the air move at its passing. Overhead, a bank of clouds slipped between the heavens and earth, momentarily blocking out the luminous glow of a three-quarter moon.

By the time the car had turned around, he was gone.

The red light was no longer flashing on the security panel inside the Donner home. The French doors leading out to the flagstone patio beyond the library were standing ajar. Outside, a wind had sprung up, bringing with it the scent of rain.

The streets were quiet. In this neighborhood, at this time of the morning, traffic was nonexistent. He liked the silence. It made him feel good. It made him feel safe. His stomach grumbled, reminding him of his hunger. Up ahead, he could see lights spilling out from a building. At the thought of food, his steps quickened, and then he saw movement from the corner of his eye. A woman walked out of the shadows, and his heart leaped.

"Mother?"

Her laugh was low and husky. "Now, honey, do I look like your mommy?"

He frowned. She didn't look like Mother. Mother had short hair and smelled good. This woman's hair was long and black, and there was a scent about her he didn't quite like. But she smiled, and he was so tired and hungry. He stopped.

She ran her hand up the length of his arm and then glanced down at the flowers and the bag he was carrying.

"Ummm-hmmm, you know just what women like, don't you, hon? You come to my place. For twenty dollars, I've got just what *you* like, too."

She held out her hand, and he took it. Because he was tired. Because he was hungry.

The stairs where she led him were steep and narrow. The door to her apartment had once been a bright, fiery red. The color had faded, and the paint was peeling, but the message was still the same. She unlocked the door and then walked inside, pulling him in behind her.

The room smelled like she did. Unwashed and smoky. He wrinkled his nose.

"Smells bad."

She frowned and then grinned wryly. "Before I get through with you, you won't care what you smell, only how Gloria can make you feel."

With that, she ran her hand down the front of his pants and unzipped the zipper, feeling him for size. As she did, he hardened beneath her touch.

"Ooh, hon, you've got yourself quite a pecker.

Normally I don't indulge, but I might want some of that myself.''

This wasn't what he'd expected, but what she was doing felt good. He forgot his hunger and stared down at her hand inside his pants, but when she lowered her head, he took a quick step backward, muttering more to himself than to her, ''No, no.''

She straightened up, her eyes narrowing. This one was jumpy, but damn, he was good-looking. It wasn't often she got hold of one like him.

''Let's put on a little mood music and make a trade. You owe me twenty dollars, big boy.'' She gave his manhood a final squeeze before turning away.

His stomach grumbled again. He looked around and sighed. He couldn't see any food, but maybe that was where she was going. Maybe she was going to bring him something to eat.

Suddenly a raucous blend of hard rock and rap shattered the intimacy of the moment.

The woman turned toward him with a smile on her face and began moving her body to the beat as she started toward him.

For him, there was no music, only a cacophony of wild sounds that to him became pain. With the wilting flowers still clutched in his hand, he threw back his head and screamed, clawing at his ears and beating himself on the head.

The woman stopped short. "What the hell's wrong with you?"

She was standing too close to his answer.

He swung blindly, wanting to stop the pain and stopped her heart instead. Thrown against the wall by the momentum of the blow, her neck snapped, and the stereo she'd turned on only moments earlier fell to the floor with a crash.

When the sound ceased, the pain disappeared. He stood in the silence, staring down at the woman in blank confusion. His stomach grumbled again. There was a small drop of blood at the corner of her lip. He squatted down beside her and wiped it away with the ball of his thumb while staring at a swath of black hair lying across her eyes.

Her blood was still on his hand, and he wiped it on the seat of his pants. He'd cut himself before and remembered that it hurt to bleed. She must be hurting, too. He looked down at his roses and then rocked back on his heels. Without hesitation, he pulled a single, long-stemmed rose from the bunch and laid it upon her stomach.

"There now. All better."

He walked out of the room without looking back.

* * *

When Gabriel opened his eyes, he found himself standing in the dark at the edge of his mother's garden with a long-stemmed rosebud in his hand. Its leaves were covered with some of the same dew that had dampened the hems of his jeans. But when he looked closer, he knew it would never open. It had been picked too soon.

As he glanced up at the house, he had a fleeting impression that it was a face and the windows its eyes, and that he was being judged and found lacking. He looked down at the rose and then suddenly tossed it away, wiping his damp fingers on his jeans as if he were wiping off something foul.

At the same time, he felt something wet on the side of his jeans. It was thick and sticky, and he stared intently, trying to make out what it was. Whatever it was looked black in this light.

Blood?

He looked down at his hands, searching for injury, but it was too dark to see what he'd done.

"What the hell is happening to me?"

All he could hear was his own heartbeat, hammering in his ears. He started toward the house, and as he did, images began to flash in his mind.

Images of a dark, ugly place and a black-haired woman lying on a dust-covered floor. Breath caught at the back of his throat as something rattled in the bushes beside him. By the time he passed through the patio doors, he was running. Only after he was safely inside did he stop to wonder why the security alarm hadn't gone off. It did nothing for his peace of mind to find out that he must have turned it off before going outside. It bothered him even more that he didn't remember anything about what he'd been doing. With a weary shake of his head, he reset the alarm and crawled back to bed.

The bathroom mirror was fogged with steam as Gabriel stepped out of the shower. His thoughts were locked into the business of the day when he saw movement from the corner of his eye. His heart skipped a beat as he spun toward the motion, and then he froze, mesmerized by what he saw. It was his own reflection, partially hidden behind the curtain of mist. The shape of his face was vague, the dark contour of his hair little more than a shadow, but there was a clear streak in the middle of the glass, as if someone had swiped across it with the palm of their hand. Eyes, dark and secretive, stared back at him, and just for a moment Gabriel felt as if he were staring at the face of a stranger.

Help. Help.

His nostrils flared, and he leaned forward in anger. "Help your damned self," he muttered, turned his back on the mirror and began to dry off.

It frustrated him no end that his mind had weakened to this state. He was a grown man. Yes, he had suffered a terrible loss in the deaths of his parents, but that didn't mean he couldn't go on with his life. He knew his parents would have wanted it and would be appalled to know what he was putting himself through. He picked up a comb just as Matty called out to him.

"Gabriel, your breakfast is ready."

He wrapped a large bath towel around his waist and stepped out of the bathroom as she looked in his doorway.

"Did you hear me? I said your—"

He nodded. "I'll be right there. Just give me a couple of minutes to dress."

At the sight of his near-nude body, the little woman threw up her hands and began to mutter. Gabriel grinned. It wasn't as if she'd never seen him butt-naked. She had been with his family since the day he'd been born and had reminded him on more than one occasion of the fact that she'd changed his diapers.

Matty glared at him and then began puttering

around his room, picking up the clothes that he'd left on the floor.

"*Madre de Dios!* What have you done to your jeans?" Her glare changed to worry as she inspected the pants further. "There is blood on them! Are you hurt? Have you hurt yourself?"

He frowned, only then remembering the wet, sticky something he'd felt on the pants last night. He shook his head.

"No, I'm not hurt. But I was in the rose garden last night. It's nothing."

She crossed herself and then left the room, muttering beneath her breath.

Refusing to let himself worry, he tossed the towel on a nearby chair and headed for the closet. A few minutes later he entered the kitchen, relishing the warm, homey smell of fresh-baked bread and hot coffee. Just for a while he would pretend that everything was normal in his world. He leaned down and kissed the side of her cheek.

"Something smells good."

Matty flushed, pleasure obvious on her little round face. "Hot blueberry muffins, just like you like them. Would you like some eggs to go with them?"

Food wasn't high on his list of priorities, but he

knew that the sooner he slid into his normal routine, the better off he would be.

"Sure, eggs would be fine," he said. "How about scrambled, and don't forget to put jalapeños in them, okay?"

Matty nodded. "The morning paper is on the sideboard with the coffee. Sit! I'll bring in your food shortly."

Gabriel thought of sitting in that long, formal dining room alone and frowned. "I'd rather eat in here with you," he said. "There's no need carrying everything in for just—"

Matty took him by the shoulders and pushed him out of the kitchen.

"I'm too old to change my routine now," she insisted. "Go! Drink my good coffee. Read the paper. Plan your day."

He knew better than to argue.

By the time he got to the dining room, his stomach was in a knot. But after a couple of sips of Matty's coffee, the knot began to unwind. He picked up the paper and headed for the table, automatically choosing the chair he'd always used. Then he looked at the chair at the head of the table—the chair his father had claimed—and after a small hesitation, sat down in it instead, telling himself it was because the light coming in from the windows behind it would make reading the paper that much easier.

He could see his own reflection on the surface of the highly polished wood. In a dark and muted sort of way, he looked like his dad, and somehow the thought made it easier to take, as if he were doing nothing more than bringing what was left of the Donner family full circle. An emptiness dug deep in the pit of his belly. Family. That was a joke. He was it. And if he didn't snap out of this mess he was in, the family would end with him. No woman would want a man who had conversations with himself. Then he stifled the thought. Women should be the least of his worries.

He took another sip of his coffee and then leaned back in the chair, making himself relax, letting go of the guilt and accepting the responsibilities that came with being left behind.

For a while he read without comprehending, scanning the surface of the stories without actually reading their content. He turned the first page, then the second, and somewhere between page three and four of the first section, he realized that the story he was reading was one he'd already read. He knew the facts, the location, even the supposed age of the dead woman they'd found. Curious, he glanced back at page one, looking at both the day as well as the date and thinking that Matty must have accidentally laid out yesterday's paper by mistake. But when he saw today's date, his frown deepened. This made no sense. It was today's paper, but then how would he have known about—

Truth hit him with the full force of a fist to the gut. Blood drained from his face as he turned back to the story and began rereading it, as if for the first time. Halfway through, he began to shake. It wasn't that he'd read about this before. Hellfire! This was his dream!

The paper fell from his hands and onto the floor as he bolted out of the chair. For several seconds he stood without moving, staring down at the newsprint as if it had burst into flames. A thin film of sweat broke out on his body as he closed his eyes, remembering in vivid and lurid detail the horror of what he'd been dreaming when he'd awakened to find himself in the rose garden.

"Oh, God." He wiped a shaky hand across his face.

But the paper didn't disappear, and deceiving himself wouldn't change the facts. Somehow he'd seen this woman die before it had appeared in this paper. And then he thought. Had he actually *watched* it happen, or had he dreamed about it after the fact? He thought of the blood on his jeans and groaned. What the hell difference did it make? Either way, he knew too much about a woman's death.

"Here are your eggs, just the way you like them," Matty announced and set the food at his place.

When Gabriel turned, he felt as if he was moving in slow motion while the rest of the world whirled past him at breakneck speed.

Hungry. So hungry.

The intrusion of the voice at this moment was the last straw. Gabriel reacted in rage.

"Shut up, damn you, shut up. Why can't you leave me the hell alone?"

Matty froze and then pulled back in disbelief. Her face crumpled as she reached for the plate to take it back to the kitchen.

"I'm sorry," she said quickly. "Maybe you'll feel better—"

Gabriel groaned and reached for her, taking the plate out of her hand and setting it aside before pulling her into his arms.

"Not you, darling, not you," he moaned. "I'm sorry I yelled. I wasn't talking to you."

Suddenly afraid, Matty clung to him. This was a side of Gabriel she'd never seen. The confusion he seemed to be suffering frightened her terribly.

"It's all right," she said gently, hugging him back. "You'll be better soon."

He buried his face against the thick graying bun of her hair.

"Ah, God, Matty. It's not all right. In fact, you have no idea how wrong everything is."

With that, he let her go and walked away without looking back, leaving her to deal with the uneaten meal and the shattered peace.

He made it to the library without coming undone, but the moment he gained access to the room, he shut himself in. He needed to be alone. He needed to think. Somewhere within this monstrous mess, there had to be an answer. But the longer he sat, the more confused he became.

A couple of hours passed, maybe more. He'd lost track of everything, including reality, rousing only after he heard footsteps coming down the hall. When he recognized the familiar shuffle of Mike Travers' footsteps, anger surfaced. Matty must have called him. Uncle Mike would want to know what was wrong. Gabriel snorted beneath his breath.

"I'd like to know what the hell's wrong, too," he muttered, then strode to the windows overlooking the back of the estate.

And that was the way Mike Travers found him,

standing with his back to the doors and staring out into the sunlight. His shoulders were tight and bunched, his legs taut and straight, as if braced to withstand a harsh blow.

"Gabriel?"

He hesitated momentarily. When he turned, his face was expressionless. "Uncle Mike."

This wasn't what Mike had expected. Caught off guard by Gabriel's lack of emotion, he was at a sudden loss for words. "I...uh, I mean, Matty thought that—"

"What? That I'm crazy?"

"Now, Gabriel, that isn't fair. I'm sure she—"

A bitter grin tilted the corner of Gabriel's mouth. "Fair? Who said anything about being fair? Life isn't fair. If it was, that damned drunk that hit Mom and Dad would be dead and buried, not them. And as for being crazy, it's probably closer to the truth than I'm willing to accept."

Gabriel stuffed his hands into the pockets of his slacks and then turned back to window gazing. Mike stood silently, debating with himself as to what he should say next, when Gabriel took the decision out of his hands.

"Do you believe in visions?"

The question took Mike aback.

"I don't know. What kind of visions?"

Gabriel continued to stare at the scene before him. Finally he shrugged. "Is there more than one kind?"

A question. Gabriel had asked a question, which meant he wanted an answer. Mike relaxed. He was familiar with communication. It was what he did best.

"Talk to me, Gabriel."

Gabriel turned, and in the moments before he spoke, Mike was startled by the expression on his face. It was like looking at a completely different man. He didn't know this Gabriel. He didn't know him at all. And then Gabriel spoke, and the thought was gone.

"Talk to you, Uncle Mike? I don't know where to start."

Mike sat down on a nearby sofa and then patted the cushion on the seat beside him.

"Start at the beginning, son. Just start at the beginning."

But Gabriel didn't move. He needed to be standing when he said this out loud.

"Ever since the accident, I've been hearing voices…seeing visions. Last night I sleepwalked during a dream. I woke up outside in Mom's rose garden. I had dressed and turned off the security alarm, and I don't remember doing either."

Mike listened without commenting, but he was worried. These were symptoms of deeper emotional problems. He'd known that losing Brent and Angela had been hard on Gabriel, but not to this extent.

"Look, son, in times of great stress, the mind can play tricks on us. It's not uncommon. I just wish you'd said something to me about this sooner. I hate to think of you suffering through this alone."

But Gabriel wouldn't budge. "How about the visions? Are they stress-related, too?"

"It isn't unusual to suffer hallucinations. Most often they are nothing more than old memories that our subconscious resurrects in an effort to recall happier times."

Gabriel frowned, then picked up a nearby phone and pressed a button.

"Matty, would you bring today's paper to the library?"

Moments later, she bustled in with the paper he had discarded, took one look at Mike, then bustled out again.

Gabriel tossed the paper into Mike's lap.

"Tell me this. How many times do your patients' hallucinations make the news?"

Mike frowned. "I don't know what you mean."

Gabriel leaned forward, placing a hand on either side of the older man's shoulders and pinning him in place.

"I don't know what I mean, either, Uncle Mike. But before you give me any more sage advice, there's something you should probably know. Remember what I said about dreaming last night and waking up in Mom's garden?"

Mike nodded.

"It's on page three of this morning's paper."

Mike's frown deepened.

"What's on page three?"

"My dream."

Three

Four hours had come and gone, and Mike was more confused about what Gabriel had just told him than when they'd started. But in spite of everything they had discussed, there was one thing that stood clear in Gabriel Donner's mind, and it was a fact that Mike couldn't shake. Gabriel was convinced that, somehow, he had witnessed a murder. All Mike had to do was prove him right...or wrong. And the only way he knew to do that with any degree of competence was to call someone better trained in that field. Psychics and psychic phenomena were a little out of Mike Travers' realm. Trouble was, Gabriel wasn't happy about letting anyone else in on what he perceived to be a monumental character flaw.

"It's a stupid idea," Gabriel argued. "And even if the guy believes me, what's that going to prove? You know what people think about psychics. They—including me—think they're nuts."

Mike sighed. "The guy I have in mind is a girl. And what does it matter what *they* think? What matters is what you think about yourself."

"Psychics are quacks," Gabriel said, and then dropped into a nearby chair, his shoulders slumped, his face drawn and weary.

"Not this one," Mike insisted. "I met her at a conference once. Her veracity is unimpeachable."

Gabriel covered his face with his hands. There was a part of him that wished he could be a child again, if for no other reason than to be able to lie down and cry without being judged weak or insane. But he couldn't give in to the notion. He'd lost so much already. If he lost control of himself, there would be nothing left.

He sighed. Maybe Uncle Mike was right. Besides, at this point in his life, there wasn't much left to lose. The words of acceptance were on the tip of his tongue when something inside him began to change. It was a transient feeling, one that he never would have been able to describe. All he knew was that he was no longer alone in his own skin. His fingers curled upon the arms of the chair in which he was sitting as a whisper began moving inside his mind.

Don't tell. Don't tell.

Time ceased. He could hear the sounds of his

own heartbeat, feel his lungs expanding and deflating as they drew in oxygen, separating it and then disposing of the unnecessary carbon dioxide in slow, agonizing exhalations. He looked out the window but didn't see the view before him. Instead he saw murky shadows and a tunnel that seemed to go on forever. He moved with the sight, stepping into the darkness and hearing the splash of footsteps as they split the stagnant puddles on the floor below. He leaned forward, following the sight in his mind.

Lost. Help me. Lost.

Gabriel shuddered. He knew lost. It was the most lonesome experience a human could endure.

Mike was waiting for more of Gabriel's argument when he happened to look up. He stopped in midthought, afraid to move—afraid to talk. The man sitting in the chair was still Gabriel, and yet somehow he wasn't. Mike caught himself taking a step backward and then stopped. *What's the matter with me?* he thought. *This is still my boy.*

Right in the middle of a breath, the voice left Gabriel, as suddenly as it had come, taking the vision and the feeling of intrusion with it. And when it was gone, he shuddered, then wiped his hands across his face as if wiping away a bad dream. All he could think was, *Sweet God.* That settled it. He stood.

"Uncle Mike?"

"Yes?"

"Call the psychic. Call her now."

Mike headed for the phone.

It was Sunday. Staff's day off. Somewhere within the bowels of the Dane mansion, a phone began to ring. The distant peal was a rude reminder to Laura Dane that she could run, but it would be impossible to hide from who and what she was. Weary from a five-day stint with the Dallas police department, she considered letting the answering machine pick up and then shook off the notion. It would only delay the inevitable need to return the call later. With a weary sigh, she headed for the library.

"Dane residence."

Mike Travers cleared his throat and shifted the phone to his other ear.

"This is Dr. Michael Travers. I would like to speak to Laura Dane."

Laura dropped into the chair behind her desk and propped up her feet, using the desktop for a footstool.

"I'm Laura Dane."

Elated that he'd gotten through to her so easily, Mike began to pace as he talked.

"Miss Dane, I'm sure you don't remember, but we met last year at the Colorado symposium on psychic healing."

Laura concentrated on the voice and closed her eyes. The image of a small, stoop-shouldered man with thinning gray hair popped into her mind. She kicked off her shoes and then leaned back again, letting her head loll against the headrest.

"About five-ten, graying hair, very academic in appearance, and you were wearing a charcoal gray suit with a missing button on the sleeve."

Mike paused in midstep, more than a little surprised by what she'd said. "My word, you have a very good memory."

Laura smiled to herself. "Not really. Your name was impossible for me to forget. You have the same name as my first-grade boyfriend. I was six. He was seven. You know how irresistible older men are."

Mike chuckled.

Laura continued. "As for remembering you and what you were wearing, I think it's because I had a run in my panty hose that day, and when I noticed your missing button, I was congratulating myself that I wasn't the only attendee who was coming undone.''

Her sense of humor was unexpected. He chuckled again, then glanced at Gabriel and winked, trying to reassure him that everything was going to be all right. To his dismay, Gabriel threw up his hands and stalked out of the room, as if unable to believe his life had come to this point. Mike shrugged, telling himself that at this stage Gabriel didn't know what was good for him.

''Well, then, let's get down to business,'' Mike said. Now that their point of reference had been established, it would be easier to talk.

Laura felt herself beginning to unwind. Her mother had always claimed that laughter was a powerful medicine. But when she heard the man on the other end of the line take a very deep breath, she tensed. Here it comes, she thought. She was right.

''I have an unusual request. But if you agree, you would be paid handsomely for your assistance.''

''Dr. Travers, most of the requests I receive are unusual, otherwise I would not get them. I'm usually a last resort, and…I don't take money for what I do.''

"Well, then," Mike said, "maybe a donation to your favorite charity?"

Laura smiled. "Talk to me."

Mike glanced toward the doorway. Gabriel was nowhere in sight. He turned back to the phone.

"Here's my dilemma. I have a patient who is also a friend. He recently suffered the loss of both parents and very nearly his own life. He is physically well, but mentally...well, that's a different story. He claims to be experiencing a phenomenon that is beyond my expertise. Will you help?"

She heard the urgency in his voice, but her instinct for self-preservation was kicking in. No matter how hard she tried, she couldn't fix everyone's problems, and she was exhausted. She rubbed at a spot near her temple where a dull pain was threatening to spread.

"Look, Dr. Travers, I've been gone for days. I just got home. In fact, I have yet to unpack. I can give you the names of several of my colleagues who might be able to—"

Sensing he was losing her interest, Mike interrupted quickly.

"Please! Miss Dane! You're the only person I feel I can trust. This man is like a son to me. I'm too close to the situation to help him, but if he doesn't get help, and soon, I'm afraid I'll lose him." His voice broke. "When he lost his parents, I also lost my two best friends. I can't lose him, too. Please! For God's sake—help me help him!"

Laura sat up, combing her fingers through her hair in weary frustration. "I understand your concern, but I don't see how—"

Mike dropped into a nearby chair, his voice filled with defeat. "I won't lie to you. Gabriel is totally opposed to this idea. He doesn't believe in psychic abilities, yet it's the only thing that explains what's happening to him. Every day I see him slipping closer and closer to the edge of reason. I'm afraid he'll fall off, and if he does, I won't know how to pull him back."

Laura stiffened as an image flashed through her mind. It was of a winged angel with two faces. One face was crying, the other twisted in agony. The abruptness of it, as well as what she saw, startled her. With nothing more than hearing the man's first name, she had connected. She knew herself well enough to know that the decision had been taken out of her hands. Now she had no choice.

"Okay, I'm listening. Where do you live?"

Mike straightened, almost afraid to hope. "Oklahoma City. Say the word and I'll overnight a first-class ticket."

"Tell me one thing," Laura asked. "Why me?"

Mike took a deep breath. "Because Gabriel claims to have witnessed a murder, and I know you've worked on such cases."

Laura frowned. "You need the police. Not a psychic."

"No, you don't understand," Mike said. "Like you, what he saw was only in his mind."

Laura inhaled sharply. She knew all too well the horror of trying to live with the knowledge of other people's deeds. And she'd had her entire life and the support of her family to help her cope with what she could do. She could only imagine the confusion and terror of trying to absorb such a skill overnight.

"Do you have a pen?" she asked.

Mike began scrambling through his pockets. "Yes."

"I need a day to unpack and unwind. This is Sunday. I can be there by Tuesday. Send the ticket to this address, and make hotel arrangements, as well."

Mike took down the information, but his mind was already moving into another mode.

"Miss Dane, the Donners had an enormous home. Why not stay here? It would be more convenient for both you and Gabriel."

She frowned. "I don't think so. That could put me and your friend in a compromising position."

"Gabriel Donner is the last person on this earth who would harm you."

Again, an image of a two-faced angel flashed through her mind, and this time both faces were crying. The information was strong, its power almost frightening. She knew better than to ignore what she was seeing.

"All right, I'll come, and I'll stay in Mr. Donner's home. But if it doesn't work out, I'll be heading for the nearest hotel."

The old man relaxed. "I'll pick you up at the airport and drive you here myself."

"Fine, then," Laura said, wondering what she'd let herself in for this time.

"Miss Dane?"

"What?"

"Thank you."

"Don't thank me yet. My skill is not an exact science. Sometimes the people I help don't like what I see."

Today the psychic was coming. Gabriel was already sorry he'd ever let himself be talked into this. In a short while, a strange woman whose single claim to fame lay in the fact that she could see into the future, would be intruding into his life. If that wasn't enough to swallow, he'd agreed to having her as a guest in his home.

"I just hope she doesn't look like some sideshow fortune-teller," he muttered to himself. "If Dad were here, he would be laughing his ass off."

He glanced at his watch and then headed for the kitchen to tell Matty there would be another guest for lunch.

Mike Travers drove carefully, letting the traffic flow around him without taking part in the race, while his passenger sat quietly beside him. Several times during the past few minutes he'd sensed her scrutiny, but until she asked, he didn't feel the need to volunteer anything.

Laura felt comfortable with Mike Travers. His demeanor was nonthreatening, his belief in her abilities comforting. And while she was curious about the man who would be her host for the next few days, she resisted questioning the good doctor about him, preferring to draw her own conclusions from their first meeting instead.

Travers shifted his wire-rims to a more comfortable position on his nose and then signaled for a right turn.

"Almost there."

Laura smiled.

"I hope you're not still nervous about staying in Gabriel's home?" he asked.

She shook her head. "No. Besides, if it doesn't work out, there's always a hotel."

Mike shook his head. "That won't be necessary, I assure you."

"We'll see," Laura said. "Just don't worry about it, because I'm not, okay?"

"Okay," Mike agreed, then he began to slow down.

Moments later he turned off the highway and shortly drove between a pair of iron gates that were standing ajar.

"We're here."

The height and mass of the gates surprised Laura. There was less iron in the gates at Buckingham Palace. Her eyebrows arched. "Here" was quite a place.

"It's beautiful."

Her gaze raked the perfectly manicured lawns before moving to view the careful elegance of the home. But when she saw the man standing on the veranda, her attention narrowed.

He's very tall. The thought was random and, by itself, of no consequence. But as Laura got out of the car, she became aware of another facet of the man. His dress was casual—gray chinos, a white knit shirt and black loafers—but there was a carelessness about the way he stood that told her he didn't give a damn about what she might think of his appearance. She sighed. His sanity might be in question, but his defenses were in perfect working order. She extended her hand as Travers began to introduce her. To her surprise, Gabriel Donner reciprocated without hesitation.

When their palms connected, his fingers curled around her hand in a firm but gentle grip. Laura stifled a gasp. She could hear Travers talking, introducing her to the man he called Gabriel, but her head felt light. When the man said her name, it wrapped around her like a whisper in the night. It was all she could do not to faint.

His mouth raked across her face, centering on her lips as his hands fisted in her hair. They clung to each other in desperation as their sweat-slick bodies moved in unison—him to her—her to him.

Someone groaned. Was it the man? Was it the woman? The rhythm of their madness was increasing with every thrust of his body as he drove himself deeper inside her. She felt him—knew him in every biblical sense of the word—from the sweat on his brow to the contortion of his features as sexual ecstasy came upon him.

She saw his face...it was Gabriel. He called her name over and over as he spilled himself into her.

Laura. He called her Laura.

The world came back into focus just as Gabriel dropped her hand. Laura staggered as the connection was broken. Mike grabbed her elbow, suddenly concerned.

"Miss Dane! Are you all right?"

"Please, it's Laura, remember?" She took a deep breath, trying to put away the truth of what she'd just seen. Somewhere in the not-so-distant future, she and this stranger would be lovers. She didn't know whether to turn tail and run, or accept the inevitable. "And yes, I'm fine. Just a little road weary, I suppose."

Gabriel made no comment other than to lead the way into his home.

She wasn't what he'd expected.

He hadn't been prepared for blue jeans and sneakers, and in any other situation, the T-shirt he could see beneath her blazer would have made him laugh. Emblazoned directly across her very ample breasts was the phrase *I know what you're thinking.*

Her hair was short and tousled, and there were freckles on her nose. Somehow, freckles and fakes didn't go together, and until he'd seen her, he'd been convinced that was what she was—a fake. But that was before he'd looked long and hard into her big blue eyes. He hadn't experienced any revelation. All he'd seen was his own reflection and an unassuming expression.

Laura purposefully fell a couple of steps behind as the two men led the way. It was obvious that they were more than friends. Concern for Gabriel was etched deeply into Travers' face, and, in return, Gabriel's head was tilted slightly to one side as they walked so as not to miss what the older man was saying. Family. That was what they were. At least, all that was left of what had once been a family.

She frowned as they entered a large, book-filled room. There was more than sadness in this house. She felt a spirit that did not belong.

Gabriel turned in time to catch the frown on her face and, somehow, knew he was the cause. If it wasn't for his uncle Mike's insistence, he would send her packing right now. This was going to be a monumental waste of time.

Careful...be careful.

Gabriel jerked. The intrusion of the voice was

unexpected. Startled, he clenched his fists and took a slow, deep breath.

Laura felt as if she'd been kicked. "My God."

He looked up. Laura was staring at him in open-mouthed wonder.

"I heard your thought," she whispered. "I heard you say 'Be careful.' That's never happened to me before."

Okay, so she's not a fake, he thought. Then he shook his head in quick denial.

"On the contrary, Miss Dane, that thought wasn't mine, and that wasn't my voice. But that's the same damned voice I've been hearing ever since the wreck. So what's wrong with me? Am I really tuning in to some other world...or am I going insane?"

It was after midnight. Earlier, Laura had bade the elderly doctor a reluctant goodbye and then watched as the housekeeper, a woman Gabriel called Matty, took her leave, as well. After that, their conversation had been stilted.

"Mr. Donner, I think it would be easier for the both of us if—"

"Call me Gabriel."

She nodded. "As I was going to say...I want you to be yourself while I'm here. Go about your normal routine. And if you begin to experience anything unusual, I will know."

"And that's supposed to make this easier?"

"I don't understand," Laura said.

"What's not to understand?" Gabriel muttered. "I'm already having a hell of a time trying to cope with what's happening to me, and now you tune in to my thoughts as easy as changing channels on a television. Hell, lady, I feel naked in your presence."

Laura froze. He didn't understand.

"I do not eavesdrop on people's lives," she said shortly.

"Then how do you explain hearing the same voice I hear?"

"Since that has never happened to me before, I'm afraid I can't."

A bitter grin broke the seriousness of his expression. "Well, that's just great. Seems to me you aren't any better off than I am."

"Don't count me out yet. I promised Dr. Travers I would help, and I will. I just can't promise that you'll like the outcome."

This time there was no mistaking the bitterness of Gabriel's mood.

"Well now, that's what I call hedging your bets. If you aren't able to produce the proverbial rabbits out of the hat, then all you have to do is claim there were never any rabbits to begin with.''

But Laura stood her ground. ''All you have to do is keep an open mind and give me—and yourself—a chance.''

He was impressed with her in spite of himself. He kept looking for flaws, and all that came out was an unswerving honesty. He sighed.

''Fine. You want a chance. You've got it. Uncle Mike seems to think you walk on water, so do your stuff.''

She smiled. ''Your uncle is charming, but slightly misled. I do not walk on water, I sink, just like everyone else. However, if there are sharks lurking about below, I just might be able to warn you ahead of time not to step in.''

He grinned. ''Fair enough. Now, is there anything you need before you retire for the night?''

''Just a place to lay my head.''

He had an instant vision of her head nestled on his chest just below his chin and forgot what he'd been going to say. In the following moments, as she walked up the stairs toward the room she'd been given earlier, he kept struggling to remember his manners. Finally he regained his sense enough to call up to her.

''Miss Dane?''

She paused and turned. "Laura."

"Then good night and sleep well...Laura."

A long moment of silence passed between them. Finally she nodded and smiled.

"Good night to you, too."

Only after she had disappeared did Gabriel realize he'd been holding his breath.

The bedroom she had been given was beautiful. He'd told her it had been his mother's favorite. The wallpaper design was a thick, rich cream with tiny pink roses flocked in random order across the surface. The matching bedspread covered a four-poster bed made from dark cherry wood and shined to a high gloss. The carpet was a pale, delicate pink, like the color of a fading rose. It was a woman's room, and in a way Laura felt protected, as if no man could endure within the confines of such fragile surroundings. She wondered if Gabriel had done this purposefully and then shrugged off the thought. Probably not. She had yet to meet a man who was that insightful.

In spite of her exhaustion, sleep eluded her. The fabric of her nightgown was sticking to her body. In a fit of frustration, she yanked it over her head and tossed it aside. At once her body felt cooler. She stretched and then yawned, reveling in the feel of cool sheets against her skin, and in that same moment she could feel Gabriel's weight upon her body and the thrust of his manhood hammering between her thighs.

She groaned and rolled out of bed, moving toward the window, searching for something else to occupy her mind. That was a thought she wasn't ready to handle. It was unsettling enough just knowing it would come.

Four

Gabriel slept, and for the time being, the woman who'd intruded upon his life was forgotten. He lay belly down across his bed, pillowing one arm beneath his cheek, the other dangling off the side. His legs were sprawled and tangled within the sheet covering the lower half of his body. Every now and then the central air-conditioning would kick in and a burst of cool air would circulate throughout the room. Other than the occasional involuntary twitch of a muscle, he hadn't moved in hours.

Outside, a light rain began to fall, freckling the flagstones on the patio below his windows. Within minutes, the shower had turned to a slow, steady downpour. Somewhere inside his mind, the peace that had taken him into sleep was being moved aside for a darker, more intense emotion.

Rain came without warning. It blew first in his face, then onto his clothes. Before long, the place in which he'd been lying was ankle deep with running water. Confused and miserable, he staggered to his feet, clutching a bouquet of limp, wilting roses and shivering with cold. Another gust of rain-laden wind blew into the tunnel in which he was standing. He picked up his bag and took a defensive step backward. His belly rumbled with hunger as he peered out. Somewhere out there he would find food, but not until this storm had passed. Thunder belched. Bile rose in his throat. He was afraid. So afraid.

Clutching his flowers a littler tighter, he turned toward the darkness and began to walk toward it, wincing as water squished between his toes. His socks were wet. Worse yet, he was walking in water. He wasn't supposed to walk in water.

Something rumbled on the street above him, and he slapped his hands to his ears, unaware that the noise he heard was nothing more than a truck barreling over the viaduct in which he was standing. Down here, below the surface of the street, it sounded as if the world were coming apart. A quick shaft of pain split the thought in his head, but it disappeared as quickly as the noise that had brought it.

After that he began to walk faster, trying to find

a place that was dryer and quieter.... And no noise...there must be no noise.

A whimper came out of the darkness ahead, and he stopped, his head cocked to one side, listening for a repeat of the sound. When it came again, he shrank back against the concrete wall of the viaduct, shivering with fright. He was no longer alone.

Moments later a small dog appeared at his feet, and for the first time since the start of his odyssey, he knew joy. Unmindful of the running water in which he was standing, he dropped to his knees. The dog, sensing no harm, licked the hand the man offered. Even after the man lifted the dog into his arms, cradling it among the limp roses, it made no attempt to struggle. Instead, it seemed satisfied within the confines of the man's grasp.

The dog was soaked to the skin and muddy to boot, but the man didn't care. He drew comfort from the touch of another living thing. Happy that he was no longer alone, he continued his journey toward the faint light now appearing at the other end of the tunnel.

As he walked out into the open, he lifted his head, sniffing the air and taking small comfort in the fact that the rain had stopped. The dog wiggled to be put down. Reluctant to let it go, he held it a little bit tighter. A large puddle beneath a nearby streetlight mirrored their passing as the man began to move.

Six blocks over, a forty-three-year-old accountant named Theodore Russell was stomping his way through the neighborhood park, dodging puddles and, not for the first time in their married lives, cursing his wife, Evie, for her dog's stupidity.

At least once a month Choo Choo managed to get lost. There were constant reports about animals who could find their way home across hundreds, sometimes even thousands, of miles. Choo Choo continued to get lost within the block on which it lived. It was his opinion that Choo Choo had the homing instincts of a fart—once having escaped, it would lose its point of origin, yet never get far enough away to ignore.

As Theodore walked beneath a stand of trees, water from the recent rainfall dripped off of the leaves and down the back of his collar. He shivered.

"That does it," he muttered, digging into his pocket for the dog whistle. "I'm tired. Five more minutes, and if I can't find Choo Choo by then, Evie can get herself another dog."

Just as he was lifting the whistle to his lips, he heard a rustling in the bushes behind him. He paused and turned. The faint glow from a nearby security light was barely enough for him to distinguish shrub from shadow.

"Choo Choo? Is that you, boy?"

He stared into the darkness, hoping to catch a glimpse of shaggy white fur, but when no dog appeared, he stuck the whistle in his mouth and blew.

Suddenly he was enveloped in a roar of great rage. Horrified, he froze, unaware he was still blowing the whistle. His hesitation cost him his life. Moments later, the roar visualized into a man of great height who came out of the bushes, blindly flailing his arms before him.

Theodore saw the blow coming and threw up his arms in self-defense. He should have run instead. A massive fist caught him square in the mouth, snapping his neck on impact and knocking the dog whistle down his throat.

Seconds later, Choo Choo came scurrying out of the bushes. The man on the ground carried a familiar scent of home. Choo Choo whined and then began licking at Theodore's face.

The other man swayed where he stood, his hands clasped against his ears as the last echoes of pain faded away. Trembling from the rush of adrenaline that had surged through his system, he dropped to his knees, rocking to and fro beneath the shelter of the trees, unmindful of the water dripping onto his face or the soggy ground beneath him.

Minutes passed. Calm settled slowly as he sat back on his heels, grateful the agony was over.

A familiar whine came out of the darkness, and he remembered the dog. He turned. When he saw the man on the ground, he fell backward in fright.

It was a stranger! He wasn't supposed to talk to strangers. He began grabbing for his roses and scrambling to his feet, desperate to get away. But to his relief, the stranger seemed to pose no threat.

Curious now, he leaned forward, giving the stranger's arm a tentative poke.

"Help me?"

The stranger didn't move—didn't speak.

"Asleep," he announced, satisfied with his assumption. Then, with the gentlest of touches, he patted the stranger's head, just as he'd patted the dog only moments earlier.

The dog was still there, lying motionless beside the stranger.

"Come," he said softly, but the dog scooted backward, just out of his reach.

He sighed. The dog wanted to stay. He stood up, and when he did, the little dog whined again, only softer. As he looked back, once more staring intently at the stranger on the ground, an impulse struck him. Pulling one of the roses from his bouquet, he laid it on the stranger's chest.

"There now," he said softly, and moved into the shadows as a steady drizzle began to fall.

Something filtered into the quiet of Laura's sleep. She awoke with a jerk. Momentarily confused by unfamiliar surroundings, it took her a few seconds to remember where she was. When she did, she groaned beneath her breath and shoved a shaky hand through her hair. Moments later, Gabriel's face flashed through her mind.

Without questioning her instincts, she knew something was wrong. She jumped from her bed, threw on her nightgown and ran to the door. The hallway was shadowed and quiet. A night-light burned at the head of the stairs, lighting the way up or down. She stood without moving, hearing nothing that would give cause for alarm, and staring into the shadows until her eyes began to burn.

Just when she thought she'd imagined it all, she heard a sound at the far end of the hall. She stepped out into the hallway and tilted her head, listening.

Someone was crying!

But not huge gulping sobs, just a quiet despair. Her first thought was that it was Gabriel, but the

longer she listened, the more convinced she became that it was a woman she heard. She walked
a little farther down the hall. The sound prevailed,
seeping into the pores of her skin and winding itself around her heart until it was part of her pulse.

Staggered by the intensity of what she was experiencing, she stopped. She couldn't put it into
words, but there was something about the sound
that made her stop in her tracks. It wasn't so much
the fact that someone was crying that bothered her.
It was the fact that there was no one up here to be
making that sound.

She spun around and started back down the hall,
increasing her speed until she was all but running
as she reached the door to her room. She dashed
inside, closing the door firmly behind her and then
telling herself afterward that it was all a mistake.
But the thought of going back to bed made her
jumpy. Rubbing at the goose bumps on her arms,
she moved toward the windows, instead.

From the second story, the lawns below looked
black. As she peered out into the darkness, she
realized it was raining. The flagstone patio glistened beneath the security lights, and she could
hear runoff from the roof moving through the
downspout near her windows. She leaned forward,
resting her forehead on the cool panes of glass and

blinking, trying to relieve the dry, burning sensation in her eyes. Her mind ran free, sorting through all that she had learned of Gabriel Donner.

He'd been more than polite. During dinner, she'd caught glimpses of the man he must have been before his world fell apart, and she knew that, in another situation, they might have been friends.

She pictured his face and then sighed. He was almost beautiful, but in the masculine sense of the word. His features had strength; his gaze was unwavering. Well over six feet tall, his dark skin, black hair and green eyes a striking combination, Gabriel Donner was an enigma.

The images she kept seeing when she thought of his name were confusing. The angel part of it she understood. Gabriel. Angel. The angel Gabriel. That made a strange sort of sense. But two faces? What did that mean? Was there another side to the man she couldn't see? Did he have a split personality of which even he was unaware? Her shoulders slumped with weariness. This trip was probably going to prove her undoing. She should have stuck to her guns after all and told Mike Travers she couldn't come. She couldn't remember the last time she'd spent two straight weeks at home. There was only so much a human body could endure. It was no wonder she thought she heard voices when no one was there.

The pulse at her temples was starting to pound in the way that it did just before the onset of one of her headaches. She frowned, hoping she'd packed her medicine, when she saw someone walking out of the trees that bordered the yard. He was bare to the waist and coming across the grounds toward the house in a slow, almost staggering walk.

She never knew when she realized it was Gabriel, but even from where she was standing, she could feel his despair. With no thought for the danger she might be putting herself in, she reached for her robe and ran out the door.

Something sharp pierced the bottom of Gabriel's foot. Awakened by the sensation of pain, he stepped backward in reflex and went ankle deep into a large and widening puddle. The sensation of water on his feet and rain on his face made him stagger, and with cognizance came memory. The memory of blood and pain and death. Again.

"God help me," he moaned, and covered his face.

Despair shattered his thoughts. There was mud on his clothes and skin, even in his hair. All he could think was to wonder where the hell he had been. And there at his feet, floating on the surface of the puddle, was a single long-stemmed rose. He stared at it for what seemed like forever and knew without picking it up that, just like before, every thorn on the stem had been removed.

Lost. Help me.

Gabriel covered his ears with the palms of his hands and then moaned.

"Help you? I can't even help myself."

"Gabriel."

His head came up, his eyes narrowing, and although he could see the woman standing before him, he wasn't sure if she was real or part of the dream.

"I'll help you," Laura said, and held out her hand.

He stared at it—and at her—for what seemed like forever. He kept waiting for her to disappear, but her image never wavered.

A frown creased Laura's forehead as she reached for his arm. "Gabriel?"

At her touch, he shuddered. "You're real?"

She took his hand as she would have a child and was staggered by what flooded her mind.

Rain, pouring into wide, sightless eyes and hammering at the petals of a rose. A small white dog, tattered and muddy, licking away the blood from the corner of a man's slack jaw.

When she moaned, Gabriel knew that she'd plugged into his mind. Horrified that she'd seen his hell, he quickly pulled away from her touch.

"Get out of my head," he said harshly. "There's already more in there than I can cope with. Besides, you can't help. It's too late. No one can help."

He tried to walk past her.

"What happened?" she asked. "Did you have another episode? Do they always happen in your sleep?"

His voice was harsh, laced with bitterness, as he stopped and turned.

"You're the psychic. You tell me."

"What did you see?" she asked.

His expression stilled. "What do you mean... what did I see?"

She touched his forehead. "In there. What did you see?"

A chill settled over Laura's body as she waited for his answer, staring absently at the way the rain ran down his face and wondering if all of it was rain, or if it was mixed with tears. His silence was more telling than he could have known, though his only visible reaction to her question was a slight flaring of his nostrils.

"Gabriel...what did—"

"Hell. I saw hell." Then he turned to walk away.

Without thinking, Laura reached for him again, clutching at him as if he—or maybe it was she— were drowning. Her hair was slick and plastered to her head. Her nightgown and robe molded to her body, and her bare feet were beginning to chill. But the fire in her voice was something Gabriel couldn't ignore.

"You listen to me, Gabriel Donner. As long as you draw breath, it's never too late. But if I'm going to help you, you're going to have to trust me."

Tension coiled in the pit of his belly as he stared into her face. He wanted to believe her. No...he *needed* to believe her.

She stood without moving, her hand upon his arm, her gaze unwavering.

Still he hesitated, looking down at the rose that lay in the puddle between them. He kept thinking of one just like it lying on a dead woman's chest, and then tonight, the rain-soaked token that the killer had once again left behind. And while it had yet to be proven that what he'd seen tonight had actually taken place, his gut instinct told him that it had. He took a deep breath, exhaling softly so as not to wake the demon that slept within him, and stared deep into her eyes.

"Miss Dane?"

"No. Laura, remember?"

He shrugged. "Laura, did you ever consider the fact that I may be going crazy?"

"Do you believe you're crazy?" she asked.

A long moment passed before he answered, but the determination in his voice was impossible to miss.

"No."

"Then the question is moot," she said.

"You could be putting yourself in danger."

"It wouldn't be the first time. It won't be the last," she retorted.

"I don't believe in psychics," he said.

A gust of rain splattered itself across her face and the front of her clothes. Shuddering, she wrapped her arms around herself.

"And I don't believe in Santa Claus."

He almost smiled. "Well, isn't this something? Two skeptics trying to play doctor in a house of cards."

Then he looked up at the sky, as if he'd just

realized rain was still falling, and tugged at her hand.

"We'd better get inside."

He stepped over the puddle, leaving the rose adrift on the ever-widening surface. In spite of the fact that he believed he'd just "witnessed" another murder, his step was light, and he knew the reason why. Laura Dane was willing to believe.

Unsure of the paths in the darkness, Laura let him lead her toward the house, and all the way there, she fought an overwhelming feeling of doom. Even after they were both warm and dry and back in their respective beds, she couldn't help but wonder if she was setting herself up for a terrible fall.

Prince Charming Killer Strikes Again!

Laura's eyes narrowed nervously as she scanned the headline of the morning paper before reading the accompanying story. As one would expect, the authorities hadn't given many details, but there were enough for her to make a preliminary judgment about Gabriel Donner's newfound powers.

She glanced up as the housekeeper came into the dining room and set a silver chafing dish on the sideboard.

"Breakfast is served, Miss Dane."

"Thank you, Matty, but I'm waiting for Mr. Donner."

Gabriel walked into the dining room on the heels of her statement and kissed Matty good morning before she could make her getaway.

"Good morning, Matty, my love," he said, grinning because he'd flustered her. Then he glanced at Laura. "No need to wait any longer, I'm here."

He picked up a warm plate from the sideboard and held it toward her, indicating that she should serve herself first.

Thankful to be doing something besides confronting Gabriel about the story he had yet to see, she set the paper on the chair beside her, then got up from her own chair and began filling her plate, all too aware of the man behind her. Just as she was dropping a spoonful of scrambled eggs on her plate, she felt his arm against her shoulder and knew that if she turned, she would be able to see herself in his eyes. She took a deep breath, trying to calm her nerves, but when his voice rumbled close to her ear, she jumped, both from his proximity as well as what he said.

"Do you like the hot stuff?"

Gabriel's fingers were tangled in the length of her hair as he tilted her face for a kiss. He tasted of cinnamon and something cold, and Laura knew that for the rest of her life, the scent of that spice would make her heart skip a beat.

She dropped the spoon back into the eggs. It hit the metal edge of the dish with a sharp, melodic clink as she turned, trying to focus on the present instead of the vision that had just played through her mind.

"What did you say?"

Gabriel was pointing to a dish just to her right. "Hot. I asked you if you liked hot food." Then he added. "Hot as in spicy, not as in heat."

Her mouth formed an inaudible O as she followed the line of his finger.

"Matty makes a salsa with habañero peppers that's great on scrambled eggs. But it's very, very hot. A little goes a long way."

Laura felt like a fool. Salsa. He'd been talking about salsa, not sex.

"Then I think I'll pass," she said, hoping her smile wasn't as lopsided as it felt.

"To each his own," Gabriel replied, toasting her with a brimming spoonful of the thick, red sauce before sprinkling it liberally onto his eggs and hash brown potatoes.

Laura arched an eyebrow. It even smelled hot. "Yes," she echoed. "To each his own."

"Did you sleep well?" he asked, and then

looked slightly embarrassed when he added, "I mean after I...after we—"

"I'm fine."

Still uneasy about sharing any part of his life with a stranger, he nodded, then looked away.

Laura glanced at his face. She could feel him withdrawing and, without thinking, yanked a conversational point out of the blue to keep him from shutting her out completely.

"So...about this Matty who makes wonderful salsa, has she been with you long?"

There was a pensive expression in his eyes as he answered. "She's been here as long as I can remember and then some." Then he grinned. "It's hell trying to be in charge of a woman who has changed my diapers and doesn't hesitate to remind me of the fact on a regular basis."

Laura laughed as she laid her napkin in her lap, thankful that, for the time being, he was concentrating on their meal and not the missing paper.

Gabriel paused, his coffee halfway to his lips as he stared over the rim to the woman sitting at his right. When she laughed, she was downright stunning. And when she bent her head toward her plate, a dark, tousled curl kept falling out of place, tumbling to the middle of her forehead like a recalcitrant child.

It reminded him of an old nursery rhyme his mother used to read.

There was a little girl, who had a little curl, right in the middle of her forehead. When she was good, she was very, very good, and when she was bad, she was horrid.

"Are you?" he asked.

Laura looked up. "Am I what?"

Stunned that he'd voiced his thoughts aloud, he flushed. "Nothing," he muttered.

"No fair," Laura said. "You can't start something and then not finish it."

The look in her eyes caught him, holding him suspended between one breath and the next as an odd tingle started to inch its way up his spine. He had a sudden vision of her lying on her back beneath him on a bed, his fingers tangling in those curls. He grunted beneath his breath, as if he'd just been kicked in the gut.

"Your hair. It made me remember something," he muttered.

Laura dropped her fork beside her plate, her eyes widening in disbelief. The smile she'd been considering stayed where it was. Hair was the last subject she'd been expecting to discuss.

"What about my hair?"

Now Gabriel felt silly. "Uh...that curl," he

said, glancing at the way it lay on her skin and wondering if it was as soft as it looked.

Laura frowned and started to push it back in place when Gabriel grabbed her hand.

"Don't," he said sharply, and then turned her loose as quickly as he'd grabbed her. "Sorry," he said, and then shrugged apologetically. "Look, I'm not insulting you. I just got caught thinking out loud."

"I don't understand."

I don't blame you. I don't understand this myself. But this time Gabriel didn't voice his thoughts. Instead, his gaze raked her face, from the delicate cut of her chin to the freckles on her nose, then back to that impetuous curl that had caused so much trouble.

"'There was a little girl, who had a little curl, right in the middle of her forehead. When she was good...'" His voice trailed off in the middle of the sentence.

Laura found herself caught in the intensity of his gaze and muttered the end of the rhyme. "'...she was very, very good, and when she was bad...'"

Gabriel finished what he had started, grinning at his own wit. "...she was better."

Laura's eyebrows arched as she hid a quick smile. "That's not the way I learned it."

Gabriel picked up his fork and dug back into his salsa-spiced eggs. "If you'd been a boy, you would have."

She rolled her eyes. "I'm eating with a male chauvinist."

He picked up a small crystal bowl and extended it toward her. "Honey?"

Laura glared at it, then at him. "Shouldn't that be an olive branch or something similar?"

He grinned. Damned if he wasn't inclined to like this woman anyway, crazy psychic or not.

"Only if you're a bird in need of a place to perch," he said.

Laura grinned back at him and took the bowl of honey he'd offered.

"You may or may not be psychic, but you're certainly a caution," Gabriel said, watching as she twirled a thin strand of the thick, amber sweet on top of her toast. It puddled on the surface like tears too thick to fall.

"Darn," Laura muttered, more to herself than to him as she licked the honey off her thumb.

Gabriel felt as if he were watching her from outside himself. When his belly tied itself in a knot, he looked away, trying to concentrate on something else besides Laura Dane's mouth and the tip of her tongue.

Suddenly uncomfortable with the pseudocamaraderie that had sprung up between them, they finished the meal in near silence. It wasn't until Matty came in to ask if they needed assistance that Gabriel thought to ask about the morning paper.

Matty looked about the room, puzzled as to where it had gone.

"I put it on the table, just like I always do," she said.

Laura flushed guiltily. "I'm sorry. Here it is," she said, and pulled it from the chair beside her. "I laid it aside when I sat down."

Satisfied that she was not at fault, Matty bustled out of the room, leaving them alone.

He held out his hand, expecting Laura to hand it over, but when she hesitated, his gut knotted. The expression on her face said it all.

"Well, hell."

Laura opened the paper, but she didn't have to look to remember what she'd already read.

"I want you to do something for me."

His eyes glittered. "Depends."

"Tell me what you remember from the dream."

"I spent most of the night trying to forget it." His voice was angry, his words sharp and bitter.

"Please," she said. "I can't help you if you won't help yourself."

His hand was shaking as he shoved it through his hair. Even as the words were accumulating themselves inside his mind, he was feeling the scar beneath his fingertips and wondering if it ran into the depths of his brain. Something had tied his mind into knots. He closed his eyes, remembering—and wishing the hell he could not.

"There's a man on the ground. It's dark where he's lying, but I see…saw…trees. Um…he had an umbrella. It's slightly beneath him…and the crystal on his watch is shattered." Gabriel shuddered and took a deep breath. "As shattered as his face. The time…his time…stopped at fifteen minutes after twelve. He's staring up toward the sky, and rain is falling onto his face and then running out the corners of his eyes like tears." He swallowed, as if the words he spoke had a bitter taste. "There's a small dog nearby. Grey…no, white, I think. And the rose." He opened his eyes. His gaze caught and then locked on Laura's eyes, staring intently, as if he was trying to measure the impact of what he was saying to her. "There's a rose on his chest, and the stem has no thorns."

When she didn't respond immediately, he leaned forward. "So…I told you. Now, you tell me something."

She picked up the paper and started to read.

"'The body of a man was found in Johnson Park by an early-morning jogger. It was estimated that he died around midnight. An unnamed source said that the man had died of a broken neck and that authorities have linked this murder to the killing of a woman a few days ago. In both cases, the killer left a single rose by the body as a signature. The killer's Prince Charming gesture doesn't change the fact that two people are dead.'"

"My God," Gabriel muttered. "I'm seeing these murders as they take place, aren't I?"

Laura laid the paper in her lap. "It would seem so."

No longer hungry, he pushed his chair away from the table and then stalked out of the room. Laura followed. She caught up with him in the hall and grabbed his arm.

"Wait," she begged.

He turned, his mouth twisted in anger. "Wait for what?"

"I think you should go to the police," she said.

He threw up his hands and all but pushed her away. "And tell them what? That I walk in my sleep and dream about murder? Hell, lady, they'll lock me up for committing them. Nowhere in the articles does it mention the fact that the thorns on the roses have been removed, but somehow I know that for a fact. And nowhere does it mention that the last victim died with a dog whistle halfway down his throat, but it's there. I know it, because I watched him swallow it."

Now Gabriel took a step forward, putting himself within whispering distance.

"You think that's something?" he said. "Then take a bite of this little fact and see how it tastes. You saw that beautiful rose garden out back?"

Laura nodded.

"It was my mother's passion. When they began to bloom, as they are right now, she kept dozens of fresh arrangements all over the house. The scent of roses was always in the air. But she had this little quirk. She thought it was some sort of crime against nature that something so beautiful should cause so much pain. It was her habit to remove all the thorns from the stems as she put them in vases."

Laura blanched. The implications of what he'd just said were startling.

"What are you getting at?" she asked. "Are you trying to tell me that you...that the killer is—" She couldn't bring herself to finish.

Gabriel's face was a study in the absence of color. His skin was ashen, his lips bloodless and thinned in frustration.

"I don't know what I'm trying to say. All I know is I survived a wreck that should have killed me, just like it killed my parents, and all I get for my magnificent intestinal fortitude is a large dose of living hell!"

In sudden fury, he picked up a vase from a nearby table and hurled it against the opposite wall before stalking out of the room.

Laura listened to the sound of shattering crystal as she watched him go and wondered if that was the way a breaking heart sounded when it finally gave way.

Five

A summer day in Oklahoma after a night of rain was nothing short of pure misery. The humidity was off the scale and did nothing for hairdos and clothes but cause them to wilt, except for the unfortunate few who had the kind of hair that went into a revolt, curling into unbelievable tangles and snarls.

Oklahoma State Bureau of Investigation agent Kirby Summers suffered neither of the problems with regards to his hair. It was too sparse and straight to go limp or tangle. However, the same couldn't be said of his suit. It was too hot for the weather. Right now, he would have willingly traded it for a pair of cutoffs and his favorite T-shirt—the old ragged one that had once been black but was now faded to a sick, foggy gray. Most of the Grateful Dead's logo had long since washed away, but the memories that came with it were still firm in his mind. He'd lost his virginity wearing that shirt.

As he turned onto Sooner Road and headed toward the crime scene, he thought of that shirt and grinned. He would always have a fondness for women named Shirley.

As for his suit, it clung persistently to his skin, outlining all too vividly his lack of bulk. Kirby Summers wasn't slim. He was out-and-out skinny. His balding head and high, wide forehead gave him a Tweety Bird look to which he'd long been resigned. At first glance, he was the epitome of a nerd, until you looked in his eyes. They were a soft, chocolate brown, sharp with intelligence, sparkling with wit. The true measure of the man.

He pulled into Johnson Park. When he killed the engine, his expression was somewhere between pissed and resigned. Pissed because his vacation had been canceled, and resigned because it was part of his job. As he got out of his car and began walking toward the investigation in progress at the back of the park, he couldn't help thinking that, but for the warped brain of some serial killer who'd decided to run amok, he would be in the Colorado Mountains right now, enjoying cool breezes and lots of fishing.

He'd planned this vacation for more than three

years, envisioning himself coming back with a trophy fish. His buddies had kidded him, saying he was leaving the city just to get himself laid. Kirby had let most of their crap slide off his shoulders, not because he was averse to arguing, but because it was too close to the truth to ignore. He stepped aside to avoid a large pile of dog poop and found himself shoe-deep in mud.

"Shit," he muttered, and then grinned at his own wit. Yes, it *was* shit. Shit on the ground. Shit that his vacation had been canceled. Then he remembered why he was here and sighed. And serious shit for the man who'd been murdered.

He flashed his badge at a uniformed officer standing beside the crime scene tape that had been strung about the area. When the officer lifted the tape, Kirby ducked and passed under.

"Morning, sir," the cop said.

Kirby nodded and kept on walking, keeping a careful eye out for further mud and shit.

The medical examiner was in the midst of his examination when a uniformed officer nudged Detective Ray Bush's elbow.

"Hey, Bush. Isn't that Kirby Summers?"

Relief settled on Ray Bush's shoulders as he looked up. He'd been expecting the OSBI agent all morning. As a homicide detective for the

Oklahoma City Police Department, Bush had been assigned to a case a few days ago involving a murdered prostitute. Being a Reno Street hooker was not an occupation that lent itself to old age, and the fact that the woman had turned up dead was tragic, but not necessarily out of the ordinary. The only thing unusual about the crime scene had been a long-stemmed rose left on her body. The fact that the thorns were missing had been odd, but not anything remarkable.

And that had been the general consensus until this morning, when a second body had turned up with a similar signature. Another dead body with another thornless, long-stemmed rose.

Serial killer.

It was enough to give even the veteran officers a knot in the pits of their stomachs. Not only could this cause a public panic, but pressure would come down heavy on them to solve the murders and solve them now.

Problem was, except for the roses found on the victims, there was no similarity between them. They were different ages, different sexes, and had definitely moved in different social circles. Bush had already checked on Theodore Russell's personal life on the off chance that he could have been one of the prostitute's clients. That hadn't panned out. When he'd been notified that the Oklahoma State Bureau of Investigation was sending one of their best men in to help him out, he'd been more than willing to share. This nut was one killer they needed to get off the streets, and fast. He would take all the help he could get.

Bush held out his hand as Kirby walked up.

"Agent Summers, isn't it? Ray Bush, Homicide. I assisted you on a case a couple of years ago."

"Yeah, the missing motel owner, right?"

"Right," Ray said.

"Pleasure," Summers said, shaking the other man's hand then glancing down at the body. "So, what have we got?"

Bush pulled out his notepad. "Theodore Russell. Early forties. Senior accountant. Went out looking for his wife's lost dog. Didn't come home. She reported him missing around 3:00 a.m. An early-morning jogger found his body around 6:00 a.m. Unfortunately, the rain washed away whatever clues the killer might have left. All we have is this rose." He held up a plastic bag, containing one very bedraggled long-stemmed red rose.

"I understand you had another body a couple of days earlier with a similar signature."

Bush nodded. "Right down to the fact that the stem is thornless."

Kirby glanced down at the body. "How did he die?"

"Just like the prostitute. A broken neck."

Kirby's dark eyes narrowed. "Does the media know about the missing thorns?"

Ray nodded. "No, sir. I made certain of that."

"Good." Then Kirby squatted down beside the body, watching as the medical examiner continued to work. "Hey, Sam. Anything you can tell me that might help?"

Sam Whitehall paused in the act of bagging some hair that he'd found on the dead man's jacket and looked up.

"He's got something lodged in the back of his throat. My best guess is that it's some kind of whistle. I'll extract it when I begin the autopsy."

Kirby frowned as he stood. "A whistle?"

Bush flipped down his list of notes. "His wife said he'd gone out to look for a missing dog. Maybe it's a dog whistle."

Summers made another note, then took a handkerchief out of his suit coat, swiping at the sweat running down the back of his neck.

"You through here?" he asked.

Bush nodded.

"I'd like copies of everything you have on both victims as soon as possible."

"You got it," Bush said.

"I'll be in touch," Summers said, and started to walk away when Bush called out.

"Hey, Summers."

Kirby stopped and turned. "Yeah?"

"Something about this gives me the creeps. Glad to have you aboard."

Summers thought about the fishing trip one last time and then nodded. "No problem."

Laura overslept. When she opened her eyes, she knew it was late by the amount of sunshine reflected on the wall opposite her bed. She lay without moving, absorbing the quiet of the house and thinking of Gabriel Donner. He made her uncomfortable in a way she'd never experienced. When she was around him, she felt out of control. It was disconcerting to know they would be lovers. While the thought wasn't abhorrent, right now it *was* frightening. The man was somehow involved in these murders. Whether it was psychically or physically had yet to be discerned. And that was why she was here.

She groaned, then rolled out of bed and headed for the bathroom. A short while later, she emerged from her room dressed in a knit shirt and slacks. The carpet muffled the sound of her footsteps as she came down the stairs. The scent of coffee still lingered in the air, but it was a quarter after ten. Breakfast had long since come and gone. Lost in thought, she didn't see the housekeeper coming out of the library until they almost collided.

Laura stopped in midstep, reaching for Matty to steady her. "I'm so sorry. I wasn't watching where I was going."

Matty smiled. "Good morning, Miss Dane, and there's nothing to apologize for. I'm fine."

Laura returned the smile. "I know it's late, but could I talk you out of a cup of coffee?"

Matty pushed her toward the dining room. "It's never too late around here. Sit! Sit! I'll bring coffee. Would you care for some eggs...or maybe some French toast?"

Laura shook her head. "No. Please don't fuss on my account. It's so near lunch that I'd rather wait for that, instead. However, I would dearly love the coffee."

Matty nodded and had started toward the kitchen when she paused and turned. "It is a beautiful morning, and the roses are in bloom. Maybe you would like to have your coffee out on the patio?"

"That's a wonderful idea," Laura said. "By the way, where is Gabriel?"

Matty shrugged. "He said he had to see a client.

He didn't say who. If you need him, you can call his office. They probably have a phone number where he can be reached.''

"I don't need him," Laura said. "I was just curious."

"Okay, then. You go to the patio. I'll bring your coffee."

Laura felt like saying "Yes, ma'am" as she headed toward the library. Moments later, she opened the French doors and stepped out on the patio beyond.

The air was warm with a promise of more intense heat later in the day, but for now it felt wonderful, like warm silk brushing against her skin. She lifted her head and inhaled deeply, savoring the scent-laden air.

Sunlight caught on evaporating dew, giving the new-mown grass a jeweled appearance. A fountain bubbled nearby as a constant stream of water spilled from a pitcher in a marble cherub's hands. English ivy covered more than two floors of the home, cloaking the walls in a dark, verdant growth.

And then there were the roses, growing in abundance and planted so that the eye was drawn to their surroundings as much as to the bushes themselves. Laura stared, transfixed by the ingenuity of the woman who had created such beauty.

Angela Donner had planned her garden well. No formal geometric plots between concrete paths for her. Her roses grew up trellises and out of pots, entwined around miniature fences and among old iron wheels. As Laura stood, transfixed by the magnificence of such an effort, she felt a shifting within her. She waited, but although the feeling persisted, nothing happened.

Uneasy, she decided to walk and stepped off the patio onto the well-graveled path leading to the roses just as Matty came out of the house.

"Miss Dane! Your coffee," Matty called.

"Set it there," Laura said, pointing toward a table. "I'll get it in a moment."

Matty did as she'd been asked and then disappeared into the house, leaving Laura alone. She turned back to the path. The urgency within her increased, until she was all but running to get to the garden.

Once inside its boundaries, the urgency disappeared, and she stood for a moment, trying to assimilate what had just happened. What had she felt? Was it nothing more than a bit of Angela Donner's spirit returning to a well-loved place, or was it something more sinister? Had that been a welcome or a warning?

She started to walk among the blooms, absorbing the serenity of her surroundings and letting her mind go free.

Sadie Husser had a penchant for pretties she didn't need. Her husband, Eli, had been dead for more than twenty years, but while he'd lived, he'd passed his love of antiquities on to Sadie, the love of his life.

At seventy-two, Sadie Husser was one of Oklahoma City's leading ladies. Her parties were social events. Everything in her world had been set and orderly until the robberies began to occur. There had been two in the last three weeks, and all within a six-block radius of her estate. Since then, she hadn't had a good night's sleep. This morning she'd made a call to Straight Arrow Security, confident that her troubles would soon be over.

Gabriel got out of his car, gazing intently at the massive structure before him. He knew Sadie Husser by reputation. In her heyday, she'd been quite a beauty. He supposed the same could be said for her home. The once grand structure looked a little worn at the seams, but he knew it wasn't for lack of money. Sadie Husser was stinking rich. As for the slightly weathered sashes on the windows and the faint cracks leading up the brick walls, he supposed Sadie cared more about what was inside than what was without.

The home had aged along with Sadie, and he doubted if she even noticed the faults. If she did, she obviously didn't care. His interest stirred as he stared up at the structure. Turning this mausoleum into a security-controlled environment would be one of the biggest tasks he'd ever undertaken. But the job didn't daunt him. Instead, he felt a strange sense of elation. It would be something on which to focus besides his troubles.

Gabriel walked across the veranda and rang the doorbell. A few moments later, Sadie's houseman answered the door. His soft lispy voice did not match his muscular appearance or his short, spiky hair.

"Yes?"

Gabriel handed him a card. "I have an appointment with Mrs. Husser."

"Oh! The man from the security thingy. I'm Stevie, the Jill of all trades around here, if you know what I mean." Then he gave Gabriel a considering glance. "Are you as straight as you look?"

Gabriel grinned. "Yep."

"Such a waste," Stevie murmured. "Oh well, I

always say it never hurts to ask. Follow me, big boy. Sadie is expecting you.''

She sat in a chair by the window like a queen holding court. The regalness of her expression was exceeded only by the upturned nose of the Pekingese draped across her lap. The moment Gabriel entered the room, it began to yap.

Continuously.

Yap. Yap. Yap.

Monotonously.

Yap. Yap. Yap.

Sadie frowned and picked up the dog, dangling it from her hands like a mop head without a handle.

Yap. Yap. Yap.

''Stevie, come get Mimi. She's being a bad girl today.''

The butler took the Peke, cuddling it against his chest as one would a child.

''Poor little Mimi. Doesn't her like the big hunk...hmmm?''

Sadie frowned at Stevie and then gave Gabriel a nervous glance.

Confident of his place in her life, Stevie cuddled the dog, ignoring his mistress's glare.

''You just come with Stevie. We'll find you a treat. Want a treat? Hmmm? Does Stevie's little sweetheart want a treat?''

"You don't give her a treat for being bad," Sadie argued.

"Oh, pooh," Stevie said. "She's never a bad girl, are you, sweetheart?" And he kissed the dog square on its flat little nose.

Sadie rolled her eyes as the pair left the room, then gave Gabriel a curious glance, assessing his reaction to her unorthodox household.

When he made no comment, the starch went out of Sadie's attitude. She leaned back in the chair and smiled. "They both ignore me, but they also suit me."

"Yes, ma'am."

Sadie stood abruptly. "Now, about this alarm system business. Explain it to me, young man. These days I'm too old to stand guard at the doors. I want to be able to sleep in my own bed without worrying about thieves."

He nodded. "That can be arranged. I'll explain the different aspects of security systems while you show me around, okay?"

Sadie slipped her hand beneath Gabriel's elbow. "It would be my pleasure."

It was ten minutes after four when Gabriel got home. He was exhausted, but satisfied with the way the day had gone. He tossed his keys toward a nearby table as he started upstairs—and missed. They fell to the floor in a clatter. Groaning beneath his breath, he went back to pick them up. As he reached downward, his hand passed through a beam of blue light.

"What the—"

He straightened, the keys forgotten, his gaze following the light to its source, and then realized it was nothing more than afternoon sunshine coming through the stained glass window over the front door. Once more he turned toward the stairs, and this time he noticed that the white tiles in the floor of the foyer were marbled with color, as well. He'd probably seen the sight a thousand times in his life, but today, it struck him as remarkable.

The colors flowed across the impromptu canvas, some bright and true, others running one into the other to make an entirely different shade. Mesmerized by the beauty, he turned toward the library, his mother's name hovering on the edge of his lips. And then it hit him. She was gone.

He took a deep breath and looked back at the floor, trying to focus through tears. Like his life, the colors had begun to blur. His heart hurt. His hands shook. In that brief moment of joy, he'd forgotten that she was dead.

Rage surfaced—at the drunk who'd destroyed

his world and at God for letting it happen. His hands clenched into fists. He took a deep, shuddering breath and lifted his chin, as if daring fate to strike another blow.

He was alone.

Laura stepped into the hallway just as Gabriel bent to pick up his keys. She started to call out to him but hesitated when she saw his expression changing from joy to rage. She didn't know why, but something had obviously triggered a memory he didn't want to face.

"Gabriel?"

He flinched. Laura. He'd forgotten she was here. Then he wondered how long she'd been watching him. From the expression on her face, long enough to know that he was rattled. It made him mad, both at himself for letting it happen and at her for being a witness to what he considered a weakness.

When Laura saw the telltale glitter of tears in his eyes, she forgot what she'd been going to say. Wanting only to comfort, she touched the side of his face, cupping his cheek with the palm of her hand.

"It gets better."

Anger continued to spill into his mind, and he let it come, because it filled the emptiness within.

Her hand was soft against his cheek, her compassion obvious, but he didn't want her kindness. He didn't need her pity. It was safer to rage—safer to hate. If he let himself weaken—even one tiny bit— he might come the rest of the way undone.

He lashed out as he moved out of reach. "What gets better? The nightmares? The loneliness? I know that. I'll tell you something else I know. Your coming here was a mistake. This psychic business is starting to get on my nerves. The way I see it, you're not much better than a voyeur. You can see what's wrong, but you can't fix it. So far, all you've done is assure me that I'm losing what's left of my mind, which I already knew."

She took his rebuke and let go of the pain that it caused her, because she knew where it had come from. He was sad and lonely—and she suspected that he was also afraid. And because she'd been where he was now, she forgave. She turned to him, her voice soft but strong.

"I never said I was perfect, and I didn't come to fix anything. I came at your uncle Mike's request, remember?"

At that point Gabriel had the grace to flush. An apology was hovering at the back of his mind, but Laura wasn't through. She fixed him with a piercing stare that tied his belly in knots.

''I know how you feel. I've been where you are. It took me several years to remember that I could no longer pick up the phone and hear my mother or father's voices. I miss them still. But you know what finally gave me comfort?''

He shook his head.

Laura's chin trembled, but her voice didn't waver. ''When they died, they left something they cherished behind.''

''What?''

''Me. They left me.''

Shamed by what she'd said, he watched as she walked away. When he looked down at the floor, the colors were gone. All the way upstairs, he couldn't quit thinking that Laura had taken more with her than her dignity when she'd left him standing.

The massive, two-story structure loomed in the darkness, a behemoth of brick and mortar with yellow eyes that glowed behind thin veils and loose shutters.

He stood within the shadows of a nearby tree, watching the silhouettes of the people as they moved about within. He pulled a cookie out of his pocket and began to eat as he leaned against the trunk of the tree. This was a good house. Maybe this was home. He wished someone would come out. If he could see their faces, then he would know. He took another bite, oblivious to the fact that the cookie was stale, and that the trash bin he'd pulled it from had also smelled of fish.

A cool night breeze ruffled his hair, playing with the thick, black strands and feathering them across his forehead. His nostrils flared as he sniffed the air, and when he stepped out of the shadows, he had to duck to miss a low-hanging limb.

Dew had dampened the hems of his pant legs, but he didn't seem to care. The roses dangling from his fist were limp. One of them had started to shed. There was a trail of petals from the tree under which he'd been standing to the doorstep on which he stopped.

Unaware of the doorbell just to his right, he knocked on the door and then waited. No one answered his call. He knocked again, harder.

Moments later, somewhere inside the big house, a dog began to bark.

Yap. Yap. Yap.

A low throb began at the back of his neck.

Yap. Yap. Yap.

His hands began to shake. The sound was coming closer.

Yap. Yap. Yap.

The urge to run was strong, but he needed to know if this was home. His memory was bad, but he felt a strong sense of self within the perimeters of this place, and he was tired of being lost.

A light suddenly flooded the place where he was standing. He blinked and then squinted, shading his eyes from the white burst of illumination. Before he could move, the door opened inwardly. At that point, his hopes fell. The man in the doorway was a stranger, but the feeling that he belonged here was stronger than his urge to run. Even though he could still hear the dog—even though the man grabbed his arm—even though... He stayed.

"Why...if it isn't the hunk! I couldn't be so lucky as to assume you've had a sudden change of mind. Did you forget something?"

"Is this home?" he asked.

The man's quick burst of high-pitched laughter that followed his question made him flinch, but his sense of belonging was so strong that he still hesitated.

Yap. Yap. Yap.

The sound was coming closer now, and he pulled away. The man followed him outside.

"Hey, Gabriel...what's wrong? I was just kidding about the come-on. Are you having car trouble or something? I'd be glad to call a tow for you.''

Yap. Yap. Yap.

Inside his head, the dog's bark had become a shrill, high-pitched scream with no end.

Reason died.

And so did the dog.

It was over in seconds.

''You crazy son of a bitch!'' Stevie shrieked. ''What have you done?''

Then he erupted in a fit of rage that ended as swiftly as the dog's bark had been silenced.

Moments later, there was only one man standing.

Tears streamed down his face as he stared at the man on the ground. His neck hurt. As he touched it, blood came away on his finger.

He shook his head. This wasn't home. Home was good. This place was bad. He knelt to gather the roses he'd dropped. One of them had lost all its petals. He discarded the stem, leaving it beside the man's body, then stood and walked away.

This hadn't been home after all. But home was out there somewhere. He could feel it.

Laura woke up suddenly, gasping for air. Her pulse hammered in her ears as she pulled the covers up beneath her chin and peered into the dark corners of the room in which she slept, half expecting Gabriel to step out of the shadows. To her relief, there was no one there. She thrust a shaky hand through the tangles of her hair, trying to get past the dream. It was impossible to forget.

Gabriel with his hands on her arms—with his hands upon her shoulders—with his hands around her neck.

She shuddered uncontrollably, then rolled out of bed and bolted from the room. If she embarrassed herself tonight, she would apologize tomorrow, but for now, she had to know where he was.

The carpet runner was soft beneath her feet as she ran down the hall toward Gabriel's room. She arrived to find the door ajar.

"Oh, Lord," she muttered, and took a deep breath. When she looked inside, his bed was empty, just as she'd known it would be. "This isn't happening. It was nothing but a bad dream."

She turned away, staring up and down the hallway, half expecting to see him coming toward his room with a book and a drink. She reminded herself that the house was huge. Just because he wasn't in his bed, that didn't mean anything. Maybe he'd been unable to sleep. Then she remembered he hadn't eaten much at dinner. Maybe he liked to indulge in late-night snacks. With a weary yawn, she started to go back to bed, then felt a rush of air against her cheek. Thinking it nothing more than a draft, she kept on walking. The sensation came again, this time more distinct, as if someone had just breathed against her skin. She stopped.

Go back. Go back.

The words came to her in rapid succession. Before she thought, she had turned around and was headed for the stairs.

This time she thought she heard a sigh, but she kept on walking. She was too tired, and it was too late, to consider the possibility of ghosts. Besides, she needed to know where Gabriel was before she closed her eyes again in this house. She started toward the stairs, praying with every step that it was going to be okay.

The piercing shriek of a siren blasted the serenity of the night. Gabriel woke with a start, wondering why his clothes were damp and his arms were cold. It took a moment for him to realize that he was lying on the ground, and another moment for the realization to soak in that he'd been asleep beneath the stand of sugar leaf maple trees at the end of the grounds.

Unable to believe where he was, he rolled over and then sat up with a groan. It had happened again. As he was willing himself to move, he became aware of a burning pain at the side of his neck and touched it gingerly. Even though it was dark, he could see blood on the ends of his fingers.

"No."

His heart started to pound.

"No."

His hands started to shake as he lowered his head on his knees and closed his eyes. How had this happened? The man in his dream had had a bloody neck. And now he did?

Shocked by what he was thinking, he closed his eyes and began to pray. Guilt, coupled with a fear he couldn't name, shook the very core of who he'd imagined himself to be.

"God help me. What have I done?"

Six

Laura turned on the lights as she entered the kitchen, but when she saw the outside door ajar, her hopes fell. Heart pounding, she stared out at the darkness, afraid to go farther and afraid to stay put. Somewhere beyond the safety of these walls, Gabriel moved within a world not of his making. She didn't know how to explain it. She just knew it was so.

In her dream, the danger had been so clear, but now she wasn't so certain. Dreams weren't always cognitive patterns for the future, not even for her. Sometimes they were nothing more than a mixture of hopes and fears. She prayed to God this was one of those times. She was just getting used to the fact that Gabriel would one day make love to her. Accepting the fact that he would also try to kill her was not only frightening, it was impossible to believe. The Gabriel she was coming to know was angry, yes. But he had a right. Those who are left behind when a loved one dies always experienced anger in some form or another. But not many channeled that anger into indiscriminate murder.

The sound of a siren's scream made her jump, and without thinking, she ran to the door, intent on slamming it shut. Then she thought of Gabriel, and her conscience pricked. If she shut the door, she would be shutting him out. Life had already slammed too many doors in his face. She couldn't bring herself to shut another.

She stepped outside, staring into the night as the siren faded in the distance. Where on earth could he be? Was he sleepwalking again, or was something she didn't want to believe, something more sinister, going on?

He'd already told her the roses left with the bodies had been missing their thorns, but the newspaper accounts of the deaths had made no mention of that fact. She didn't know if it was something he had just imagined, or if it was true and the police were withholding it. Denuding the stems of their thorns was something his mother had practiced. Maybe that fact had gotten mixed up with everything else he was experiencing until he believed it was so. And then again, maybe not.

So far, the victims had all died of broken necks,

reportedly from a single blow to the head. Only a person of great size and strength would be able to accomplish such a feat. Gabriel Donner was very tall...and very, very strong.

She shuddered. She couldn't believe, wouldn't let herself believe, that he could be capable of such rage. If he was that kind of man, she would have known...wouldn't she?

Then she sighed. She wouldn't get any answers by second-guessing herself. She lifted her chin and stepped out into the grass.

Dew dampened her feet and the hem of her gown. A faint night breeze molded the fragile lingerie against her skin, outlining her legs, as well as the narrow indentation of her waist.

Her senses heightened as she moved beyond the halo of light spilling from the open doorway. In the dark, everything seemed more pronounced, from the brush of fabric against her body to the cooling breeze on her face. Even the rustling of the leaves sounded like whispers. Secrets. The world was full of secrets.

She moved farther into the darkness, tilting her head to listen—both to the whispers on the wind and the whispers in her mind. A sense of anxiety drew her farther and farther away from the house—

away from safety. She had to find Gabriel, and quickly.

Long minutes went by as she searched the immediate grounds surrounding the house. Although her search came up empty, she refused to panic.

Five minutes became ten. Ten became twenty. She wanted to give up, to go back inside where it was safe, but a sense of urgency prevented her from following her instincts. She continued to search until more than thirty minutes had passed. Just as she was about to give up, she saw him in the distance, and the posture of his body was proof of his despair. On his knees, with his head thrown back and his neck arched in silent agony, he looked to Laura like a man awaiting a death blow from an unseen executioner.

"God help me," she whispered, and started to run.

The grass felt like wet silk between his toes. The air moved across his face like a lover's breath. The scent of roses was thick, drugging his senses and filling his mind with bittersweet memories. Moisture fell onto his cheeks, and he flinched.

Rain?

He opened his eyes to the sky. It was cloudless. Stars dotted the darkness above him, tiny pinpoints of light too far away to illuminate anything but a soul.

There was a knot in his belly and another in the back of his throat, threatening to choke him. That was when he knew it wasn't rain on his face, it was tears. With a groan, he pulled himself upright. As he felt the dampness of the grass beneath his feet, the hopelessness of his situation suddenly struck.

"Ah, damn."

The urge to hide was overwhelming. He turned, intent on going back to the house, then forgot what he'd been thinking.

He thought she was a ghost. With the hem of her nightgown brushing the grass, she seemed to be floating, rather than running, across the grounds. It took a few seconds for him to realize it was Laura and not the ghost he had first believed.

He watched her coming, puzzled by the urgency with which she ran. It wasn't until she came closer and he could see her face that he realized her concern was for him. Touched that she cared enough to come in search of him, his eyes suddenly burned with fresh tears.

At that point, emotion hit. Hard. Fast.

Remembering the death he'd just witnessed, his hands curled into fists. He drew a deep, shuddering breath, fighting a sudden need to feel life, to re-member that he was alive. He wanted to take her in his arms and make love to her. Over and over. Without promises. Without regrets.

She was closer now. So close that he could see the motion of her body beneath her gown, the bounce of her breasts, the flat of her belly. He no longer saw her as the psychic who'd come to lay blame but as the beautiful woman she really was.

Yet there was an obstacle between them that he couldn't ignore. No matter what she was willing to offer him, she was little more than a stranger.

His heart began pounding, his muscles tensing. He tried to call out to her. To warn her to go back, because right now he needed more from her than she had come here to give. But hesitation cost him. Within one heartbeat and the next, she was reach-ing for him.

"Gabriel?"

He heard fear in her voice. It cooled the fire in his blood in a way nothing else could have. He and fear were on an intimate basis. The last thing he would willingly do was pass it on to a fellow hu-man being. Again he thought of his dream—of the man at the door and the dog that had been silenced forever—and wondered if he was kidding himself. Unless he was terribly wrong, there was every possibility that he'd already passed on more than fear. God help him, but the man at the door had been Sadie Husser's houseman, Stevie, and Stevie had recognized his killer. He'd called him by name. He'd called him Gabriel.

He looked into her face and just for a moment pictured it broken and lifeless, like that of the man in his dream. Just the mere thought of causing her harm made him sick with fear. Seconds later, his fear turned to anger, both for her and himself.

"What the hell are you doing out here?"

Laura froze. The anger in his voice startled her. Every rational thought she had told her to turn and run, but her instincts held her fast. She stared into the shadows, intently searching what she could see of his face, needing more than the tone of his voice before she would let herself panic.

"Looking for you."

"And now you found me," he growled

She took a step forward.

"Be careful," he warned.

"Of what? Of you?" She grabbed him by the hand. "First you wanted my help and now you want me to leave. What are you afraid of, Gabriel?"

He slid out of her grasp and then took her by the shoulders, moving them both until they were out of the shadows of the trees and standing fully beneath the glow of a three-quarter moon.

"I'm not the one who should be afraid," he said harshly, all but shaking her to make her understand. "You're the one treading on unfamiliar ground. You don't know me." His laugh was a bitter expletive of sound. "I don't even know myself."

But Laura wouldn't budge. "Then let me see where you live," she said softly, touching first his heart, then his head. "Will you trust me enough to let me come in?"

Her question took him aback, and as the meaning of it finally sank in, his first reaction was to refuse. Then he thought, what the hell? The way he figured, he was already damned. Having it confirmed might actually be a relief.

"How?"

She took him by the hand, urging him toward a nearby bench at the perimeter of one of the rose gardens. He complied. Not because he trusted her, as she'd asked, but because he was tired of fighting.

Laura pushed him down and then sat beside him.

"Don't you think we should be doing this inside?" he asked.

Her voice wrapped around him like silk, soft but

binding. ''Darkness gives its own measure of anonymity,'' she said.

He frowned. She was right. He felt somewhat easier just knowing that she couldn't clearly see his face.

''What do I do?'' he asked.

''Just sit. The rest is up to me. Now give me your hand.''

He did as she asked, but when she lifted his hand to the side of her own face, his heart skipped a beat.

''What are you—''

''Trust,'' she said softly. ''It's all about trust. You must relax. Don't concentrate on anything but the sound of the wind in the trees and the grass beneath your feet.''

''I hope you know what you're doing,'' he muttered.

She didn't respond but merely shook her head, clasping both his hands and then holding them as she would have held an injured bird, cradled against her breast. When he settled, she took a deep breath and closed her eyes.

Her touch was light, her fingers small in comparison to the size of his own, but Gabriel could no more have torn himself away than he could have stopped his own heartbeat. Her head was tilted slightly toward the moon, as if searching for light by which to see, but her eyes were closed. It was a staggering thought to know she needed no light to see truth. At least not now. Not this time. Not when the place she was looking was inside him.

As he stared at her face and the intensity with which she seemed to be focusing, he caught himself holding his breath. He relaxed, exhaling on a shiver.

Although she didn't look up, she shook her head, as if remonstrating him to silence.

For Gabriel, it was almost impossible. He forced himself to focus on her frown, then the shape of her face, then her lips. When his gaze fell below the level of her chin and began measuring the fullness of her breasts and imagining what their weight would feel like in the palms of his hands, he suddenly flinched. Had she *seen* what he was thinking? If she had, what would she do if he acted upon the thought?

In that moment, his defenses went down and Laura Dane slipped into his mind.

To Laura, the union of one mind with another was a little like flying. There was the sensation of weightlessness, coupled with the intimacy of having been separated from earth. She let herself go,

accepting the images that came to her without trying for identification, knowing that the time for that
would come later.

*The blur of a woman's face. Her soft gasp as a
man's hand moves upon her breast, touching, then
caressing. Roses spilled upon the ground...
no...upon a grave. A barking dog.*

Laura stiffened. The images she was receiving
went almost immediately from sensual to sinister.
It was like standing in a doorway and looking into
a room, then past that room into the room beyond—one room light and beautiful, the second
dark and threatening. The urge to stop was strong,
but for Gabriel's sake she stayed, determined to
see as far as he would let her go.

Once more she focused, letting herself move
past the obvious to what was hidden within his
thoughts.

*Fear...no...pain. Terrible, terrible pain. A
stranger's face. Smiling...then questioning...then
dead.*

Silence. Blessed silence.

She moaned, unintentionally tightening her grip
on Gabriel's hands.

As he watched the changing expressions on her
face, his eyes narrowed thoughtfully. Either she
was damned good at pretending or—

Get out!

Both Gabriel and Laura jerked. The intrusion of the second voice into Gabriel's head startled him as much as it did her.

She blinked and then swayed where she sat, staring at him in quick confusion as he tore away from her grasp and stood.

"That wasn't me," Gabriel said harshly, and walked away.

She followed him, running to catch up.

"Wait!" she begged.

He spun. "Wait for what? People are dying! I can't live with this anymore. I'm going to the police in the morning."

She grabbed him by the arm. "And what are you going to tell them?"

The words were there in the back of his mind, but they wouldn't come out. Twice he tried to form his thoughts, and both times he failed. He hit his leg with his fist in frustration.

"Hell if I know. But I can't just sit back and let these people keep dying when I may be responsible."

Laura froze. For a moment, words failed her. She could tell by the look on Gabriel's face that there was something more. Something he hadn't told her.

"What are you saying?" she whispered.

He took a deep breath. "The man in the dream…the one I saw die tonight."

"Yes?"

"He knew his killer."

Laura's eyes widened, and she reached for Gabriel's hand. "That's wonderful…and you're right. This *is* something we can take to the police."

But Gabriel didn't seem elated.

"What?" Laura asked. "And don't tell me it's nothing. I can tell by the look on your face that you're not telling me everything."

Again he started to turn away, but Laura refused to let him go.

"Please, Gabriel, don't. Talk to me. I can't help you if you aren't honest with me."

He stared down at her in the darkness. Her face was little more than a series of shapes and shadows, and yet he could sense the intensity of her stare. He could hear her trying to catch her breath. Her hand was gentle upon his arm, yet he felt as if he were bound by iron chains.

Laura persisted. "Gabriel, what is it you aren't saying?"

"Before he died, he called the killer by name."

Moments passed. Laura caught herself holding her breath.

The words tasted bitter on his lips, and he spit them out in haste.

"He called him Gabriel. In my dream, the killer was me."

Kirby Summers squatted beside Sam Whitehall, the medical examiner, as he went about collecting evidence on the body of the most recent victim.

"So, Sam, what do you think?" he asked.

"I think he's dead," Sam said, without looking up from what he was doing.

Kirby snorted beneath his breath. "Your sense of humor leaves much to be desired."

Whitehall shrugged. "Sorry. When *I* know something, *you'll* know something."

"Good enough," Kirby answered, and then stood and stepped back, staring intently at the crime scene, which, oddly enough, included the carcass of a small dog. Although some things were different about this scene as opposed to the others, he knew the murder had been committed by the same man.

Once again a rose had been left with the body. But in this case, the rose was also one of the differences. The rose was devoid of petals and looked as if it had simply been discarded. There was a trail of petals from a nearby tree. Proof of where the killer had stood, obviously watching the house.

He frowned as he continued to gaze about the area, trying to picture what the killer had seen. What in hell was the killer looking for? He didn't steal. He didn't vandalize. He just killed. And not with a gun or a knife. According to the medical examiner, the perp used his fists, and yet not one victim had been beaten to death. Death had come from a single blow to the head.

Sudden.

Instantaneous.

Final.

In an uncharacteristic gesture of frustration, Kirby stuffed his notebook in his pocket and kicked at a small rock with the toe of his shoe.

"Well, hell," he muttered.

"My sentiments exactly," Ray Bush said.

Kirby turned, nodding his greeting to the homicide detective.

"Good morning, sir," Ray said.

One more time, Kirby glanced toward the body on the ground. "Not for him, it isn't."

Ray nodded. "Same M.O. as before."

Kirby shrugged. "Yes and no."

Ray looked surprised. "How so? Do you think we've got ourselves a copycat?"

Kirby shook his head. "No. It's the same man all right, but something feels different about this one. There's the dog. Why kill this dog and not the one with the man in the park? And the rose. This one wasn't lying on the body like the others."

"Maybe it blew off in the night," Ray offered.

"I don't think so," Kirby said. "Besides, all the petals are missing. This one looks as if it were simply discarded."

Ray frowned thoughtfully. "I see what you mean." And then he grinned wryly. "Sort of like the last bunch of flowers I tried to send to my wife when I forgot our anniversary. They wound up in the trash."

Kirby pivoted, his face alight. "That's it! That's what I've been feeling but couldn't put it in words. The killer was angry with this man. He wasn't asking for forgiveness by leaving behind a rose. In fact, after he broke this man's neck, he continued to show his disdain by leaving a rose that was no longer of use to him."

Ray's eyebrows rose as he looked back at the scene. "Damned if I don't think you're right."

Whitehall suddenly stood, motioning for his assistants. "Bag him," he ordered as he stripped off his surgical gloves and stuffed them in his pocket.

Kirby turned. "Well?"

"Best estimate...he died around midnight, and although I'm no vet, I'd guess so did the dog. But we may have gotten lucky on this one. There's blood and tissue beneath the victim's fingernails. I'm guessing they don't belong to him."

Kirby's pulse shifted gears, suddenly flushing his neck and face with a quick surge of new blood.

"I want a copy of this report on my desk before morning."

Whitehall rolled his eyes. "Damn, Summers. That's the fourth time I've heard that request this morning. I've got news for you. There was a killing down on Reno. A gang-related shooting over on Twenty-third, and some farmer out feeding his calves found a decomposing body in a road ditch between here and Edmond. You'll get the report when I can get to it and not before."

Kirby wanted to argue, but common sense told him not to piss off the M.E.

"Sorry, but you know how it is. The press is playing this for all it's worth. The mayor is nervous, so he's breathing down everyone's neck, which in turn makes everyone else as nervous as hell."

Whitehall nodded. "I'll be in touch," he said, and walked away.

At that moment Kirby noticed an old woman a

distance away, standing at the corner of the house. Her expression was pale and stricken, her gaze constantly straying to the place where her loved ones had lain.

"Who's that?" Kirby asked.

"The owner of the property. The man who died was her houseman. The dog was hers, too."

Kirby checked his notes. "I didn't get her name."

Ray sighed as he watched the old woman turn and disappear into the home.

"That's Sadie Husser," he said.

Startled, Kirby glanced up. "The first lady of Oklahoma City herself?"

Ray nodded.

Kirby's eyes narrowed. "How's she taking this?"

"Just about like you'd expect," Ray said, then added, "And it's the damnedest thing. Only yesterday she had contacted a security business to have an alarm system installed."

Kirby shrugged. "Sometimes it happens that way."

Ray Bush took a pristine white handkerchief from the hip pocket of his slacks and wiped the sweat from his face, then looked at his watch.

"Man. We got the call on this a little after five, and it's almost nine. I haven't had breakfast yet."

"Me, either," Kirby said.

"Then let's make a run on McDonald's."

Kirby made a face.

"I'm buying," Ray added.

A rare grin broke the somberness of Kirby's expression. "I changed my mind."

Ray rolled his eyes. "Why am I not surprised?"

Gabriel hung up the phone just as Matty announced Mike Travers' arrival.

"I'm sorry," Mike said. "I didn't know you were busy."

Gabriel picked up his glass of iced tea and took a long drink, not trusting himself to answer right away. For him, the tea had no taste, but it was wet. He drained it right down to the cubes.

"I'm not anymore," he said shortly. "That was Sadie Husser. She just canceled her contract to have a security system installed, and I can't say as I blame her."

Mike knew he was missing something, but he couldn't figure out what.

"What do you mean?" he asked.

Gabriel clutched the empty glass until his knuckles turned white, but the expression on his face never changed.

"Last night, while she was sound asleep in an upstairs wing, someone killed her houseman and her dog. She's so rattled about the incident, she says she's selling her home and moving to Europe."

"That's too bad," Mike said. "I've met her on more than one occasion. She's a grand old lady."

An image flashed in Gabriel's mind—of her slow smile, her obvious tolerance for Stevie's wit and her pleasure in her little dog. Suddenly it was more than he could take. He turned and flung the glass, ice cubes and all, into the open fireplace. Glass shattered, and ice cubes scattered.

Mike jumped as if he'd been shot. "Gabriel! What on earth did you—"

Gabriel pivoted. "If I had died in that wreck, too, none of this would be happening."

"You're wrong!" Mike said. "Just because you claim to be *seeing* these incidents, that doesn't make you responsible."

Gabriel shook his head. "Yesterday morning I might have agreed with you, but not now."

There was so much pain on Gabriel's face that Mike wanted to cry. He reached for him, wanting to hold him, needing to let him know that there were people in his life who still cared, but Gabriel moved away.

"Please, son. I can't help you if you won't talk to me. Tell me what's wrong. What is it today that's so different from yesterday?"

But Gabriel wouldn't answer, and Mike didn't know what to do. At that point Laura entered the room. Mike could tell from the look on her face that she'd heard most, if not all, of what was going on. However, she seemed bent on ignoring Gabriel's presence.

"Good morning, Dr. Travers."

Mike sighed. It was everything *but* a good morning.

"Laura."

"Thank you for coming," she said softly.

He nodded.

Gabriel spun. "So *you're* the reason he's here. I might have known."

He would have stalked out, but Laura stepped in front of him, almost daring him to push her aside. He stopped, only inches away, and as they stared into each other's eyes, Laura could feel the heat of his breath upon her face. She tilted her chin at a determined slant and met his gaze with a straightforward glare.

"Someone has to talk some sense into you. You

wouldn't listen to me. I thought maybe you would listen to your uncle Mike.''

Mike was frustrated and feeling every one of his sixty-seven years as he thrust a hand through his gray and thinning hair.

''Will someone please explain what this is all about?'' he asked.

She looked Gabriel straight in the eyes. ''Will it be me, or do you want to do the honors?''

''You started this,'' he said, turning his back on them both. ''Feel free.''

Laura's voice softened. ''I didn't start anything, Gabriel, and you know it. But I came to offer help in any way I know how, yet every time I try, you shut me out.''

The anger went out of him all at once. When he turned, there was a droop to his shoulders that hadn't been there before, and the tone of his voice was so quiet that Mike had to strain to hear what he said.

''Can you blame me?'' he asked.

There was so much sadness in his eyes, so much defeat in his posture, that Laura wanted to hold him. But she stayed her ground, aware that what had to be said must come from him.

Gabriel shuddered, then wiped a shaky hand across his face as he turned to Mike.

"Last night, something new was added to my dreams."

Mike didn't move, but he could tell by the way Gabriel was talking that it wasn't going to be good.

"I'm listening," he said.

"The murder victim knew his killer."

Mike frowned. "Then that would mean you could go to the police, maybe give them a description—at the least a name. Why is this not good news?"

"Because, in my dream, the killer was me."

Seven

It was Mike Travers who came up with the plan. All they had to do was just lock Gabriel in his room each night. If and when another incident occurred, Laura would be witness to the fact that Gabriel had not left his room and that in no way could he have committed the crime. It was a crude and drastic move, but Gabriel's sanity was riding on its success.

Laura was more than a little troubled by what they were about to do. At first she'd been shocked by Mike's suggestion and had argued vehemently against it, reminding them that the house was wired with a state-of-the-art security system, which Gabriel still managed to bypass. And then Gabriel stated the obvious.

"The lock will be on the outside of my door."

"That's dangerous," she argued. "What if there's a fire or a—"

Gabriel's eyes narrowed angrily. "Damn it,

Laura. People are dying! If I'm responsible, then I hope to God I *do* burn."

Mike felt obligated to intervene before they could come to blows.

"I think you're both being a bit overdramatic," he said quietly. "It's not like it will be forever. It's only until Gabriel is confident that he's innocent, which I firmly believe he is."

Gabriel glared at Laura while she chewed on the edge of her lip.

"Well?" Mike asked.

Laura shrugged. "Fine."

Gabriel relaxed. "I'm going to the hardware store to buy a padlock. Anybody want to come with me?"

Laura turned without saying a word and stalked out of the room.

There was a thoughtful expression on Gabriel's face as he watched her go.

"I'd say that was a no," he drawled.

Mike scratched at the bald spot on the back of his head and smiled.

"She's quite a lady, isn't she, boy?"

Gabriel grabbed his keys from the desk and headed for the door. He didn't want to talk about his feelings for Laura, even though they occupied a good deal of his conscious mind.

"You coming?" he asked, giving Mike a considering look.

"Oh, I don't know. Maybe I'd better—"

"I'm stopping at Braum's to get ice cream on the way back."

"You talked me into it," Mike said.

Gabriel put his arm around the old man's shoulder.

"When it comes to fudge ripple, you're a pushover, and you know it."

Dinner that night was more like a wake than a meal. Mike had done his best to keep a civil conversation going, but it seemed to be a lost cause. Gabriel had little to say to Laura, and she had even less to say to him. But Mike was beginning to believe that the strain between them had nothing to do with locking Gabriel inside his room. He'd seen the way Laura looked at Gabriel when she thought he wasn't watching. And he'd caught Gabriel stealing glances at Laura off and on all night. Their lack of conversation had nothing to do with animosity and everything to do with a growing attraction they were trying to ignore.

As soon as it was decent, he made his excuses and bade them good-night. Laura followed the men into the hallway, escaping up the stairs before either one could object. Gabriel watched her go without comment, but Mike could tell by the look on Gabriel's face that his mind was not on the business at hand. In his own opinion, this day was long overdue. It was about time Gabriel Donner invested something of himself into a personal life.

The thought made Mike smile all the way home.

The clock in the upstairs hallway was striking eleven when Gabriel knocked on Laura's door.

"Come in," she called, then watched the door swing inward, her eyes widening with apprehension.

It was Gabriel. Right on time. He dangled a key and a lock in the air.

"I'm heading to bed. Come do your duty."

The skin crawled on the back of Laura's neck, but she did as he asked.

They walked side by side toward his bedroom without speaking. Each locked into their own thoughts. Each struggling to come to terms with a growing attraction to the other that neither could afford.

Laura's hair was still damp from her shower. Wisps of short curls stuck fast to her forehead and the sides of her cheeks. Gabriel wanted to touch them, to see if they were as soft as they looked.

Her bathrobe was belted loosely, revealing far too much of the dainty pink gown beneath for his peace of mind. His fascination with this woman was increasing on a daily basis. He alternated between admiration for her gutsy attitude and a growing desire to explore the woman she was.

She walked with her head held high and a slight swagger to her steps, like a woman who was sure of her place in the world. Once Gabriel had been the same way. He wanted that life back and was willing to do anything it took to reclaim it. Even to the point of being locked up each night like a criminal, which he feared himself to be.

But Laura was still ambivalent about the whole idea and felt compelled to speak her mind one more time. She paused in the middle of the hallway near a recessed light, unaware that the glow had cast a halo around her head, or that Gabriel seemed stunned by her sudden angelic appearance.

"Gabriel, please reconsider. What if the house catches on fire? You would be locked inside your room with no way of getting out."

He knew she was upset, but it was all he could do to tear his gaze away from the light in which she stood. It was only after he felt the touch of her hand on his arm that he was able to answer.

"You would call the fire department and then come let me out," he said.

She persisted. "What if something happens and I can't get to you? What if—"

The halo seemed to be spreading, like a white-hot fire, enveloping her head and shoulders. He needed to touch her, wondered if it would burn him if he did. But he didn't move.

"And what if nothing happens? Or what if it does and you *do* get to me?" he countered.

She took a step forward, and as she did, the halo seemed to engulf her whole body, leaving her framed from head to foot in the light.

"But what if—"

He couldn't breathe, couldn't swallow. Suddenly the urge to fall into her fire and let himself be consumed was too strong to deny. He took her by the shoulders and pulled her close, then closer still, until their lips were separated by little more than a breath.

"What if I kiss you—right now—before you have time to slap my face?"

Someone gasped. Laura thought it was herself that she heard. But after his mouth had descended and their breaths, then their lips, had merged, she wasn't so sure. After that, the thought of answering him had been impossible...and unnecessary. It could have been his swift intake of breath that she'd heard, or the groan that had ripped up his throat as she willingly returned the kiss.

Finally one of them had taken a slow step back. She didn't remember who had made the first move, but it must have been her. Surely she had better sense than to get mixed up with this man and his problems.

Surely.

Gabriel was torn between what he wanted and what he knew he should do. The last thing he wanted was to let her go, but right now, he had no choice.

"Laura, I—"

"Don't say a word," she muttered, then opened the door to his room and almost pushed him inside. "Don't you dare ruin what just happened with some pissant apology that will make me sorry I ever set foot in this house. Right now, I don't want to hear anything out of your mouth but good night."

Gabriel stood without moving, watching the expression on her face as she closed the door between them. Only after he heard the padlock snapping in place did he punctuate her last remark.

"Laura..."

She paused in the hallway. His voice was soft,

just above a whisper, but she heard it all the same. "What?"

"Good night," he said.

She splayed her hand on the door, as if by wish alone she could still touch him.

"Yes, good night." Then, loath to break the tenuous tie between them, she added. "Sleep well."

She was almost out of earshot when she heard him call out to her again.

"Laura."

She sighed. He wasn't making this easy for either one of them, and she suspected that he knew it. She turned and walked a few feet back to his door.

"What?"

The taste of her was still on his lips. He closed his eyes and leaned his forehead against the door.

"We're not finished with that."

"Not finished with what?"

"With that kiss," he whispered.

Her cheeks flamed, and her knees went weak, but Gabriel couldn't see her reaction. All he could hear was a surprising acceptance in her voice.

"I know."

It wasn't until later that it dawned on him to wonder what else she might know, but it was too late to ask. She was already gone.

* * *

Three days later, the peculiarity of their lives had become routine. She was now his jailer. And for a while the dreams were absent and the recurring voice he'd heard was blessedly silent. Gabriel was starting to believe the past few weeks had been nothing more than an aberration caused by his injuries. He went to work each day and came home with a smile. He was beginning to relax. He was beginning to believe that what had been happening had been nothing more than his mind playing games.

On the night of the fourth day, someone changed all the rules...again.

He glanced at the sky with apprehension. The sun was going down. It would soon be dark. He was afraid of the dark.

His stomach grumbled, and he frowned. He was hungry again. He had never been hungry before. At least, not before he got lost. He was so tired of being lost.

He scratched his face, uncomfortable with the days' old growth of whiskers. They were sharp and prickly. He should find a razor. Mother didn't like prickly things. He looked down at the roses in his hands and nodded to himself with satisfaction.

They wouldn't hurt her. The thorns were already removed.

He stepped out of the alley in which he'd been hiding and started walking down the street. Even though it was all but deserted now, he was still uncomfortable. Yet in spite of his fears, he kept on walking. The inner magnet guiding him toward home was getting stronger, but his patience was growing thin. The desire to feel his mother's kiss upon his brow and to see her gentle smile was almost more than he could bear. Added to that, the roses he'd taken days ago were falling apart in his hands. He didn't know what to do. Mother loved roses. He needed his mother.

He glanced down at the flowers, his frown deepening. These flowers were no good anymore. He had to find some new ones. Maybe he would find some tonight.

The faint glow of a security light shone through the curtains at Gabriel's window, casting a dim slice of white on the pale blue carpet. The jeans he'd been wearing earlier were hanging over the back of a chair. One tennis shoe was under the chair, the other one upside down beside a nearby table. The book he'd been reading was on the floor next to his bed. He'd used a sock to mark his place before casting it aside.

He slept on his belly with one arm over his head and the other pillowing his face, still dressed in the gym shorts he'd pulled on after his shower. It was a calm, unremarkable scene.

Four doors down the hall on the right, the glow of the security light wasn't visible. Except for a butterfly night-light in the adjoining bath, the room was in darkness. Everything was in its proper place, including the woman asleep in the bed.

Laura lay curled on her side, hugging a pillow. She hadn't moved in hours. Her robe was folded neatly and hanging over the back of a chair. The soulful sound of a country music station was playing softly in the background from a radio she'd been listening to when she'd fallen asleep. Her body was at rest, her mind at peace.

In spite of the distance between them, the crash that came echoing down the hall was as startling and abrupt as if it had sounded right next to Laura's bed.

She was awake within seconds and running for the door. Even before it happened again, she knew what she'd heard.

It was Gabriel.

He was trying to get out.

* * *

The shriek of the train whistle coincided with the fat woman's scream. Backed into the alley near the Dumpster where she had been rummaging for cans, there was nowhere left for Bella Cruz to run.

It was a terrible thing to look into the eyes of a killer and see nothing but your own reflection, but that was what she saw. Moments later, there was little to mark his passing but a handful of dead roses that he'd left in the crook of Bella's arm.

There in the darkness, with nothing but a single burning lightbulb above the back door of a closed bar to light the way, the old woman's body seemed serene in repose.

She lay on her back, cradling the limp and shedding roses as she might have a child. The felt hat she'd been wearing now pillowed her head. In the daylight, her stained and tattered dress would have been looked upon with disdain, but here in the shadows, the damage to the woman and her clothes was subdued.

A couple of blocks over, a policeman in a cruiser briefly hit his siren and lights before pulling over a speeding car. It was nothing unusual for this time of night in this part of town. Several stories above the alley where the old woman lay, the angry sound of a couple fighting could be heard spilling out an open window. But the sounds of the train were long since gone, just like the man who had ended Bella Cruz's life.

Laura reached Gabriel's door just as another crash sounded inside the room.

Her hands were shaking as she jammed the key into the lock and gave it a quick turn. When the padlock came loose in her hands, she let it fall to the floor as she darted inside.

He was standing at the windows with both arms raised. Within the seconds it took for her brain to comprehend what he was about to do, she had dashed across the room and grabbed at his wrists, swinging on them with all her weight. Panic flooded her body, along with a surge of badly needed adrenaline, and still it was barely enough to keep Gabriel from flinging himself through the window.

She kept screaming his name in desperation, trying without success to wake him. He struggled against the weight of her body and Laura knew it was only a matter of time before his superior strength put them both in danger. With only seconds of her own strength left, she gave it one last try. Wrapping her arms around his waist and then locking her hands together, she fell backward. The unexpected move caught Gabriel off balance. Together, they fell to the floor with a thud.

Lost between what he'd been dreaming and the fact that he'd woken up on the floor, Gabriel's reaction was instinctive. He rolled, pinning Laura beneath him. It wasn't until he heard her soft groan that he realized what he'd just done. He bolted up within seconds of cognizance, pulling her up with him.

"My God!" he muttered. "What the hell just happened?" He turned on a lamp and dragged her closer toward the light. "Are you all right?" Just the thought that he could have caused her harm made him sick. He cupped her cheek with the palm of his hand. "Talk to me, Laura! Did I hurt you? Are you all right?"

She splayed a hand across the middle of her belly and drew a slow, painful breath.

"I'm fine...I think."

Gabriel dropped to the side of the bed, taking her with him.

"Sweet Jesus," he muttered, and buried his face in the curve of her neck. "Don't ever do that again."

His breath was ragged against her skin, his pulse hammering beneath her fingertips. She laid her cheek against the springy texture of his thick black hair and closed her eyes. That had been close—too close.

A minute passed. Sixty seconds of time for Gabriel to contemplate the scent of her shampoo, the thrust of her breasts against his chest and the erratic beat of her heart. Again, he'd watched someone die. He was so very, very sick of death. The need to feel life—and to feel alive—was overwhelming. He wanted to experience the inescapable surge of passion between man and woman and then lie replete in her arms.

He lifted his head.

Laura sensed his change of mood. It had gone from panic to passion so swiftly that it scared her. There was no escaping what she saw in his eyes. She'd seen it before, in a vision, on the day they'd met.

She sighed, and it was a gesture of relief and also of acceptance. Acceptance of what he offered. Acceptance of her fate.

He put a hand on her shoulder.

She cupped the side of his cheek.

He traced the shape of her with his gaze, from the tousled curls framing her face to the imprint of her body beneath the thin fabric of her gown.

She whispered his name.

He pushed her backward onto the bed and hooked his finger in the top of her gown.

She heard it rip and closed her eyes as a surge of longing hit her deep in the belly.

He straddled her legs and leaned down, bracing himself above her with a hand on either side of her head. His voice was ragged, thick with an emotion he couldn't control.

"Look at me."

Calmed by the inevitability of this moment, she did as he asked.

His manhood was thick and hard, surging against the inside of her leg as he struggled with the words that had to be said.

"All you have to do is say no."

"I can't," she whispered. "It's too late."

His arms were shaking as he lowered himself upon her. "I don't want to know what that means," he said. And he kissed her.

After that, reason blurred. There were moments of sanity when she could feel his hands in her hair and on her body, when she could think to savor the wild tenderness of his kisses. And then it would fade into an all-consuming emotion as she was swept away by this man's passion.

For as long as Gabriel could remember, there had been an emptiness within him that he couldn't identify. But no more. When he'd taken her, a belonging had filled his heart. The sensation of being one with this woman was blinding in its intensity. He didn't want it to end. Yet with each stroke of his body, the inevitability of that happening became more and more impossible to deny.

Her breath scattered against his face; sometimes sweet sighs, sometimes short gasps, always urgent. Her hands were soft against his back. Her legs were wrapped around his waist. And still it was not enough. He needed more. He wanted to be deeper inside. He wanted her—

Suddenly she dug her fingers into his back and arched. At that point, thought ended. Her climax shattered around him, and he lost control, spilling himself into her depths in one blinding wave after another until there was nothing left but the aftershock of what had been a true and frightening passion.

Afraid to let go for fear one of them—maybe her, maybe him—might disappear, he collapsed with a groan, then rolled with her still in his arms, pulling up the covers and sheltering her with his body.

He could feel her shaking, even heard the catch in her breath. And when he brushed a kiss across the crest of her brow, he tasted the salt-sweat of her body.

Before he'd known only her name.

Laura.

Now he knew the woman she was.

His.

Startled by the ferocity of that feeling, he tightened his grip, and a quiet silence came upon them.

She doesn't belong.

The voice came out of nowhere. Gabriel felt Laura start, which told him that she'd heard it, too.

"Shh," he whispered, gentling her with a sweep of his hand across her brow.

Only after he felt her relaxing did he let himself answer the voice, and for once, he reacted with reason, not fear.

You're wrong. She does belong. She belongs to me.

Just before morning, Laura started to dream. At first it was nothing more than a replay of the lovemaking that she and Gabriel had shared, beginning with the instant when she'd pulled him away from the window. She shuddered. Unbeknownst to her, Gabriel sensed her unrest. Thinking she was chilled, he pulled the covers up over her shoulders, then held her close, cradling her against the warmth of his body. When it seemed as if she had settled, he relaxed. A few minutes later, he'd fallen back to sleep with Laura still in his arms—still lost in her dream.

A short while later her breathing pattern changed, and a frown furrowed her forehead. The dream was shifting, changing from what had really happened to something different—something ugly and deadly.

Gabriel was coming toward her with arms outstretched. There was a terrible fear on his face, and she sensed it was for her. He was saying something to her that she couldn't understand, but she sensed it was a warning. She tried to run, but her legs wouldn't move. And then, right before her eyes, he began to change. The love in his eyes disappeared, and the warning he'd been trying to give turned to rage. She felt herself falling, falling, deeper and deeper into the eternal silence of death.

She sat up with a jerk, dislodging Gabriel's arm from around her waist and sending the covers onto the floor as she turned to stare at him in disbelief. That wasn't real. It couldn't be real. She wouldn't let it be a portent of things to come.

Gabriel woke suddenly.

"Laura, what's wrong?" he asked.

When she covered her face, a knot began to

form in the pit of his stomach. From the way she was behaving, it had to do with him. This wasn't the morning after that he'd imagined. He began rubbing her back, then her shoulder, hoping to ease her fears.

"Can you talk about it?"

She shook her head.

He almost smiled. This morning, without makeup and with the tousled curls, she looked far younger than her years. But all he had to do was remember the passion with which they'd made love and he knew good and well Laura Dane was old enough for anything he wanted to give. He frowned, tossing her own words back in her face.

"I can't help you if you aren't willing to let me."

A low moan slid out between her teeth as she turned and threw her arms around his neck.

"Oh, God," she whispered, savoring the feel of his arms as they settled around her, taking courage from his strength, as well as his gentleness.

"Laura...baby, please talk to me."

She took her hands and placed them on his face, feeling each feature as a blind person might *see* another, telling herself that she knew this man, that he would never do to her what she'd seen in her dream. And even as she was doing so, her mind was racing, trying to map out a plan that would stop the inevitable from happening.

When he turned his head and kissed the palm of her hand, her heart dropped.

She was wrong. Dear God, she had to be wrong.

"Make love to me," she whispered.

His eyes glittered darkly as he rolled, pinning her beneath him on the bed with his great strength.

"It would be my everlasting pleasure," he said softly, and began to do as she'd asked.

For a while, time stopped. There was nothing in her world but this man and the way he could make her feel. The climax came suddenly, breaking what was left of her apart in tiny pieces and then scattering the pieces within her heart for sanity to reassemble.

In the midst of the joy—in the midst of the beauty of their love—the thought returned.

And when it came to her visions, she was never wrong.

Kirby Summers sat at his desk, staring at the pictures before him, trying to find a connection between the discovery of Prince Charming's latest victim and the others he'd left in his wake. Bella Cruz, his latest victim, had been a sixty-eight-year-old homeless woman. His first victim, a twenty-seven-year-old prostitute, had lived on skid row. There was the fact that they were both females who'd ended up on the wrong side of the tracks. But the difference in their ages was drastic.

Then there was the second victim. He didn't fit into any category. A middle-aged married man out looking for his wife's lost dog, who had died with his own dog whistle in the back of his throat. The third victim, a gay male, had died in the doorway of Sadie Husser's home with the carcass of the family pet beside him.

As far as he could see, the only connections between any of the victims were those damned roses the killer left behind. The only clues they had to his identity were blood and tissue samples, and until they had a suspect to match them to, they weren't going to help. Nothing made sense. Why had the victims died? What was it that set the killer off?

Finally Kirby tossed his pen on the desk and laid the file on top of the others. Pressure was mounting on all sides. They needed a break in this case, and they needed it now. Four deaths in less than two weeks. Four random acts of violence, with four acts of contrition left behind as penance. He kicked back in his chair and closed his eyes. Roses without thorns. What the hell did that mean?

* * *

Mike Travers rang the doorbell, then stood on the doorstep, waiting for Matty to let him in. The call he'd gotten from Laura this morning had been brief but revealing. According to the news, Prince Charming had left another victim in his wake, but it could not have been Gabriel. She knew because she'd been at his side through the entire night.

She hadn't elaborated further, and he didn't intend to ask. What mattered most was getting Gabriel back up to par, and if Mike gained a niece along the way, then better yet.

Eight

The elation Gabriel felt in knowing he was innocent of murder was only slightly less startling to him than the realization that he'd fallen in love with Laura Dane. It didn't make much sense.

He'd known her for less than two weeks.

Her touch made him weak.

Her claim to be psychic was still foreign to his beliefs.

Her kisses made him whole.

She lived in New Mexico.

Her laughter was a balm to his crippled heart.

His home was in Oklahoma.

And last night he had lost his mind in her arms in a way he would never have believed possible. They had connected on a level beyond passion. It was only after she'd come apart in his arms that he'd regained any sense of himself. In a way it had been frightening, but on another level, it had been the most overwhelming bond he'd ever known.

At least one good thing had come out of this hell. He'd found Laura Dane—or she'd found him. Either way, he was no longer alone.

As far as dealing with the voice, he was learning how to cope. It was simply a matter of tuning it out. But he didn't know how to tune out the dreams. Watching murder in progress was a hell he wouldn't wish on anyone. And, if he was truly experiencing psychic phenomena as Laura and Uncle Mike believed, then he felt obligated to tell the police. He didn't know how or if it would help their investigation, but he was sure it would help him, if for no other reason than to alleviate the distant guilt of being a voyeur to death.

They were all going out to dinner tonight. He would bring up the subject of contacting the police again. But right now, if he didn't hurry, he was going to be late for a consultation with a new client, and he was taking Laura with him.

"Last week I get robbed. Second time in three months. Windows old. Walls thin. I want first-rate security system. Silent alarm. Whole thing. You can do?"

Gabriel listened as the tiny Oriental man continued to pace back and forth behind the counter of his restaurant, Wok on Inn. He sympathized with the owner, but the restaurant's problem wasn't in the design of the building. It was in the location.

"I'll do what I can, Mr. Loo, but you have to realize that your location is a large part of the problem."

"I know. I know. Soon I get enough money to relocate. You help me?"

Gabriel nodded. "I can help you."

"Good, good. You come back to my office. We talk."

Gabriel glanced at Laura, who had remained silent ever since their arrival. "Laura?"

Startled by the sound of her own name, she blinked. "What?"

Gabriel frowned as he touched the side of her face. "We're going back to his office to sign some papers. Are you all right?"

"I'm fine," she said quickly.

But she wasn't. From the moment she'd set foot in the restaurant, she'd sensed a feeling of impending danger.

"We won't be long," Gabriel said.

"She have tea. Maybe egg flower soup. I order. My treat," Henry Loo said, but Laura stopped him.

"No, please," she said, intending to thank him. But the longer her fingers stayed on his arm, the more his face began to blur.

Unaware that her gaze had gone blank, or that her grip was tightening with every passing second, she continued to stare past him into the scene in her mind.

Piercing screams…no, not screams…the intermittent shriek of a car alarm.

A dark figure moved out of the shadows…the glow of the streetlight slashed across a face—a very dear, very familiar face.

Laura froze, unaware that Gabriel was talking to her, or that he was trying to free her hand from the little man's arm.

Another figure appeared, a small Oriental man, moving toward the car and the constantly sounding alarm. It was Henry Loo.

Laura whimpered, "No, Gabriel, no," and fell to the floor in a faint.

The drive home was silent. Gabriel had managed to calm Henry Loo and revive Laura without causing much fuss. But he'd known from the moment she'd come to that something had scared her to death. She was pale and shaky and wouldn't look him in the eyes. Add the fact that she'd called out his name as she'd fainted, and he was pretty damn sure whatever she had to tell him wouldn't be good.

He waited for her to start talking, but she remained mute. And every time he touched her, she flinched. This whole business was beginning to scare him. Her eyes were red-rimmed and brimming with unshed tears. Her chin was trembling, and every so often he saw her biting her lower lip to keep from crying.

"Damn it, Laura, either tell me what happened or let it go."

She turned in the seat until she was facing him. "I saw Henry Loo die."

It was the last thing he'd expected to hear. "The hell you say!"

He glanced at her quickly, trying to judge her state of mind. But it was impossible. Was this how real psychics worked? His stomach turned as he returned his attention to the streets and the traffic through which he was driving. Now what?

And then, right in the middle of a turn, he remembered.

"But if it was Henry Loo you saw die, then why did you call out my name?"

Tears brimmed and spilled, rolling unchecked down her cheeks. At that moment she wished she'd never set foot in Oklahoma or met and made love to this man, because this was breaking her heart.

"Because it was you, Gabriel." Then she covered her face with her hands and started to sob. "I saw you kill Henry."

Oh, Jesus.

Everything faded around him except the sight of his own hands curled around the steering wheel. The scent of his own fear was strong within his nostrils, and the hammer of his heartbeat loud inside his ears. He kept hearing that damned dog of Sadie Husser's, barking and barking. He kept seeing the look on her houseman's face when he'd opened the door. Gabriel. He'd called him Gabriel.

Somehow he managed to get the car to the curb. He shoved the gear in park and then got out, his legs shaking and his stomach muscles jerking. Nausea hit him belly high. The urge to throw up was strong. He inhaled sharply and started walking, drawing in huge, refreshing draughts of air, trying to flush away the horror of what she'd just said.

This didn't make sense. A woman had died last night, and he'd been locked in his room. Laura could verify that. That had been all the proof he'd needed to convince himself that he was innocent. So, what the hell did her vision mean? Who had he been fooling? Himself—or her?

The moment the car stopped, Laura knew she'd done the wrong thing by blurting it out like that.

And when he got out of the car, she began to panic. It was evident by the expression on his face that he was in shock. Her hands were trembling as she grabbed for her seat belt, trying without success to set herself free. By the time she got out of the car, Gabriel was more than half a block away, and from the way he was moving, she was going to have to run to catch up.

"Gabriel! Wait!" she cried, and she started to run.

He didn't so much as pause. She shouted louder.

"Gabriel, please!"

By this time she doubted he was even hearing her. He was walking like a man in a trance—and he was almost at the street corner. Traffic was swift and heavy. She wasn't sure he would stop, and if she didn't reach him in time...

Fear clawed at her conscience as she screamed his name and then broke into an all-out sprint.

The long blast of a car horn pierced the shroud around Gabriel's senses. He jerked and then paused in midstride just as Laura grabbed his arm

The yank she gave him sent them both staggering backward, and once again she found herself flat on her back, pinned by the weight of Gabriel's body. Still fearing for his safety, she wrapped her arms around his upper body and held on for dear life while saying his name aloud, over and over.

"Gabriel, oh, Gabriel, you scared me to death."

Only after she felt the tension flowing out of his body did she dare to relax. Moments later, he rolled off her and stood, then reached down and pulled her to her feet. His eyes were glittering, and there was a muscle jerking at the side of his jaw. His voice was low, his lips drawn tightly, as if stifling unwanted emotion.

"Are you all right?" he asked.

She brushed at a stain on the elbow of his jacket, needing to hold him, telling herself not to cry.

"I should be asking you that."

His eyes narrowed. "You're asking *me* if I'm all right?" He looked past her into the distance. "I haven't got a clue."

The absence of emotion in his voice frightened her.

"Gabriel."

"What?"

"I'm sorry. I shouldn't have blurted it out like that."

He shrugged. "If it's the truth, it makes no difference how it's said."

Laura felt lost. Never in her entire life had she thought to question herself as she was doing now.

But this didn't make sense. She knew this man. Or at least she thought she did. She'd seen how gentle and caring he was with Matty, as well as with Mike Travers. She'd witnessed firsthand the devastation he still suffered from the loss of his parents.

She'd known from the first that they would make love. But she hadn't known until now how deeply she had fallen in love. Surely to God she couldn't love a man who was capable of murder.

Surely.

"Maybe I was wrong," she said softly. "Maybe I misinterpreted what I saw."

"And maybe we're both just plain crazy," Gabriel snapped. "However, this is the first time there's been any warning about who's the intended victim, and I'm going to the police."

Laura's heart sank as he swung around and started back toward the car. A few yards away, he paused and turned.

"Come on," he said sharply. "You're coming with me, and you're going to tell them what you saw. And then someone needs to warn Henry Loo to hire a bodyguard."

Kirby Summers' car skidded as he turned off the street into the OCPD parking lot. He got out on the run, praying all the way into the building that the call he'd gotten from Ray Bush was the break they'd been waiting for. The message he'd received was that someone had walked into police headquarters claiming to have information on the Prince Charming murders. All he could think was, Please, God, don't let this be a scam.

Laura's mood alternated between panic and the inevitability of this moment, while Gabriel seemed resigned. The longer they waited, the calmer he became. She didn't understand that it was relief he was feeling. By coming here and telling his story, Gabriel was giving the responsibility of saving Prince Charming's victims to someone else.

When they'd arrived at headquarters, the detective they'd been directed to was quite obviously busy. But it hadn't taken long to get Ray Bush's attention. Three little words, *Prince Charming murders,* and they had his undivided attention— until Laura said the word *psychic* and Gabriel said something about dreams. After that, Ray's enthusiasm had waned noticeably. He'd asked them to wait, telling them that an OSBI agent named Kirby Summers was officially in charge and that they needed to tell their story to him

Gabriel shifted in his chair, glancing at Laura and trying to gauge her apprehension. He knew she was worried for him, and in a way, he knew he should be worried about himself. But he wasn't. Whatever happened after this, it had been the right thing to do.

He'd seen the skepticism on the detective's face, but he didn't give a damn whether the man believed him or not. He needed to tell what he knew. After that, it would be out of his hands.

And then there was Laura. He couldn't quit thinking about the timing of her appearance in his life. It was almost as if fate were trying to slap him back down by showing him a new kind of love and then yanking it away. He'd survived a deadly car crash, even survived the loss of his parents, although there had been days when he'd wished for the opposite. But he *had* survived, while battling a loneliness he could never have envisioned.

Then Laura Dane had entered his life, daring him to accept not only who she was, but *what*. When he thought back to how reluctant he'd been for her to come, he almost laughed. Now he couldn't imagine life without her. He didn't know what his future held, but he would never regret loving her. Her presence alone had done more toward healing him than any medicine could ever have done.

A telephone rang on a nearby desk. Gabriel

watched as Ray Bush got up to answer it. As soon as the man was out of earshot, Gabriel looked at Laura and then took her hand. She was trembling, and her skin was cold…ice-cold.

"Laura, look at me," he demanded.

She did as he asked, telling herself that, under the circumstances, this was the right thing to do. But she was afraid, so afraid for Gabriel that she could hardly think.

"It's going to be all right," he said softly. "Either they believe me or they don't."

Laura nodded. "I know. And it's the only thing we could have done. Henry Loo's life is at stake."

Gabriel grimaced. "You saw how the detective reacted when you told him. He didn't know whether to laugh or throw us out on our butts."

She bit the edge of her lower lip as her shoulders slumped. "It's nothing I haven't experienced before."

Gabriel touched her mouth with the tip of his finger. "Hey," he whispered. "If you want that bitten, wait for me."

She met his gaze, remembering last night and the passion that had erupted between them.

"Gabriel?"

"What?" he said.

"Everything is happening so fast."

His eyes narrowed thoughtfully. "Are you referring to what happened between us, or what we're doing here now?"

She dropped her gaze and shrugged. "I don't know. Maybe a little of both."

"Are you sorry?" he asked.

She didn't answer.

"Laura, look at me," he said.

She looked.

"Are you sorry?" he repeated.

Her gaze moved from the promise of passion she saw lurking in his eyes to the cut of his mouth, remembering how soft his lips had felt on her body, and then how demanding they had become, coaxing things from her she would never have believed herself capable of.

She reached out, tracing the shape of his shoulders, then the length of his arm, remembering his strength and the tenderness with which he'd held her. She looked into his eyes with a straightforward gaze.

"No. I could never be sorry about last night. But, oh God, I wish I'd never seen the—"

"Stop right there," Gabriel said, his voice low and harsh with a demand she'd never heard. "Never be sorry for who you are, or for the fact that, by coming here, we could be saving a man's life.''

Don't tell. Must not tell.

Gabriel jerked. That damned voice. Why now? And why the warning?

Laura tightened her grip on his arm as Gabriel turned to her. ''Did you hear?''

She nodded. ''What does it mean?''

Gabriel rolled his eyes. ''You're the psychic,'' he muttered. ''You tell me.''

Suddenly Ray Bush was standing before them. Laura looked up.

''Here comes Agent Summers now,'' he said.

They both turned to look. Kirby Summers was a skinny caricature of a cross between Don Knotts and Detective Columbo, wearing a suit that hung on his overthin frame and a wrinkled beige raincoat flapping at his heels.

''Sorry for the delay,'' Summers said, as he reached Bush's desk. ''It's starting to rain.''

Then he glanced down at the couple sitting at Ray's desk, telling himself they looked reputable enough. Elation continued to bubble. This was the break they'd been waiting for, he could feel it.

''Agent Summers, I'd like you to meet Gabriel Donner and Laura Dane. They have something they want to tell you,'' Ray said.

Kirby frowned. There was a tone in Ray's voice he didn't think that he liked. He looked at Ray. When Ray rolled his eyes, his hopes dropped. Damn. Damn. Damn. But he maintained control and held out his hand.

"Mr. Donner. Miss Dane. I'm Kirby Summers, OSBI. I understand you have some information on the Prince Charming murders?"

Gabriel shook the man's hand, while Laura just nodded.

Kirby glanced around the room and then back at Ray.

"Is anyone using the interrogation room?" he asked. When he saw Laura stiffen, he added with a smile, "It's just quieter, you understand?"

But Laura wasn't pacified. They didn't know she'd been through this drill many times before, seen sometimes as a credible psychic and sometimes as a quack, depending on who had asked for her help.

A few minutes later they were sitting around a table in a small, windowless room. Gabriel glanced at the mirror on the opposite wall and knew that it was probably a two-way. He didn't care. The more the merrier.

"I'll be recording our conversation," Kirby

said, looking from Gabriel to Laura and back again. "Is that all right?"

They both nodded.

"If you don't mind, would you verbalize your response?" he asked.

Both Gabriel and Laura said yes.

"Fine," Kirby said. "Now tell me...who witnessed what?"

Gabriel looked at Laura. "Where do we start?"

Kirby answered for her. "How about at the beginning?"

Gabriel shrugged. "Okay. I was in a car wreck a couple of months ago. My parents died. I was in a coma for several weeks. When I woke up, I was the same...but also different. Things started happening to me that I couldn't explain."

Kirby leaned forward. "I'm sorry for your loss, but what does this have to do with the Prince Charming murders?"

"I've seen every one of them happen."

Laura groaned beneath her breath. There was only one way the police were going to interpret that statement. Guilt. Pure guilt. She wanted to take Gabriel's hand and run, but she sat without speaking, waiting, praying that she would be able to make them understand later on.

Kirby stood abruptly, tilting his chair onto the

floor with a loud crack. He righted it without taking his eyes from Gabriel's face.

"Where were you when these murders happened? Are you confessing? Were you an accomplice?" he asked, glancing quickly at Laura before turning his attention back to Gabriel.

Gabriel shook his head. "No...I don't think I had anything to do with them, although one of the victims called out my name."

Laura interrupted. "Gabriel, you're not explaining yourself. You're misleading Agent Summers as to how you witnessed the crimes."

Kirby resisted the urge to glare. "Are you his lawyer?"

"No, I'm his—"

"She's a psychic," Gabriel said. "And she's right. I've been living with this hell for so long that I forgot to make myself clear."

Kirby bit his lip to keep from cursing aloud. *Psychic. Great! This is why Ray rolled his eyes.* He braced his hands against the flat of the table and leaned forward, telling himself to stay cool.

"Then I suggest you do so," he said softly. "This has been a very long day, and it's not over yet."

"Sorry," Gabriel repeated. "As for where I was when the murders occurred, I was at my home.

And no, I am not the killer or an accomplice. The killer works alone.''

"How do you know that?'' Kirby growled.

Gabriel looked at the man without blinking an eye. "Because I saw the murders in my dreams. Every one of them. From the prostitute down on Reno to the last, a homeless woman in an alley.''

Kirby didn't know whether to kick them out now or let the tape run for a good laugh later on.

"That's not news,'' Kirby said. "All of that was in the papers. So far, you haven't told me anything new, and quite frankly, visions and dreams don't stand up in court.''

Gabriel nodded. "I know. But there are things that I saw that weren't in the paper. If I'm wrong, I'll be one happy man tonight.''

"Like what?'' Kirby asked, and then saw Laura touch Gabriel's hand in a warning fashion. But the man didn't waver.

"I don't know why he kills, but I see what he does,'' Gabriel said.

"And that would be?''

Gabriel closed his eyes, letting himself slide back into the memories he'd tried so hard to forget. Then he took a deep breath.

Kirby Summers was still waiting.

"Mr. Donner?''

"His fists. He uses his fists. It's always one blow."

Kirby started to tense. This was close to what they'd suspected, but then he began to relax. The newspapers had said the victims had died of a broken neck. The man could be guessing.

"Go on," Kirby prompted.

"After it's over, I feel a sense of profound sadness. I think that's why he leaves them a rose. I think he's sorry it happened."

Kirby frowned. Again, this was close to what their profiler had suggested.

"Mr. Donner, any intelligent man could have come to any of these conclusions just from reading the newspapers."

Gabriel tensed. "I know. But there's something else that I see that hasn't been in the news. I don't know whether it's real, or whether it's something from my life that has somehow been interwoven into the truth."

Kirby glanced at his watch, telling himself it was about time to cut them loose.

"What would that be?" he asked.

"The roses he left. The stems don't have any thorns."

Kirby froze. *Sweet Jesus.* He stared at Gabriel Donner until his eyes began to burn, and then he looked past him toward the mirror on the wall, well aware that Ray Bush was listening on the other side.

"How the hell did you know that?" he asked softly.

Gabriel leaned forward. "I told you. I saw it in my dreams."

Two hours and three additional detectives later, it was just as Laura had feared. The interview had turned into a full-fledged interrogation. So when Kirby Summers' questions began to be echoes of the same ones he'd asked over an hour earlier, she snapped.

"Look, gentlemen!" Laura said. "If you don't have any new questions to ask, you won't get any new answers. That's the way truth works."

Ray Bush had forgone the two-way mirror and come inside hours ago, and he had to give it to this woman. If she was a fake, she was as good as they came.

"Settle down, lady," he said shortly. "Agent Summers is only doing his job."

But Laura wasn't willing to budge. She could tell by the way the questions had turned that they were considering putting Gabriel under arrest. She started digging through her purse. A few seconds later, she pulled out a small red notebook.

"Here!" she said shortly, and handed the notebook to the detective. "There are more than forty-five names and numbers in that book. A large portion of them are police departments and the detectives with whom I've worked. Call one. Call them all. They will vouch for me. I am not a liar. I am not a quack."

Kirby took the notebook from Bush and started turning pages. To his surprise, he recognized some of the names. He glanced up.

"You've worked with these people?"

She sighed. "That's what I said an hour ago. The truth hasn't changed."

Kirby tossed the book to one of the detectives. "Make a few calls."

Then he looked back at Gabriel. The man seemed impervious to all that had transpired. In fact, for a man so close to being arrested, he was as laid-back as they came. Either he *was* telling the truth, or he was one hell of a con artist. What Kirby couldn't figure out was, if Donner was guilty, then why this scam? What did he have to gain?

"Okay, Mr. Donner, let's take this in another direction. If everything you've told me is true, then why have you waited to come forward?"

Gabriel shrugged. "Look around. You're treating me…us…like we're freaks, and believe me, I feel like one. Only an idiot would welcome this kind of treatment."

Kirby had the grace to flush.

"However," Gabriel continued, "when Laura saw Henry Loo as the next victim, it changed everything. I only saw the murders as they were happening. Laura's precognition may just save a man's life."

Kirby's belly grumbled, reminding him that it had been hours since he'd eaten. But food was the last thing on his mind. Getting a killer off the streets was more important than losing another pound, whether he could afford it or not.

"I understand that," Kirby said. "And, as you requested, we did send someone to speak to Mr. Loo. But you should know that he's taken the warning with a grain of salt. Said something to the effect that one's fate cannot be changed."

Laura groaned. "No," she muttered, and suddenly stood.

Gabriel reached for her hand. "Don't worry," he said softly. Then he looked up at Kirby. "Agent Summers, I wonder if you might do me a favor."

The request was so unexpected that Kirby stifled

a grin. The man was something all right. Cool. Still in control.

"And what might that be?" he asked, curious as to what possible favor he could do for a man in Gabriel Donner's shoes.

"Run my picture through your computer system. See if there is a criminal on file who looks like me. And then put me in jail for the night."

Kirby frowned. "And why the hell would I be doing something like that?"

Laura inhaled sharply. Gabriel squeezed her hand as he answered.

"Because Laura saw Henry Loo's killer."

Kirby's eyes narrowed as he shifted focus from Donner to the woman at his side.

"So, something new *has* been added to this mess. Exactly who is supposed to do the killing?"

Laura paled, but her voice never wavered. "Gabriel. I saw Gabriel kill Henry Loo."

Nine

Mike Travers was beside himself. He'd gone to get a haircut and come home to find a message on his machine that Gabriel was in jail. After talking to Laura, he was only a little bit less panicked than when he'd first dialed the phone. The fact that Gabriel had not been arrested was good news. However, he couldn't help but worry about the conclusions the police were bound to draw. With a serial killer on the loose and no clues to speak of, having someone walk in off the street claiming he'd witnessed the killings in a dream was nothing short of suicide.

Henry Loo was too worried about lost revenue from the second robbery to pay much attention to what the man from the police department told him a few hours ago. A psychic had predicted he would die tonight? It had been all he could do not to laugh.

His big concerns were staying in business long enough to be able to move out of this terrible location. The food was excellent, the service even better, and he'd cut his prices to rock bottom to draw customers. It was paying off. Only a couple more months—without any more robberies—and he would have plenty of capital to make the move to a new location.

He was excited. It was a classy spot on the northwest side of town, with plenty of parking and businesses on both sides that would complement his restaurant, not detract from it. The only reputable business in this entire four-block area besides his restaurant was a one-woman flower shop two doors down.

As he counted out the day's take, he glanced at his watch. It was five minutes to eleven. A little over an hour to midnight. He'd promised his wife he would try to get home early tonight. The grandchildren were visiting, and he'd hardly had a chance to see them. The Closed sign was already turned, and the last of his employees had gone home over fifteen minutes earlier.

Ten. Twenty. Thirty.

He set the stack of one-dollar bills with the other money that would go back in the register for tomorrow's till and zipped up the bank bag that he would drop in the night deposit slot on the way home.

With one last look at the empty room, he turned out the main lights and headed for the back door and the alleylike area beyond, where he and his employees normally parked. As he was reaching for the knob, a loud clatter sounded on the other side of the door, and just for a moment he thought of the police and the warning he'd had.

Then he scoffed at the notion and patted his pocket, taking comfort in the handgun's bulge. Those robbers weren't the only ones who could be cagey. If they were out there again, this time they would get more than they bargained for.

With thoughts of his wife and grandchildren foremost in his head, he opened the door and stepped out into the alley, giving the area a careful look before closing the door behind him. It was only after he started across the lot toward his car that he realized the security light under which he normally parked was out. He frowned and reached for his gun. Darn kids. Always breaking something. It was Henry's opinion that children today had no respect...except for his grandchildren. They had been raised in the old ways. For Henry, the old ways were best.

Another sound of metal to metal echoed within

the confines of the small enclosure, and he clutched his money bag close to his chest and spun, aiming into the darkness.

"Who's there?" he shouted. "Don't come any closer! I have a gun!"

Although he saw no one, he began backing toward his car while fumbling for his keys. A little nervous, but still convinced that he could make it to his car okay, he continued to back up while fumbling for the fancy key ring that went to his new car. One push on a particular button and his door would be unlocked. Then all he had to do was jump inside and speed away. They would never reach him in time.

He glanced over his shoulder, judging the distance he still had to go. As he did, out of the corner of his eye he saw something moving inside the shadows. He panicked. His first mistake was when he started to run. His second was hitting the wrong button on the key ring. Instead of the button that unlocked the doors, he hit the one marked Panic. Within a second, his car horn began to honk.

Loudly.

Constantly.

Reverberating within the enclosure like an echo gone mad.

And even for Henry, who realized instantly what he'd done, the sound was deafening.

Suddenly a roar sounded behind him, somewhere between a scream of great pain and a howl of rage. In a panic, he turned toward the sound, and in doing so, dropped his keys. The keys that would get him to safety. Within the periphery of his senses he could hear them clattering to the pavement, and he groaned. The time for getting in his car had passed.

The man was coming toward him now, waving his hands and shrieking like a demon from hell. The gun. He still had his gun. He took aim, his hands shaking as fast as his heart was pounding. A quick spurt of wet warmth slid down the inside of his leg. It shamed him to know he was wetting nimself as the first shot rang out.

Somehow he'd known before the bullet ricocheted off the opposite wall that the shot would go wild. He pulled the trigger again and again, emptying the gun without taking clear aim, continually missing his target.

"No! No!" he screamed, and threw the money bag across the lot toward the oncoming man 'Take money. I not care. Take money and go!"

To Henry's shock, the man swung at the money

bag as it flew by his head. In that moment, he thought of the warning and knew he was dead.

Gabriel lay on the bunk, staring at the ceiling and wondering if this was the biggest mistake he'd ever made. Laura had been right. The police hadn't believed the psychic theory, and there was a good chance they were going to try to pin the murders on him. Yes, they were cooperating right now by locking him up for the night as he'd asked, but they'd also asked if he would submit to blood and tissue samples so they could run a DNA test. He'd done so, knowing there was no way he could refuse and still maintain his innocence. Besides, there wasn't any real reason why he should worry. He hadn't been a crazy killer before the accident that killed his parents, therefore a knot on the head shouldn't have changed his personality so drastically that he would be capable of taking another person's life now.

Yet with every passing minute, he couldn't quit thinking of the look on Sadie's houseman's face when he'd opened that back door. He'd known his killer.

Gabriel swiped his hands across his face, as if trying to remove the memory.

Why would he think it was me? I wasn't there.

I couldn't have been there. It's more than a mile from the Husser home to mine.

Then he remembered waking up with that scratch on his neck.

I was wandering all over the garden. I probably scratched it on a rosebush or something.

Laura's face flashed through his mind, and he rolled over on his side, absently watching a cockroach as it disappeared into a crack running up the wall. He inhaled slowly and closed his eyes, picturing her off-center smile and the way her eyes gleamed when something made her happy.

He'd known her for less than two weeks, and she'd gotten under his skin in a way he would never have believed. He'd had one unbelievable night with her in his arms, and even if he could repeat the act for the rest of his life, it would never be enough.

What the hell am I going to do if I can't fix this mess? I haven't figured out how to live without my parents yet. How am I ever going to live without Laura?

He rolled over on his back, his mouth grim with anger.

Even more to the point, why would I want to? I'm tired of losing people I love.

His eyes burned with unshed tears, but he refused to give in to the weakness of the emotion.

In fact, I'm so damned tired of it, I could—

A chill ran through him as the thought ended suddenly. What was it? What terrible threat had he been about to utter that his conscience wouldn't let him voice? He lay there for a moment, all but holding his breath as certainty slithered through him.

Kill?

Was that it?

Did he feel so guilty for living when his parents had died that he was trying to die and take everyone with him? Then he frowned. Not only no, but hell no. He wasn't going to let his mind play those games. A few minutes later he dozed off.

Laura stood naked in the lamplight, her arms outstretched, her body trembling with desire.

"Gabriel, make love to me. Take me where you took me last night."

Gabriel opened his arms, and when she walked into his embrace, he picked her up and carried her to his bed.

She lay beside him, whispering words he could not hear. Now she was begging...begging.

"What?" he kept asking. "What's wrong? What's wrong?"

Finally, unable to make him understand what she was trying to say, Laura pointed. Gabriel followed the line of her finger until he caught himself staring at a reflection in a mirror.

He smiled. It was him and Laura.

Then he frowned. Something was wrong. Yes, it was him and Laura, but they weren't in bed. This didn't make sense. They were right here. Lying in each other's arms. But their reflection showed an entirely different scene.

He looked down at Laura and frowned, but she had started to cry. He looked back at the reflection. It was starting to fade. But he could see clearly enough to recognize what he was doing. He was reaching for her neck. He jerked and looked down. The tears were still fresh on her face.

Gabriel tried to wake up, but the horror of the dream wasn't over. Suddenly he was no longer in bed with Laura. He found himself standing in an alley beside a Dumpster. The scent of flowers was strong. He looked down. There were flowers everywhere. Limp ones. Broken ones. Shattered ones. Where were the roses?

He started to dig.

A short while later, he suddenly groaned beneath his breath and then came off of the bunk on which he was sleeping, swinging his arms and screaming like a man in deep pain. Seconds later, the jailer bolted through a doorway and began running down the hall toward Gabriel's cell with his gun drawn, shouting for help as he ran.

When the phone rang beside Kirby's bed, it was years of being wakened in such a manner that made him answer in his sleep. But when the man on the other end of the line started talking, it didn't take long for him to come fully awake.

"That's impossible," he muttered, as he reached for the light.

"Maybe so, but the guy nearly tore the cell apart before they got to him. You're not gonna like this, but he had himself another one of those dreams."

Kirby's belly knotted as he shoved a hand through his hair.

"There's not a likeable thing about this whole damned mess, so get it said," Kirby ordered.

"You know that man, Henry Loo? The one that woman warned you about?"

Kirby closed his eyes. Ray was right. He wasn't going to like this a bit.

"Yeah, what about him?" he muttered.

"They found his body in the alley behind his

restaurant about half an hour ago. He's seriously dead.''

Kirby closed his eyes. "Oh, damn."

"Yeah," Ray echoed. "And, Kirby…"

Kirby groaned. "There's more?"

"Yeah. There were roses everywhere. Looks like the killer had been doing a little shopping in the Dumpster behind a nearby florist. There's a trail of them all the way from the back of the florist to Henry Loo's face.''

Kirby knew he needed to start dressing, but his legs felt weak. He couldn't quit thinking that this was all his fault. They'd been warned. And then he shook his head in disbelief, warned by a psychic, for God's sake. Who could have known?

"Are the roses missing any thorns?"

"Only some of them. It looks as if Henry surprised the man before he had time to finish the job.''

"Okay," Kirby said. "I'll be right there."

"You have the address?" Ray asked.

"Somewhere," Kirby said. "But give it to me again.''

Ray did as Kirby asked and then disconnected, leaving Kirby with the certain knowledge that had he taken Laura Dane as seriously as she'd expected, one small Oriental man who'd been trying to go home to his family would still be alive.

Sam Whitehall was just finishing his investigation as Kirby walked up.

Kirby took a sip of the coffee he'd been nursing and nodded at an officer he recognized.

"Hey, Sam. What do you think?" Kirby asked.

Whitehall looked up from where he was squatting. "That he should have ducked."

A wry grin broke the somberness of Kirby's face. "You're awfully witty for someone who got dragged out of bed."

Whitehall stood, wincing as pain shot through his bad knee. Damn, but he hated getting old.

"Sorry," Whitehall said. "Sometimes it's either make jokes or cry."

The grin slid off of Kirby's face. "Yeah, I know what you mean. So, was it the same killer?"

Whitehall shrugged. "It's hard to say for sure, but I'd lay odds that it was."

Kirby glanced around at the roses scattered all over the place and nodded. Then his gaze moved from the body being moved onto a gurney to a nearby car.

"What the hell happened to that car?" Kirby asked.

Whitehall pointed. "I only do human bodies, not car bodies. Ask him."

Kirby turned. Ray Bush was heading his way.

"Sorry to get you out like this," Ray said.

Kirby pointed toward a car parked beneath a streetlight, though the light was out and the car was sitting in shadows.

"What's the deal with the car? It looks like someone took a bat to it."

Ray shrugged. "Kids, maybe. Who knows?"

Kirby frowned. The hood of the car was all but destroyed. Huge dents peppered the entire surface. But something about it didn't sit right.

"I don't think it was kids."

Ray looked up. "Why not? There's plenty of them down here who would willingly do worse for less reason than the fact that it was here."

"I know, but it just doesn't fit. You're asking me to believe there were two separate crimes here. Vandals hammered a car, and then someone whacked Henry Loo...or vice versa. Whichever came first."

Ray flipped through his notes. "I've got several reports of hearing a car horn go off."

"You mean, someone was honking a horn?"

"Not honking per se. Honking like this."

Ray pulled the keys from his own pocket, aimed

them at his car and pressed a button. Immediately the horn began to sound in a loud and intermittent blast. He pressed it again, and the horn went silent.

Kirby glanced at the car again as Ray continued.

"We think maybe Henry Loo hit the Panic button, hoping for help. Obviously, help didn't come fast enough to save him."

Kirby's frown deepened. "Maybe the killer bashed the car, trying to silence the alarm."

Ray glanced over his shoulder to the woman standing at the edge of a crowd.

"Why don't you ask her? She said this was going to happen. Maybe now she can tell you why."

Kirby spun around, instantly picking Laura Dane out of the gathering crowd.

"It's four minutes after three in the morning. What the hell is she doing here?"

Ray shrugged. "She came with that old fellow over there. Got here about fifteen minutes after I did."

'Who called her?"

"As far as I know, nobody. Hell, Kirby. She's got a line of communication going that I don't understand. Maybe she's on the spook hotline. Besides that, we got some information back on her that you might like to know. You know those calls you wanted made on the names and numbers in her book?''

"Yeah, what about them?''

"Not only does she have a sparkling reputation, but she's rich as sin. One of the detectives said that every cop he talked to about her swears she's for real. It seems she'd helped every one of them in solving dead-end cases.''

Kirby stared at her for a long, intense moment, then took a deep breath, as if he'd just made a painful decision. He started toward her with fixed intent.

"Miss Dane.''

Her face was pale. Every now and then she bit at the edge of her lower lip, as if trying not to cry. Her eyes were wide and filled with horror as she watched the coroner's car leaving with what was left of Henry Loo.

"Why did you let this happen?'' she whispered. "I warned you. I warned all of you.'' Mike Travers put his arms around her. Weak from spent emotion, she leaned against him and covered her face. "Why don't they ever believe me?''

"Come along, Laura dear. You've seen enough,'' Mike said softly, trying to urge her toward the car.

"Who are you?'' Kirby asked, eyeing the older

man closely and trying to picture him in the act of breaking necks with one blow. No matter how hard he looked, the image wouldn't come. In fact, the old man looked as if a strong wind would knock him off his feet.

"I'm Dr. Michael Travers," he said. "Gabriel Donner is like a son to me, and I'm the one who called Miss Dane into this mess. In a way, we're colleagues."

"Are you claiming to be a psychic, too?" Kirby asked.

Travers shook his head. "Only a psychiatrist."

Kirby frowned. In his mind, they were one and the same.

"How did you two come to be out here in this part of town at this time of the morning?"

Mike looked down at Laura. "She called me, very distraught and pleading for a ride. I gave her one."

Kirby glanced back at Laura. "Why, Miss Dane? How did you know to come out here? Who called you?"

"Only hours ago, I told you what would happen. No one had to call me. I already knew." It was evident by the tone of her voice that she was angry. It was all she could do not to scream at him. Then she shuddered. "I went to sleep around ten. When

I woke up, I knew it was over. I had to come see for myself.''

"How?" Kirby persisted. "Did you—"

Still angry, she said, "I'm not the one you need to be questioning. I already told you all I know. You chose to disregard it. I doubt there's anything else I can say that would be of interest to you."

He stared at her, remembering what Ray had just told him and trying to understand what it would be like to live with an ability like hers.

"Look, Miss Dane, you have to understand something. I deal in facts, and—"

She interrupted. "One fact is certain. Henry Loo is dead, and Gabriel is still behind bars."

Kirby frowned. "What does that last fact have to do with the first?"

Laura wrapped her arms around herself and swallowed, trying to calm her nerves.

"Obviously nothing, now," she said shortly. Then she glanced back at the scene of the crime. "The car. Who did it belong to?"

Kirby's frown deepened. "The victim. Why?"

She worried at the edge of her lower lip again and then looked at Kirby with new intent. "May I touch it?"

Her request took him aback. "What? The car?"

She nodded.

"Why on earth would you want to?"

She almost smiled. "If I told you, you wouldn't believe me. Please. May I?"

Kirby shrugged and then lifted the yellow crime scene tape for her to slip under.

"Come with me. I'll see if forensics is finished."

Laura was right at his heels, with Mike not far behind. Moments later, she was standing in front of the car and absorbing what was left of a rage she couldn't understand.

Ray Bush cocked his head to one side and then leaned down and whispered in Kirby's ear. "What's she doing?" he asked.

Kirby scratched at the bald spot on his head. "Beats me. Said she wanted to touch the car. Far as I'm concerned, she can pretend she's the damned hood ornament if it will get her off my back."

Laura took a deep breath, laid the flat of her hand on the car and then closed her eyes. The surrounding noise faded into the background as her mind slid into another place. A long, silent minute passed, but Laura was unaware of the time.

Kirby began to fidget, wishing he'd run her ass off instead of playing this game. Ray Bush stared, curious as to what made someone like her tick.

Mike Travers felt every one of his sixty-seven years and then some, and wished he could turn the clock back to a happier time. To a time when Brent and Angela were still alive, and Gabriel didn't question his own sanity every time he took a new breath. One second ticked into another and another, so when Laura suddenly spoke, it startled them all.

"He did it," she said softly. "He did this with his fists."

All three men stared at the car, trying to picture the strength it would take to put dents the size of grapefruits into the hood of Henry Loo's car.

Ray surprised himself by asking, "Who did, Miss Dane?"

"The killer. The man who looks like Gabriel."

Mike Travers took a step forward and placed his hand on Laura's shoulder. A muscle flinched beneath his fingers as her body adjusted to his touch.

"Why, Laura? Why did he do it?"

Her head dropped forward, as if she were falling asleep. "The noise. He was trying to stop the noise."

Ray snapped his fingers. "The alarm that Henry set off! By God, he was trying to stop that horn!"

"That doesn't make sense," Kirby argued. "If you've just killed someone, you don't beat the shit out of some car. You run."

Laura sighed, and the sound came up and out of her like a faint but clear wail. "He wasn't angry. He was in pain. Sound causes pain."

She slumped forward, and if Mike hadn't been standing so close, she might have fallen.

Kirby started to scoff, but there was a look in her eyes that stopped him cold. Damned if he wasn't starting to believe her.

"Miss Dane, I've got a favor to ask of you."

Laura wiped a shaky hand across her face and then looked up. "Yes?"

"Would you consider coming to my office to look at some pictures?"

Her stomach turned. She knew what the pictures would be, and the thought of looking at the rest of Prince Charming's handiwork made her sick.

"Not tonight."

He accepted that. "Okay, but soon."

She looked at Mike. He shrugged, as if to say this had to be her call.

Kirby couldn't believe he was even doing this, but at this point in the case, he had little else to go on.

"I have to be in Enid by three tomorrow afternoon. Give me a call when you're ready."

"All I want now is for you to let Gabriel go."

* * *

It was five minutes to five in the morning when Gabriel entered his home. He glanced at the security alarm and grimaced. It hadn't been set. Damn. He hadn't thought about it beforehand, but his grandstand demand to be locked up last night had meant that Laura would have had to spend the entire night in this house alone. Sometimes the place even intimidated him, and he'd been raised here. He could only imagine how uneasy she must have felt, alone in a house this size.

Suddenly the need to see her, to touch her, to assure himself that she was all right, overwhelmed him. He tossed his keys on the hall table and started upstairs. With every beat of his heart, her name sounded in his head. Stronger than the intruder's voice—stronger than the fear that had become a constant companion.

Laura. Laura. Laura.

Ten

Dawn was breaking as Laura stepped into the shower. She had yet to go to bed. She'd come home from the scene of the crime with only one thought on her mind, and that was to bathe away the stench of that alley in which Henry Loo had died. As soon as Mike Travers had dropped her off at the Donner estate, she'd entered the house, locking the door behind her. Before she was halfway up the stairs, she had her clothes unbuttoned. By the time she'd reached her room, she was carrying her shoes. She stopped outside the door and began stripping off her clothes, tossing them aside to be carried to the laundry room later. Right now, all she could think about was ridding herself of any reminders of what she'd seen.

A few minutes later she stepped beneath the shower without waiting for it to heat, letting the water pepper her skin. The first burst of the spray was cold, but the need to be free of that murder scene was stronger than the chill, and so she stayed. It wasn't long before a steady stream of warmth began engulfing her, steaming the stall and causing her hair to curl even closer to her head. Closing her eyes, she took a step closer to the spray and lifted her face, welcoming the warm, even flow upon her body.

One minute passed into the next, and then the next, as she tried to get past the sight of Henry Loo lying on the street near his car.

In her mind's eye, she could still see the way his eyes had appeared. Earlier today they'd been sparkling with wit. Tonight they'd been little more than sightless slits in an aging face. His mouth, so easy to tilt into a smile of welcome in greeting customers, had been swollen and puffy. The smile on his face had died with his heart, leaving him with nothing but some blood drying near his chin.

She turned around, letting the spray pelt her back as it kneaded the tension-filled muscles in her neck and down her spine. But when she opened her eyes, the floor seemed to tilt. She grabbed for the walls to steady herself, but it was no use. Her legs gave way. She sank to her knees. Burying her face in her hands, she started to cry.

Gabriel found her that way, drenched and sobbing, unable to stop either the flow of water or her tears. Overwhelmed with guilt for having involved her in this hell, he opened the shower door and turned off the water. He reached for her with one hand and for a towel with the other. Wrapping her in its warmth as he would have a child, he lifted her into his arms and carried her to the bed.

"Ah, baby, don't cry. Don't cry. I'm so, so sorry we got you into this mess."

Laura threw her arms around Gabriel's neck and buried her face against his chest while the tears continued to fall.

"Why didn't they believe me?" she sobbed. "No one ever believes until it's too late."

Gabriel hurt. He hurt for her, and for himself, and for a man named Henry Loo.

"It's not your fault any more than it's mine," he said, and lay down beside her.

She curled into him, fitting herself to his body and holding on as if she might never let go.

Her panic worried him. It was apparent that Laura's world was very unstable, although up until now, her demeanor had seemed just the opposite. He'd only had to live with this "knowing" for less than a month and couldn't imagine having to live within such parameters for the rest of his life. This whole mess was so damned bizarre he could hardly think. There wasn't anything he could say that would make it better, because right now, there was no end in sight.

They lay without moving, without speaking, until heartbeats slowed and the aftershock of Laura's breakdown was little more than an occasional shudder.

Laura felt numb. She couldn't think past the feel of Gabriel's hands upon her back—of his breath upon her face. She closed her eyes, remembering what it felt like to come apart in his arms. Outside, another day was just beginning, but for Laura, yesterday would never be over. She shifted closer to Gabriel and buried her face against his chest. She wanted to feel alive, to forget what death looked like, if only for a while.

His heartbeat was strong against her cheek—as strong as the hold he had upon her body. She sighed. Dear God, how she loved this man, but the way things were going, there was no guarantee that they would both survive to explore that love.

She'd *seen* herself about to die at his hands. But she'd also *seen* him killing Henry Loo, and that hadn't happened. She'd never been this wrong before, but she wasn't about to question her fallibility. This time she wanted to be wrong in the very worst way. Ignoring the last of a lingering shudder, she rose up on one elbow to gaze into Gabriel's eyes.

"Gabriel?"

His eyes filled with wonder as he looked upon her face. She was so damned beautiful it made him ache. He traced the path of a tiny blue vein along the side of her neck and then cupped the side of her face. His voice was soft, his touch gentle.

"What, baby?"

"I'm afraid."

"I know. Sometimes so am I."

Then he pulled her back down into his arms and began combing his fingers through her short, damp curls, marveling at the silky feel of them upon his skin. But when she tensed and then started to shake, something occurred to him, something she'd said before, something bad, something ugly.

"Laura?"

She shifted in his arms, her voice muffled against his chest. "What?"

"I know you're afraid…but please God, tell me you're not afraid of me?"

Her hesitation was brief, but it was enough to make him sick. He turned her loose and had started to roll out of bed when she caught him by the arm. The plea in her voice and the terror on her face were enough to give him pause.

"Don't go! For God's sake, don't leave me now. I feel like I'm dying inside." Her voice caught on a sob as a fresh set of tears suddenly blinded her. "Make love to me, Gabriel. I'm so tired of death. Make me remember what it feels like to live."

He rolled, pinning her to the bed with both his body and a hard, intent stare.

He cursed beneath his breath, resisting the urge to shake her. "Why, Laura? Why me?"

She encircled his neck with her arms and then tugged, urging him back to her.

"Because I can't help it. I love you, Gabriel. If you can't return the favor, then lie to me, because right now I don't think I could stand knowing the truth."

His expression mirrored hers—torn with indecision and filled with grief, both for the victims they couldn't save and the horror they couldn't escape.

"Considering the situation we're in, making love to you is probably the biggest mistake we can continue to make," he said harshly. "But it damned sure won't be a lie. You're in my blood. Your scent envelopes me. I want to be so deep inside of you that—"

She tore the damp towel from between their

bodies and tossed it onto the floor, then started taking off his clothes.

"Then do it. Make love to me, Gabriel. Make me crazy in love."

He did, and created a magic that lasted just over three days.

A warm beam of sunshine broke through the overhead clouds, piercing the leaves of the trees under which he was sleeping and centering on the curve of his strong, handsome face. There was a healing cut on his cheek, a weariness to his features that even sleep could not disguise. His clothes were the worse for wear, and his shoes were still wet from the last place he'd been hiding. His bag lay nearby, the contents slightly scattered, as if it had dropped and spilled when he'd slid to the ground in exhaustion.

Other than his dirty clothes, it didn't contain anything of consequence—a couple of used, disposable razors he'd dug out of the trash and a comb he'd picked up off the street. A single rose lay near his cheek, the scent engulfing him as he slept. He'd taken it from a bush less than two hours ago, before he'd stumbled onto this place and collapsed, nearly blind from lack of sleep. And now he dreamed with the sweet smell guiding him.

The dream was simple. One he'd had many times over in his life, but never with more meaning than he dreamed it now. He was walking with his mother in her garden. The garden was filled with roses. Roses growing up trellises, abundant on bushes, in as many colors as a rainbow. And then the dream began to change. He was still in the garden, but his mother was nowhere in sight. He began to run, from one path to another, crying out her name.

He shifted restlessly in his sleep. He was lost. Even in his dreams, he was lost. He needed to find home. If he could find home, he could find his mother. Mother would know what to do. Mother would fix everything.

The muscles in his shoulders began to twitch, and he shifted again, readjusting his great size to accommodate the small space in which he was lying. He was tired, so tired. Tired of running. Tired of hiding. Tired of being afraid.

A few blocks over, a gaggle of preschoolers walked hand in hand down the sidewalk with the attendants from their day care. Seventeen tiny bits of life that were just starting to live. As they neared the park, anticipation shone in the sparkle of an eye, the curve of a smile, the hushed whispers of shared joy. Once there, they knew they would be allowed to run free, if only for a while. They ran from the swings to the slides, running and squealing if for no other reason than the joy of being alive.

A short while later, the children were playing at full tilt. Their periodic shrieks could be heard all over the park. Most of them were gregarious little individuals with definite goals. To always be first.

And then there was Lelly. A tiny, blue-eyed charmer with a sweet, baby face and a foot that just wasn't right. Lelly ran with the others and played just as hard. But she could never, would never, be first. Once in a while, like today, she would withdraw from the melee and find her own peace in her own special way.

Billy T. had taken her ball, only to run away screaming in pretend terror and leaving Lelly with no option but to sit and wait for him to come back. One minute turned into another and another, until it became evident to Lelly that Billy T. wasn't going to bring back her ball. Silent tears pooled in her round, baby eyes as she turned and limped away toward the shade trees at the edge of the park

She sat down on a log and then started to cry in

earnest. One silent sob after another, the tears rolled.

Crouched behind the bushes that separated the play area from the trees, he watched in consternation as the little girl began to cry. In his way, he recognized the misery for what it really was. In spite of his reticence toward people, he sensed a kinship with the child he could never have explained. Without thought of the consequences, he slipped through the bushes, coming to within mere feet of where she was sitting.

Startled by the sounds behind her, the child turned. Silently she stared at the giant on his knees who was only a short distance away. Her first instinct was to run. But when he neither moved nor spoke, her eyes widened in curiosity, and her tears ceased.

From the time Lelly could remember, she'd been taught repeatedly not to talk to strangers. But when this one smiled, for some unexplainable reason, she sensed a kindred spirit. Somehow, this time the warning didn't apply.

He touched his cheek and then pointed at hers. Lelly sniffled and then swiped at the tears with the palms of her hands.

"Been cryin'," she said, rather matter-of-factly.

His dark eyes suddenly glistened with unshed tears, and he rocked back on his heels, listening intently.

"Billy T. took my ball."

He looked toward the children in the distance. Even from here, the noise of their play made him nervous. But the little girl's plight was strong enough to make him stay for a brief moment more.

From across the way, Miss Smith, Lelly's teacher, began calling for them to gather. She sighed and then stood.

"I goin' now," she said.

Then a soft whisper stopped her. "Wait."

She looked nervously toward the gathering children, then she sighed and looked back at the man. Again her nervousness dissipated as he extended his hand.

"For me?" she asked.

He nodded and smiled.

Her tiny fingers curled around the thornless stem as she lifted the bloom up to her nose. She sniffed deeply as she'd been taught to do and smiled when the sweet scent of fresh rose filled her nose.

The teacher called out again, and this time Lelly broke free and ran, clutching the rose to her breast. For now it no longer mattered that her stride wasn't smooth, or that Billy T. had taken her ball. She had something special.

Marie Smith was an old hand at taking care of children. She had worked at County Day Care for over seven years and was counting heads for the second time when Lelly slipped into line. She rolled her eyes and then sighed.

"Leslie Morgan Dean, where have you been? Didn't you hear me calling?"

Lelly ducked her head. When Miss Smith called her by her entire name, she knew she was in big trouble.

If Billy T. hadn't pulled at Lelly's hair, causing her to yelp, Marie might have missed seeing the rose in the little girl's hand. But she did see it, and the incongruity of its presence prompted her to ask, "Lelly, where did you get that? You're not supposed to pick flowers without permission."

Lelly's chin began to quiver again. "I didn't pick it. He gave it to me," she said, pointing toward the trees.

He? Marie pivoted, staring intently toward the place where Lelly Dean was pointing, but there was no one there. She stared down at the rose in the little girl's hand as thoughts of child molesters sprang forth. And then something clicked, and her mind made the jump from child molester to serial killer. Dear God! A rose! It was Prince Charming's signature.

She gasped and spun around.

"Children! Hold on to your partner's hand and don't move! I'll be right back!"

She called out to a co-worker to come watch her group and then started to run toward the pay phone at the entrance to the park. It was a parent's worst nightmare, but for a day care worker who was in charge of many parents' children, it was even worse. Within minutes of Marie Smith's call, the park was swarming with officers and Lelly Dean was more important than she might ever have wished.

But the man who'd caused all the uproar was nowhere to be found. There was nothing left to mark his passing except the one single rose dangling from Lelly Dean's small fist.

Dr. Harry Wallis drove through the gates of Reed House, grimacing slightly as he maneuvered along the winding road and up to the employee parking lot. He kept telling himself it was good to be back, although right now, he wasn't so sure.

After being away from this place for the better part of two months, he'd almost forgotten how beautiful Reed House was—and how different the lives of the people who lived here, although none of the patients who resided in Reed House came from indigent families. On the contrary. Reed House was the kind of place where the wealthy put away their family embarrassments. It wasn't just a home for the aged, nor was it a place where people with broken bodies or hearts went to heal. Only those missing necessary bits and pieces of their minds need apply.

Harry considered it a privilege to work with the mentally challenged, and on that rare occasion when one of his patients took the initiative and did something without being told, he rejoiced. However, the job and the people who lived at Reed House were a considerable source of wear and tear on his own gentle mind.

The vacation had been his first in over ten years and from the shape he'd been in when he left two months earlier, long overdue. But now he was back and well-refreshed from a cruise. He parked and got out, telling himself it was good to be back and trying not to think about the fact that yesterday he'd been in the Caribbean.

"Good morning, Dr. Wallis."

He looked up. A gardener was waving at him from behind the hedge he was clipping.

"Morning, Alfred. Long time no see."

Alfred grinned. "Got yourself quite a tan," he teased.

Harry waved as he headed inside. "Almost as good as yours," he called back.

Both men laughed aloud.

Alfred's skin was a dark chocolate brown, compliments of his African ancestry. Harry's tan was closer to red than brown, but such was the fate of fair-skinned, redheaded people.

As he entered the building, he was struck by a scent he had never noticed before. In spite of the perfectly designed interior, there was a slight smell of decay, the likes of which one might encounter in a fine old home. He sighed. No matter how finely turned out Reed House might be, there was no way to disguise the depth of disappointment that hung within these walls.

He continued down one long hall and then turned the corner. Two doors down and to the right and he would be in his office. If he was lucky, he wouldn't have to greet the administrator until after he'd had another cup of coffee. Only a few more steps and he—

"Good morning, Dr. Wallis. I see you finally deigned to make an appearance. We were beginning to wonder."

Damn. He pasted a smile on his face and turned.

"Good morning, Althea. I trust you've been well in my absence."

She sniffed and then tilted her head, eyeing him in a semijudgmental manner.

"You're sunburned," she said shortly. "Staff meeting in half an hour. See you there."

His smile was sharp, but he didn't bother to respond to her cutting comment. Yet when he entered his office, he slammed the door behind him just loud enough to make a statement. He glanced in the mirror beside the door and frowned. It wasn't a sunburn—at least not anymore. Damn Althea Good and her opinions anyway.

An hour later, he was leaning on a pile of papers and trying not to yawn. It wasn't until Althea Good shifted topics and began referring to the list of recently released patients that he came to. He shuffled a few papers and then found the page. Around here, no one was ever released.

There were the exceptions, but in those cases, the patients weren't actually released, but rather moved. Sometimes when people's jobs and lives took them elsewhere, they moved their family members to other facilities similar to this. But because of the problems and conditions of the patients who resided in Reed House, the only people who actually left here were the ones who died.

Harry skimmed the names on the paper with absent interest, and then one name caught his attention. He bolted to his feet and then leaned across the table, unable to believe what he'd just read.

"What is the meaning of this?" he asked, pointing to a name halfway down the list.

She glanced at the name, hiding a quick surge of anxiety. There was no way they could be allowed to know.

"Meaning of what?" she asked.

"Releasing my patient without my consent."

"You were gone a long time. Things happen."

"Like what?" Harry asked.

The answer was pat, one she'd used countless times before. "In his case, the parents were killed in an auto accident. I suppose the executors of the estate had their reasons. At any rate, they had him sent elsewhere."

Harry felt sick to his stomach. "Did you read his file? Did you make sure they knew of his special problems?"

Althea picked up her pen. "That's their responsibility now, not ours."

She pointed to the next item on the agenda, but Harry Wallis wasn't satisfied. "Althea…do you know what that man was capable of doing?"

She shrugged.

Harry groaned beneath his breath as he headed for the door.

"Where do you think you're going? This meeting is not over," she called.

"It is for me," Wallis said. "I've got to find out what happened to him." He reached the door and then paused, making no attempt to hide his disdain. "I don't suppose you've done a follow-up, just to make sure he settled in okay?"

Her eyes were a cold, distant green, but the high flush of color on both cheeks gave away her emotion. She was as angry as a woman could get without screaming.

"You aren't the only competent doctor on the face of the earth. You're behaving as if he were some unpredictable animal. I'm sure that, wherever he is, he is in capable hands."

Harry Wallis's face was as red as his hair. His voice was shaking with pent-up fury when he said, "Without that medicine he's been taking for the past twenty-odd years, he *is* an animal. If anything bad has happened, it will be your fault."

At that point, Althea Good began to panic. This needed to stop before it went any further.

"Look, Harry, come back and sit down. I'll make a few calls and let you know personally."

Harry shook his head. "If anyone is making calls, it will be me." Then he started out the door.

"Where are you going?"

"To the Donner home to pay my respects. Regardless of what happened to their son, they were fine people. I'm sorry I was gone when they died."

Althea paled. This was going too far. "But that's silly," she argued. "There's no one there. I told you, they died."

But Harry was through listening. He was too worried to delay any longer. Until he knew for sure that his patient was receiving the finest care, he wouldn't be able to rest. Surely someone there could give him some answers.

With the address in his pocket and his cell phone at his side in case he got lost, he took off in haste. Almost an hour later, he arrived.

It was obvious to Harry Wallis as he turned through the gates that the Donners' worth was substantial. But why, he wondered, would they have left orders for their son to be moved? Reed House was the only home he'd known. If they were dead, it only stood to reason that they would want him where he would be best cared for. None of this made any sense.

Matty put the finishing touches on the salad she'd just chopped. The roast was in the oven and warming. Scalloped potatoes and new green beans were cooked and ready for reheating whenever Gabriel and Laura got hungry. A few more minutes and then she would be on her way home, and none too soon.

She glanced over her shoulder, making sure she was still alone. Ever since the Donners' deaths, there had been many strange things happening in this house. Things that didn't make sense—like small objects being moved from room to room, and the lingering scent of Angela Donner's perfume when it shouldn't be there. Add a psychic to the picture and Matty was very unhappy.

So when the doorbell rang, she jumped in sudden fright and then made the sign of the cross as she scurried toward the front of the house. Too many things were going on in this house. Too many things she didn't understand.

Preoccupied with her own set of troubles, she opened the door and glowered at the stranger on the doorstep.

"Yes?"

Harry took a deep breath. The sooner he asked his questions, the sooner this meeting would be over.

"I'm Dr. Harry Wallis, chief of staff at Reed House. May I speak to—"

Matty blanched and then started to cry.

Stunned by her behavior, Harry took an instinctive step backward, hoping that distance would give her a measure of reassurance.

"Please, I meant no harm. I was only—"

The door swung suddenly inward. Harry and the maid were no longer alone, and Harry could do nothing but stare at the man looming in the opening. He was tall, well over six feet, and his dark skin and black hair were terribly familiar, as were the shape of his face and those piercing green eyes. Harry had the feeling that the man would happily deck the first person who dared come any closer.

Gabriel's expression was cold. The glint in his eyes a warning. "What's going on here?"

Harry Wallis took one look at the man in the doorway and exhaled. "My God," he said softly. "I never knew."

Gabriel frowned. "Have we met?"

"I'm sorry," Harry said, extending his hand. "Dr. Harry Wallis, chief of staff at Reed House."

That meant nothing to Gabriel. He remained silent, waiting for the man to explain further.

Matty glanced nervously at the men and then scurried away.

Harry shrugged. "I don't know what I said to upset her, but whatever it was, I'm truly sorry."

Gabriel nodded, reserving forgiveness.

"I came to express my sympathy for your loss," Harry said, "and to inquire about your brother's welfare."

Gabriel frowned. "You must have me mixed up with someone else. I don't have a brother."

Harry felt like a drowning man who'd been tossed into a lifeboat without any oars.

"I was referring to Garrett," he said. "I've been his doctor for some time now. Surely your parents mentioned me?"

Gabriel shook his head, then he heard footsteps and turned. It was Laura.

"I'm sorry," Laura said. "I didn't know you had company. I'll just—"

"No, don't go," Gabriel said, and held out his hand.

Laura slipped her fingers through his, smiling as he pulled her close.

"Dr. Harry Wallis," Harry said. "I work at Reed House." Again he was surprised by their lack of recognition.

Gabriel was tired. The last thing he wanted to

do was deal with more business, but it was obvious this man wasn't going away.

"Dr. Wallis, I appreciate your condolences, but I'm afraid you have my family confused with someone else."

Harry shook his head, like a dog shedding water. He'd known plenty of families who wanted to ignore the kind of people who resided in Reed House, but he'd never met any who denied knowing them to the patients' own doctor. When he answered, his voice was louder and more defensive than normal.

"There's no need pretending with me," he said shortly. "You forget, I've been responsible for his care. In fact, that's partly why I came. I respected your parents very much, but I cared deeply for your brother, as I do all of my patients."

Laura was standing quietly within the shelter of Gabriel's arm, but the moment she heard the doctor say *brother,* she flashed on the image she'd had of an angel with two faces. Suddenly it all made sense. She grabbed Gabriel by the arm.

"My God...of course! Two! There are two of you."

Gabriel stared at Laura as if she'd just lost her mind.

She wanted to hug the doctor. This was the best news she'd had in her life.

"They're not just brothers, are they, Dr. Wallis? They're identical twins, aren't they? That's why I kept seeing Gabriel's face. But why, Gabriel? Why didn't you know?"

The skin on the back of Gabriel's neck began to crawl. Somewhere in the back of his mind, something dark and ugly began pushing itself forward.

"No," he muttered, and turned quickly away, afraid to let anyone see his deep fear.

Harry Wallis's mind was scrambling for answers. He was stunned that the man hadn't known. And then another fact hit him hard, sucking the breath from his body and the blood from his face. If these people hadn't known about Garrett, then what had happened to him? Althea had said that the family had moved him. But the family couldn't move someone they knew nothing about.

"Look," Harry said. "I came because I'm concerned about Garrett's welfare. I was told that the family had him moved to another facility. Is that so?"

Gabriel was fighting panic. He had a brother? Even more than that, an identical twin, and he didn't even remember him?

"I have no idea," Gabriel mumbled.

Laura stepped in to explain. "Gabriel was only recently released from the hospital himself. He was in the wreck that killed his parents."

Harry blanched. "Oh. Oh my. I am so very, very sorry. And I've bumbled in here and dumped all of this on you, as well. Still, you must understand my position. I have to know that Garrett is all right. People's lives could depend on that."

Gabriel's stomach turned. People's lives. Oh, God.

"How so?" he asked carefully. "Is he dangerous?"

Harry sighed and then nodded. "He can be." It was so hard to explain someone like Garrett.

Gabriel kept thinking of the violence he'd witnessed and the people who'd died. He felt sick all the way to his soul.

"I did not have him moved," he said.

Harry shuddered.

Gabriel took a step closer, needing to hear something that would make this okay.

"If he was put in your care, why don't you know where he is?"

Harry's voice was shaking. "Our administrator said that you had him moved."

Gabriel's voice had lowered to a low, angry

growl. "But how could I move someone I knew nothing about?"

Harry was at the point of panic. "I don't know."

"So," Gabriel continued. "Let me see if I've got this straight. I have a brother who isn't right in the head. And you people lost him. Is that about right?"

Harry groaned. "I was gone on vacation," he mumbled. "I only got back today."

"When would he have been released?" Gabriel asked.

Harry hesitated, but there was no use lying. "More than a month ago."

Gabriel closed his eyes. That would be about the same time he started hearing the voices.

Oh, God.

His brother had been calling out for help, and Gabriel had shut him out of his mind. Slow anger began to build, both at God for letting this happen, and at his parents because they'd never told him.

"They must have had their reasons," Laura said.

Gabriel jerked. It was disconcerting to know that the woman he loved could read his mind. His fingers curled into fists. One more push and he could easily explode.

And then Laura touched the side of his face. "Look at me," she urged.

Gabriel did, and within seconds was left with nothing but an overwhelming sadness.

"Lost. He kept saying he was lost. Dear God, he was just trying to get home."

Before anyone could react, they heard sobbing at the end of the hallway. It was Matty.

Gabriel felt weak with relief. Matty would know. She would help them understand.

"Matty?"

Once again, her face crumpled, but this time she didn't look away. Without having said a word, Gabriel found himself staring into a truth he didn't want to believe.

"Matty, for God's sake!" he said. "Talk to me!"

"You were both so beautiful. Tiny little *niños* with so much black hair and such healthy appetites. You grew so big so fast." Her eyes brimmed with unshed tears, but she kept on talking, purging herself of a secret she'd kept for almost twenty-six years.

"By the time you were both three, we knew something was wrong. Garry—that's what your mother called him then—didn't talk. Autistic. That was the first diagnosis. Then they changed that to something else, and then something else again, until no one had a name for what was wrong. All they could say was that he would never be right.''

"But why?" Gabriel asked. "Why don't I remember him?"

"Because when you were five, you and Garrett were on your way outside to play baseball. You fell down the stairs and broke your arm. When you started screaming with pain, Garrett went crazy. He hit you with the bat he was carrying so many times, you almost died. It was then your parents knew they'd been fooling themselves. Garrett had been violent before, but never like that. Your mother made your father promise that if you lived, they would put Garrett in a place where he could never hurt anyone again. When you woke up, you never asked for him—never even spoke his name.''

Gabriel turned away to stare out a window at the oncoming darkness, trying to imagine what that little boy, who was already crippled in his mind, must have thought when they took him out of the only home he'd ever known.

"It wasn't your fault," Laura said softly.

Gabriel turned, unable to quit staring at her face. Again she'd shown an amazing knowledge of what he was thinking. He held out his arms.

Laura stepped into his embrace, wishing she

could give him peace, but knowing that he would have to come to terms with this revelation on his own.

"He didn't hate you, Gabriel. It was the sounds that set him off, not a lack of love. His hearing is very acute. Noise causes him pain, not anger."

Harry couldn't hide his surprise. "Miss Dane, I don't know how you know these things, but you're right. That's why I was so concerned when I learned he'd been released."

Gabriel interrupted. His voice was tinged with despair.

"He's lost, you know."

Harry's hopes dropped. "We've got to find him before he does any harm."

Gabriel turned, his eyes blurred with unshed tears. "It's too late. Haven't you been reading the papers?"

Harry's belly began to knot. "I've been out of the country for the past two months."

Gabriel pointed toward a bank of windows in the adjoining room and the rose garden visible beyond.

"My...our...mother loved roses. She had a habit of picking the thorns off all of her roses before she arranged them."

Harry caught himself holding his breath.

Gabriel's gaze locked on the doctor's face.

"During the last two weeks, five people have been murdered in the greater Oklahoma City area. According to police reports, they died from a blow to the head. Most of them from broken necks."

Bile began rising in the back of Harry's throat. He wanted to run. He wanted to hide. He couldn't move.

"The killer—the press has named him Prince Charming—leaves a rather remarkable calling card with each victim."

Harry closed his eyes and tried to picture the color of the Caribbean at sunset, but nothing would come. He couldn't get past the ugliness of what Gabriel Donner was saying.

Gabriel continued, needing to get it all said before he came undone.

"He leaves a rose with each victim. And the damnedest thing...something the police have not made public knowledge, but it's something I know—the stems have no thorns."

Harry Wallis's face was as white as his shirt. "Oh, God! Oh, dear merciful God. What have we done?"

Eleven

When Harry Wallis could think without needing to throw up, he staggered to the nearest chair and sat down. Gabriel was sitting on the staircase, his hands covering his face. Laura was beside him, uncertain of what to say. At this point, there wasn't anything Harry could say that would help. He'd already done enough.

The housekeeper had slumped into a nearby chair and was sobbing quietly. The knot in Harry's belly tightened as he stared at the trio. They were suffering, and mostly because of what his colleagues had done. He couldn't fix what had already happened, but he knew how to stop it from happening again.

"Mr. Donner, I need to notify the police. Garrett must be stopped before anyone else suffers. They'll need a picture of him, but I'm not sure we have a recent copy on file."

Gabriel looked up, his expression still blank with disbelief.

"I don't suppose they could use one of mine?" he asked.

Harry's eyes narrowed thoughtfully as he stared at Gabriel. He'd seen Garrett Donner every day of his life for the past fifteen years, and he wouldn't have been able to tell them apart.

"Yes, I suppose they can."

Even though Harry Wallis had made the decision to call the police, he couldn't bring himself to walk away...at least, not just yet. Gabriel Donner's pain was almost palpable. Harry caught himself watching the man without figuring out why. It took a bit for him to realize that he was expecting Gabriel to react as Garrett would have done. Then he shook off the feeling. Just because the two men looked alike, that didn't mean they would react in the same manner. He needed to remember that Garrett was the one who kept coming unglued.

Gabriel wanted to lie down and never get up. Only Laura's presence right now was keeping him sane. And yet, as badly as he needed her to be here, he couldn't face her—at least, not yet. He could only imagine what she must be thinking. He wouldn't blame her if she got on the next plane and never looked back.

As for Matty, he couldn't bring himself to even look at her. In a way, he felt as if she'd betrayed him, too. Truth was, he didn't want to talk to anyone. What he wanted was to find the man—he amended the thought: find his brother—before anyone else died.

Gabriel pushed himself up from where he was sitting and walked to the windows at the front of the house.

The yard needed to be mowed. He needed to remember to call the lawn service tomorrow. He glanced up at the sky. It was getting dark. He could hear the others talking, making plans, trying to guess and then outguess what this lost man might do, but he couldn't focus.

Guilt gnawed at him.

A brother.

He had a brother, and he'd forgotten him—tossed his memory away like an unwanted toy. As he stared out the window, he began to see his surroundings for what they truly were. He turned, looking up at the grand staircase and the opulence of the decor in the room beyond. His gaze traveled from that to the paintings hanging on the walls, a passion his father and mother had shared. For the first time in his life, he looked at his surroundings and realized that he'd taken the excess and comfort for granted. He'd led a privileged life. What about Garrett?

"Dr. Wallis?"

Glad to have something to do besides breathe, Harry jumped to answer. "Yes?"

"Reed House. Is it nice?"

Harry sighed. He understood what Gabriel Donner couldn't bring himself to ask.

"It's beautiful," he said softly. "Garrett had his own room. Your parents had it decorated especially for him and visited at least twice a month, sometimes more."

It was impossible for Gabriel to hide his shock. He knew he was staring, but he couldn't help it. It would seem his brother hadn't been the only well-kept secret in this house. Obviously he hadn't known his parents, either.

Matty knew Gabriel all too well. She could only imagine what he must be thinking. And in spite of her reluctance to interfere, she knew she was the only one left who could help. She shifted nervously and then cleared her throat. Everyone looked at her, but her attention was focused entirely on Gabriel.

"I heard them once, talking about telling you."

"Then why didn't they?" Gabriel asked.

Matty shrugged. "I don't know. Your father

wanted to. Your mother did not. But they loved him dearly, as dearly as they loved you. That is all I know."

Gabriel frowned. It would seem that he wasn't the only one who'd been irrevocably affected by their premature deaths. He couldn't quit thinking about the brother he didn't know. He could only imagine how confused and frightened Garrett must have felt when his parents never showed up. And no matter what bullshit the people at Reed House were trying to sell, something awful had happened to him there. Gabriel could feel it.

He couldn't get over the image of a child trapped in a grown man's body, trying to fend for himself on the streets. One did not just...lose an entire human being without a reason. It was more than Gabriel could stand. He suddenly erupted.

"That's bull! If Mom and Dad loved him so much, then why didn't they make provisions for him? I didn't know about Garrett, but our lawyer should have. This shouldn't have happened."

He walked away without looking back.

Harry glanced at his watch. "It's getting late. I should call the police." Then he thought of all the parameters concerning this case and shifted mental gears. "On second thought, I think I'd better go in person. This is too complicated to explain over the phone.''

Laura's first instinct was to follow Gabriel, but getting Harry Wallis's information to the police seemed more pressing. She grabbed the doctor's arm, begging him to wait.

''Before you leave, let me give you the name of the officer in charge of the case.''

Gabriel was standing on the patio overlooking the rose garden when he heard the sound of a car engine starting. He didn't bother to look. It would be the doctor leaving.

He closed his eyes, inhaling deeply and then exhaling slowly. When he looked up, Laura was standing at his side. She didn't speak. He tried to smile, but it just wouldn't come. There was too much pain in his heart.

''Ah, God, baby, what a monumental mess.''

She laid her head against his arm and began rubbing her hand up and down the middle of his back in slow, measured strokes. He shuddered as the tension in his body began to subside.

''Is Matty gone?''

Laura nodded.

He started to speak and then paused. Laura felt his hesitation.

"What?" she asked softly.

"My whole life has been one big lie. The people I loved and trusted most have been lying to me. And why? I'm not a little kid. Why would they think I couldn't handle this?"

He turned and pulled her into his arms, burying his nose against the curls on her head.

"Maybe it wasn't about you as much as it was about them," Laura said.

Gabriel stilled. "What do you mean?"

"Well, Matty said your father wanted to tell you but your mother refused. Look at it from her point of view. From the time you and Garrett were babies, I'll bet she found herself watching every move Garrett made in order to protect you."

It was a direction he hadn't considered. He straightened, listening carefully as Laura continued.

"If Garrett was as easily provoked as the doctor said, then I'll guarantee that cracking your head with a baseball bat wasn't the first time you suffered at his hands."

It made sense, yet Gabriel still couldn't let go.

"Okay, but look at me now. I'm past thirty years old and nearly six and a half feet tall. I have shoulders like a pro linebacker, and I've been all but running the security business single-handedly for the past four years. I'm not weak, and I'm damned sure not helpless.''

Laura smiled gently and then shook her head. ''No, Gabriel, you still don't get it. A mother may grow old and feeble, but in her eyes, her children never grow up. I think it was that instinct to protect that kept her silent, and if your father was anything like his son, he loved her too much to deny her what she wanted.''

In a strange way, what Laura said helped. A weight lifted from Gabriel's heart as he took her in his arms, hugging her close and then placing kiss after kiss on her face.

Laura closed her eyes, savoring the taste of him on her lips. For a time, the world slipped away. But there was too much at stake for her to stand silently by. It wasn't long before Gabriel carried her to a chaise longue and sat down with her in his arms.

Night closed around them. Out on the lawn, fire-flies began to make an unannounced appearance onto evening's darkening stage. Gabriel held her close, partly because he loved the feel of her near his heart, and partly because he needed to hold on to someone warm—someone sane.

A car honked. The faraway squawk of a siren drifted through the air. The scent of charcoal was in the air. Someone was barbecuing their evening meal. In the midst of it all, an emptiness within Gabriel's heart began to expand, growing wider and deeper with each oncoming breath. And in that second, between the exhaling of one breath and the drawing of another, Gabriel knew that what he was feeling belonged to someone else.

Garrett.

It struck him dumb. *Ah, God. I thought I knew what lonely felt like...until now.*

"Laura?"

"What?"

"How will we ever find him? The city is so big, and he's so damned lost."

She hadn't known until he asked, but the moment the words were given life, she knew what the answer was.

"I don't think we have to," she said.

Gabriel frowned. "Of course we have to."

"No, you misunderstand," she said. "What I meant was, we won't have to find him. I think he will find us."

"What do you mean by that?"

"Think about it, sweetheart. He's connected to you in a way we don't understand. At times your thoughts are the same. You hear his voice. You see what he sees."

"Yes. So?"

Laura slipped an arm around Gabriel's waist and leaned into his strength. "You know what I think? I think that he's locked onto you like a homing device. I think he will find his way home through you."

For the first time since Harry Wallis had knocked on his door, Gabriel felt a measure of hope. "Really?"

She nodded.

But then his hopes crashed. "Even if he gets here, look at what he's facing. They'll never let him go back to Reed House, and he'll never understand why."

Laura turned in Gabriel's arms, cradling his face in the palms of her hands. "One worry at a time," she said softly. "Remember, Dr. Wallis is on his way to the police. The decision is out of our hands. All we can do is pray. Tomorrow…if we have to…we worry."

Gabriel turned his face into the palm of her hand, tracing her lifeline with the tip of his tongue. As badly as he wanted her here, the fact that she was made him sick with worry. He kept remembering that she'd seen her own death at, she'd thought, his hands. Now they both knew she'd been wrong. It was Garrett who would try to kill her.

"I should send you home on the first plane out tomorrow."

But he cupped her face, then her breast, teasing the nipple until it peaked into a hard, achy nub. She swayed with a sudden longing. The flashfire of need that swept through her was staggering. Leaving was the last thing on her mind.

She leaned forward, whispering against his ear, "I'd much rather you took me to bed."

His eyes glittered dangerously, his nostrils flaring with need. He gathered her into his arms and then stood.

Love. He loved Laura Dane.

Then he thought of Garrett. Who did Garrett love? Could Garrett love? He groaned as Laura's arms slid around his neck.

Ah, God, love was good. He urged her toward the door, for the time being shutting Garrett and everyone else from his mind.

Acting more on instinct than reason, he got them both inside, set the security alarm, and then headed upstairs with the blood pounding against his eardrums.

He stripped her standing and then laid her on his bed. He watched her eyes grow heavy, her breath coming in shudders as he stripped off his own clothes, leaving them in a pile upon the floor. His body was hard and straining toward her, his pulse ragged with need. He buried his face between her breasts and then took a deep breath, making himself calm, forcing himself to regain some control.

Laura's hands were shaking as she tunneled her fingers through his hair.

"Gabriel, I—"

She gasped as he slid downward, leaving a trail of kisses to mark his passing. When it dawned on her what he was about to do, she froze. Could she? Should she?

"Oh! Oh, Gabriel, I don't think I can—"

His voice was ragged, his cheeks high with color as he raised his head and met her wild gaze.

"Yes."

One word. But it was enough to push her over the edge. She took a deep breath and then sighed.

"Close your eyes," he whispered.

She did as she was told and felt his lips upon her belly, then on the inside of her thigh. Well aware of what was coming, she tensed nervously. Then out of the darkness, she felt his hands upon her hips and heard his voice, beckoning, demanding, promising.

"Laura."

Her answer was little more than an exhalation of sound.

"Don't think...just feel," he said.

She let him all the way into her soul.

Gabriel was still awake long after the madness had stopped, long after Laura had fallen asleep in his arms. He lay without moving, staring thoughtfully at a parting in the curtains and watching the light that spilled through making wild, nightmarish patterns on the wall and the ceiling. But there was nothing nightmarish about what he was feeling. His heart was full, so full of love for this woman he held. She shifted in her sleep and then sighed, and he felt her breath against his chest. At that moment he knew that he would do whatever it took to keep her safe and alive, even if it meant risking his own life.

Yes, love was good. When it was good, it was very, very good. Then he thought of Garrett. And when it was bad, it was horrid.

Harry Wallis turned left, heading under the overpass to get back on I-40. His mind was racing from explanation to explanation that he might offer the authorities, and all the while wondering how much culpability Reed House was going to have to shoulder. The only thing that gave him any measure of satisfaction was knowing that Althea Good was going to have to answer for what she'd done. But his concentration was shattered by the sudden pop and then wobble of his car.

Blowout!

Adrenaline shot through his system like a bullet through butter as he struggled to steer to a nearby exit ramp. Relief came as he maneuvered to a side street and put the car in park.

He peered through the windshield, trying to figure out where he was. Nothing looked familiar, and what he did see looked seedy and rundown. It figured.

He leaned back in disgust. There was no such thing as a convenient accident, but there *was* modern technology. All he had to do was call road service, get the tire fixed, and he would be on his way. He reached for his cell phone and started to punch in the numbers when he realized something was wrong.

"Damn, damn and double damn," he muttered. The battery was dead.

He popped the trunk and got out with a grunt, cursing every step to the back of the car. As he leaned inside the trunk, he heard the rush of crunching leaves and stopped and turned, staring nervously toward the bushes at the side of the road. But when no one emerged, he scoffed at his own fears and began to remove the spare.

Time passed. Harry was squatting beside the jack, giving the last lug nut a final twist and cursing car manufacturers in general for that joke they passed off as a spare, when the skin on the back of his neck began to crawl. From the corner of his eyes, he saw movement. He tightened his fingers around the lug wrench and started to stand, but he was a moment too late.

He never saw the mugger's face or knew what was happening after the blow to his head. Minutes later, Harry's unconscious body was dumped into a nearby ditch. The thief sped away in his car, leaving nothing to mark what had happened but Harry Wallis's body and a set of smoking tire tracks on the pavement.

Before, he'd been afraid of the dark. Now dark was his friend. Negotiating streets and alleyways at night wasn't easy. He couldn't see street signs, which didn't much matter, because he couldn't read many words. But he could write his name, and he could say his prayers. His mother had taught him to say his prayers. He thought about his mother and wanted to cry. They hadn't come back like they'd promised. Before he got lost, they had always come back.

Up ahead, a car suddenly turned the corner and started down the street toward him. He froze in the oncoming glare like a spotlighted buck. A horn sounded, breaking the trance in which he was standing and sending a piercing pain throughout his skull. He threw back his head and screamed. The undiluted sound of pain and rage sent a cat on the hunt up a nearby tree and brought an old woman to her window to peer out. All she saw was a speeding car. Afraid of drive-by shootings, she quickly turned off the lights and went to bed an hour and a half early.

The teenagers shrieked with delight as they sped past, laughing and pointing at the screaming giant.

When the fire was no longer behind his eyes and the wolves had quit taking bites of his mind, he moved deeper into the shadows. Tied to an invisible bond that only his heart knew well, he continued to move ever closer to the other half of himself. And as he walked, he began to recite the verse his mother had taught him.

"'Now I lay me down to sleep. I pray the Lord my soul to keep. If I should die before I wake, I pray the Lord my soul to take.'"

* * *

At exactly five minutes after eight the next morning, Kirby Summers walked into his office. Outside, it was threatening rain, and his expression was only a couple of shades less grim than his mood. The media was having a heyday with Prince Charming's latest victim. They had interviewed an FBI profiler, as well as a Texas serial killer who was on death row, awaiting execution.

And, everyone had an opinion as to why Prince Charming had given a five-year-old child a rose and then let her walk away, when he'd killed other innocent people for no obvious reason at all. Pressure was coming at the police from all sides. They were facing mass hysteria from metro citizens. They needed to make an arrest. They needed someone in jail. They needed someone to blame.

Reports were already sifting into OSBI headquarters that gun sales in the greater Oklahoma City area had gone up three hundred percent. The jump had begun right after the first victim was murdered and soon after the police had been unable to come up with even one good suspect.

Kirby took off his jacket and loosened his tie before reaching for his coffee cup. His mind was in limbo as he walked out of his office and down the hall to the break room, his nose wrinkling as he walked through the doorway. The coffee smelled burned, which meant it was probably re-heated from last night. He was, however, in need of caffeine too badly to care. He poured himself a cup and then took a slow, careful drink, sipping at the thick, black brew as if he were taking medicine.

"Hey, Summers. Did you see the report I put on your desk? It's the top file in your In basket."

Kirby looked up. Red Anthony, a fellow agent, was standing in the doorway.

"What report is that?" he asked.

"The DNA you had run on that nut who wanted to be locked up."

"Already?" he asked.

"It's an early report. The in-depth one comes later, but I think you'll find it interesting," Red said, and then grinned as he walked away.

Kirby bolted for his desk, juggling the hot coffee and a big case of anticipation. Something was up or Red Anthony wouldn't have bothered to mention it.

It was there, right on top, where Anthony said he'd put it. He set down his cup and slid into his chair as he opened the file. Within moments, he began to read.

His eyes widened, and his heart began to pound. There was no misinterpreting the information. The blood and tissue samples taken from under the fingernails of Sadie Husser's houseman matched the blood and tissue samples taken from Gabriel Donner.

"Son of a—"

He set down the report and then took a deep breath, trying to calm his racing pulse as he calculated the data he had left. He didn't know how to explain the fact that another victim had died while Gabriel Donner had been locked in an Oklahoma City jail, but he figured there was a way. They'd just assumed it was the same guy. Maybe it was a copycat killer. He loosened his tie and reached for a pen.

Gabriel Donner had walked in of his own accord, claiming he'd been having psychic flashes into the killer's mind. But what if Gabriel Donner *was* the killer? What if he was playing games with them? What if he'd planned the whole jail thing just to put them off the track?

Then he frowned. That didn't make sense. They'd had absolutely *no* clues until he'd walked in with that crazy story. Still, Kirby was a realist, and facts were facts. Gabriel Donner's DNA matched the samples they'd taken from one of the victims. It was enough.

He reached for the phone. "Chief, I need an arrest warrant. We just got a break on the Prince

Charming case.'' He paused. The smile on his face was genuine. "Yes, sir. I'll be right there.''

Mike Travers was all smiles as he rang the doorbell. Not even the threat of an impending thunderstorm could ruin his day. When Matty answered, he bolted into the house and grabbed her around the waist, dancing her about in the hall as if it were New Year's Eve.

A pink flush moved up Matty's neck and onto her cheeks as she struggled to free herself.

"Dr. Mike, have you lost your mind?''

He stopped in a patch of light spilling through the stained glass window behind them, unaware that the purple and green colors settling on his hair had given him a punk rock look and that the exertion of their dance had put a youthful expression on his face.

"Good news is always a cause for celebration.''

Still haunted by the secret she'd kept all these years and the revelations that had come out last night, she couldn't think of anything to celebrate. Tears sprang to her eyes, and she pressed her fingers to her lips to keep them from shaking.

"Good? Secrets are never good, Dr. Mike. You of all people should know that.''

With that cryptic statement, she turned and left, leaving him confused and alone in the hallway.

"Well now," he muttered. "What *didn't* they tell me when they called?"

He smoothed the top of his hair, shifting the purple side back toward the green where it belonged and then moved out of the light. At once the bizarre appearance disappeared and he became the graying, stoop-shouldered man that the years had made of him. He went in search of Gabriel and Laura.

A few minutes later he spied them in Angela's rose garden. He could tell by the expressions on their faces that something was wrong. Then what, he wondered, had they meant when they'd left a message saying Gabriel was definitely cleared of any part in the killings? It would have been obvious to a blind man that everything wasn't okay. He stepped out onto the patio and waved to get their attention.

Laura saw him first. "Gabriel, your uncle Mike is here."

Gabriel pivoted angrily and started toward him. He wanted the truth. All of it. Even if it meant learning that Uncle Mike had been part of the great deception.

Well aware of how hurt and angry Gabriel was,

Laura started running to catch up, hoping to stop something from being said that couldn't be taken back.

Gabriel never even said hello. He just started talking, spitting out the bitter words without hesitation.

"Were you in on it, too?"

What was left of Mike Travers' smile withered. He took a deep breath and then headed for a nearby chair.

"Where are you going?" Gabriel asked.

"To sit down. It's too early in the morning for inquisitions."

Gabriel was so angry he was shaking. "Early? From where I'm standing, it's pretty damned late. About twenty-five years too late."

Mike's belly turned. This was bad. Very bad. His fingers curled around the arms of the chair in which he was sitting as he braced himself for whatever was coming.

"I don't know what you're talking about," Mike said. "But if you'll tell me, I'm sure we can work something out."

A cold smile broke the planes of Gabriel's face. "Don't give me any of your damned—"

Laura bolted up the steps and grabbed Gabriel's arm. He stopped in midsentence, his face contorted with fury. But when he saw the unspoken warning in her eyes, he began to relent. Anger shifted, leaving him with nothing but a wall of hurt he couldn't get over.

"Let's sit down," Laura said softly. "Don't rush to judgment, okay?"

He nodded, then slid into a chair across from his uncle and took a slow, deep breath. "Maybe I should start over."

Mike managed to smile. "That sounds like a plan to me."

Gabriel leaned forward, resting his elbows on his knees as he pinned the old man with a stare. "Did you know about Garrett?"

Mike frowned. "Who's Garrett?"

Something tight and binding that had been there since last night snapped loose inside of Gabriel's chest, and the relief that came with it was weakening.

Gabriel put his hand on his uncle Mike's knee. "You really don't know?"

Mike Travers shook his head. "No, son. I don't know. I don't know that name, and I don't know what you're talking about. I got a phone call from Laura saying that you'd been definitely cleared of any part of the murders. I thought that was a reason to celebrate. I don't understand what—"

Gabriel leaned back suddenly and covered his face with his hands. Deception from this man, too, would have been his undoing.

"Thank you, God," he whispered.

Puzzled, Mike turned to Laura. "Look. Would someone please tell me what's going on?"

Laura was standing behind Gabriel's chair. She touched his hair, then leaned down, briefly hugging his neck.

"Let me," she said softly. She began to talk.

A short while later, Mike Travers got up from where he was sitting and walked off the patio and out into the garden without speaking.

They watched him go, knowing that he, too, was struggling to come to terms with the fact that his two best friends in the world had not trusted him enough to share their burden.

Laura's heart went out to both men. "Go to him," she told Gabriel. "You love each other. You can heal each other."

Can't find you.

Startled by the intrusion of the voice at this particular moment, they stared at each other in total silence.

Gabriel's voice was bitter as he thumped himself hard in the chest.

"But who's going to heal him, Laura? Who's going to heal my brother?"

He walked away with a heavy heart.

Twelve

It was threatening rain when Harry Wallis came to, and his first thought was, Daylight...thank God it's daylight. It wasn't the first time he'd awakened, but it *was* the first time he'd been able to see where he was.

Twice during the night, he remembered hearing traffic on the road above, and each time he'd tried unsuccessfully to make himself known. He could only assume he was in a deep ditch or they would have been able to see him. And now, with the impending dawn, he could tell his assumption was right.

He was flat on his back, faceup to a mist that was starting to fall, and all he could see was gray sky above him and dirt and grass all around him. His head hurt terribly, and his right leg felt as if it were on fire. Although he was a doctor of psychiatry, he remembered enough about medicine to guess that it was probably broken.

Get up. I've got to get up. But when he tried, he fell back in the ditch with a groan. Something was wrong with his shoulder, too. Dislocated, he thought.

The mist was soaking into his clothes and his hair. He began to shiver. This wasn't good. He lifted his head, then had to close his eyes momentarily until the world stopped spinning.

Carefully, he took several deep breaths, trying to prepare himself for another move. By his estimation, he'd been out here most of the night with untreated injuries. As if that wasn't bad enough, it was starting to rain in earnest.

He gritted his teeth. ''Lord, help me.'' Then he rolled until he was lying on his belly instead of his back. Inch by inch, he began to crawl, using his good arm and uninjured leg to maneuver. In spite of the chill of the drenching rain, he broke out in a sweat born of pain. If he didn't get help soon, he would be adding pneumonia, at the least, to the problems he already had.

And then thunder ripped the heavens, belching through the elements. Harry jerked in reflex, groaning from the pain of the unexpected motion. But in that same deafening crash of uncontained fury, he remembered something he'd left undone.

Garrett Donner!

He had to be found before he took another life. With superhuman effort, Harry surged forward, emerging to the crest of the ditch. At that point his hopes dropped. He didn't see any signs of people—no houses or traffic—only a ribbon of potholed pavement and a thick line of trees on both sides of the road. Fighting back despair, he began to call out for help.

Sometime later, he thought he heard voices, but by then he was too weak to care. He never heard the arrival of the first police car, or felt the pitch and roll of his body as he was strapped onto a gurney and shoved into the back of an ambulance. It was only after the siren began to sound as the ambulance sped away that Harry Wallis came to again.

He opened his eyes, blinking at the unexpected lights. There was so much confusion and so many strange faces. He hurt. Why was he hurting? And he was cold...so cold.

"His BP is dropping."

Harry turned toward the voice. He knew what that meant. Blood pressure...his blood pressure was dropping. The faces hovering over him began to fade in and out of focus. He tried to think. There was something he needed to do.

"How long?" a paramedic shouted toward the driver up front.

"A minute, maybe two," the driver answered back.

Harry's heart skipped a beat. Did that mean he only had a minute or two to live? No. That didn't make sense. Why would they ask the driver?

"We're almost there," the driver yelled out.

Something clicked in Harry's mind. The hospital. They were talking about the distance to the hospital. That was a good joke on him. If he hadn't been so sleepy, he would have laughed. Someone was talking to him. He kept trying to listen, but they were talking too loud...no, too soft. He licked at his lips. They weren't the only ones who had something to say.

"P'lice. Gotta call p'lice," he mumbled.

A paramedic leaned toward him. "Sir, can you tell me your name?"

Harry's mind was stuttering. They were asking him one thing, he needed to tell them another. He shook his head from side to side and tried to reach for his pocket. To his dismay, he couldn't move his arms. It took several seconds for him to realize that he wasn't paralyzed but merely strapped down.

Another voice came at him through the fog in

his mind. "Sir, are you allergic to any medications?"

This time he knew the answer, and although his words were slurred, they understood what he was trying to say.

"Codeine. 'ergic to codeine."

"That's good, buddy, that's good. Can you tell me your name?"

Harry took a deep breath, making himself focus on saying the words. People were depending on him to fix things. Those same people needed to know where he was.

"Wallis. Harry Wallis. Need p'lice. Tell p'lice."

"We've got you, sir. You're going to be all right."

"No, no," Harry muttered. "P'lice. Call p'lice. Need 'talk to p'lice."

But no one was listening. And by the time they wheeled him into the operating room, he was in no condition to talk.

Kirby Summers turned off the highway and headed up the drive leading to the Donner residence. Three Oklahoma City police cars, as well as two other agents from the OSBI, followed him up to the house. When he parked and got out, the others followed.

Across the street, a neighbor in the act of trimming his hedge saw the array of vehicles turning in through the Donner gates and momentarily lost his focus by taking one snip too many, leaving a huge dip in the top of the shrub. When he realized what he'd done, he grimaced and threw down the shears in disgust. Now his wife was going to pitch a hissy fit for sure.

Kirby knocked, then rang the bell, too, patting his coat pocket and checking to make sure the arrest warrant was safely in place.

Matty saw the array of vehicles as she headed toward the door. Panic shafted through her. The last time officers had been standing on this doorstep, they'd come to tell her that Brent and Angela had died.

Kirby flashed his badge. "Ma'am, we have a warrant for Gabriel Donner's arrest. Is he here?"

Matty gasped. Before Kirby could react, her eyes rolled back in her head and she dropped to the floor with a thud.

"Well, hell," he muttered, and bolted inside.

Laura was standing out on the patio when she happened to turn. All she could see through the French doors were some people standing in the hallway and Matty lying on the floor.

Fear swamped her as her heart skipped a beat.

She began waving and shouting at Gabriel, who was at the other end of the grounds, until she made him look up.

"Something has happened to Matty!" she screamed, and pointed toward the house.

When she saw him starting to run, she bolted inside without waiting for him to catch up. Within seconds, she was on her knees at Matty's side and trying to figure out why Kirby Summers was there.

"My God," she gasped. "What happened?"

Kirby grabbed Laura's arm. "Where is Gabriel Donner?"

But Laura was too worried about Matty to do more than point.

Kirby glanced up, saw Donner coming in the distance, and rocked back on his heels. Time enough for the man to come to them.

Laura continued to feel for a pulse and rub Matty's hands in a panicked motion. "What happened to her? Have you called for an ambulance?"

Kirby felt slightly embarrassed, but at this point it was too late to start over. This arrest wasn't going exactly as planned. And although he didn't think Laura Dane was the fainting type, he still decided he would wait for Donner before repeating why he'd come.

"She fainted," he said shortly.

Laura could feel Matty's pulse. It was strong and steady. Still, no one fainted without reason.

"Maybe we should call an ambulance. With the deaths of Gabriel's parents and then the strain of his recovery, she's been under a lot of stress."

Kirby knew he was right in coming here, but he wasn't feeling as good about this trip as he had when he started.

"I guess it was the surprise," he muttered.

"What surprise?" Laura asked, but before Kirby could answer, Gabriel was on his knees beside Laura, cradling Matty's head in his lap.

Pale with worry and slightly out of breath, he brushed a gentle hand across the old woman's face. Her skin felt warm, her pulse steady. But he'd already lost more of his family than he could afford to; he didn't think he could face losing her, too.

"What happened?" he asked, without looking up.

"They said she just fainted," Laura said. "Should we call for an ambulance?"

Gabriel brushed a small strand of gray hair from her forehead. "Matty...Matty...can you hear me?"

When she didn't respond, he glanced up at an officer who was standing in the doorway and pointed toward the powder room across the hall. "In there. Bring me a wet towel."

The officer glanced toward Kirby, a little uncertain as to whether he was supposed to be following orders from the man they'd come to arrest. But Kirby nodded, and the officer did as Gabriel asked.

Moments later, with the wet cloth against her face and neck, Matty began to revive.

"What happened?" she mumbled, as Gabriel pulled her to a sitting position and leaned her against the wall.

"You tell me," Gabriel said gently, still mopping at her face and neck with the damp towel.

"My head hurts. Why does my head hurt?"

Matty reached for the back of her head, groaning at the knot beneath her fingertips. As she looked up, her gaze fell on Kirby Summers. Although she was shaky, there was no mistaking her anger.

"Him! It was him!"

Kirby flushed and then stood, trying to regain his composure, but Gabriel stood with him, and the look he gave Kirby was not friendly at all.

"What the hell did you do to her?"

Kirby reached into his pocket and pulled out the warrant. "I didn't do anything to her, and I'm sorry she fell before I could catch her." Then he took a deep breath and shifted mental gears. "Gabriel Donner, I have a warrant for your arrest for the murder of Stevie Ray Hampton, houseman for Sadie Husser.''

Gabriel froze.

Laura bolted to her feet and jumped between Gabriel and Summers. "No, you're making a mistake!"

Kirby smiled. "There's no mistaking the test results of the DNA we took from Gabriel. It was a perfect match for what we took out from under Stevie Hampton's fingernails.''

"That's because it was Gabriel's twin...his identical twin. Didn't Dr. Wallis tell you?"

The muscles in Kirby's belly began to tighten.

"I was given to understand that Gabriel Donner was an only child, and now you're claiming he has a twin?"

"But it's true. Dr. Wallis was—"

Kirby held up his hand. "Who's Dr. Wallis?"

Laura was frantic. She knew how absurd this must appear, but what in the world had happened to Harry Wallis's testimony? Why hadn't he done as he promised?

"Cuff him," Kirby ordered.

Laura spun around, frantic to stop this mistake before it got any worse.

"We didn't know about the brother ourselves until yesterday evening," she argued.

Kirby kept on walking.

She followed them all out the door.

"You don't understand. His name is Garrett. He looks just like Gabriel, but he's mentally disabled. Dr. Harry Wallis of Reed House is Garrett's doctor. He left here last night and said he was going straight to the police."

Kirby shook his head. "You're pushing your luck, Miss Dane. I still have some questions about that crazy story you two fed me about psychics and dreams."

Laura wanted to shake him. "It wasn't crazy. Henry Loo did die, remember? And Gabriel was locked in your jail when it happened."

Kirby spun sharply, pointing a finger in Laura's face. "That's just what I mean. You're not out of the clear, either. If I find you two staged that stunt with some copycat killer to try to throw us off Gabriel Donner's trail, you'll be charged with aiding and abetting."

Laura groaned with frustration. "You're making a mistake."

"And you're pushing your luck," Kirby retorted, then slid behind the wheel of his car. Just before he started the engine, he added, "Oh, and Miss Dane...don't leave town."

An officer pushed Gabriel's head forward as he folded him into the back seat of the cruiser.

"Watch your head, sir," he said.

But Gabriel was more worried about Laura than he was about bumping his head. She couldn't stay here alone. Garrett was still out there, and if Laura was right, he was slowly heading toward this place like a pigeon searching for home.

"Laura, listen to me! Call Uncle Mike and then get out of this house."

Laura reached for him, but someone pushed her out of the way and then closed the door in her face. Moments later, the police unit began to drive away, but she could still see Gabriel mouthing the words: *Get out of the house. Get out of the house.*

She started running alongside the car, shaking her head in vehement denial.

"I'm not leaving you. I won't leave you, too."

Gabriel dropped back against the seat in a panic. Laura had seen her own death. She'd also seen the face of the killer. He had to make somebody believe him before it was too late.

Laura was starting to get scared. The receptionist she'd just talked to had probably told Laura more than she should have, but she had been so desperate for news that she'd encouraged her to talk. According to the woman's story, Dr. Wallis hadn't shown up for work this morning, and everyone at Reed House was in an uproar. It seemed that he and the administrator, a Miss Althea Good, had had words yesterday, and Dr. Wallis had stormed out in a huff. They didn't know whether he'd quit, or whether he was just forming a new plan.

"A plan for what?" Laura had asked.

At that point the receptionist's information became sketchy. She wasn't really sure why a plan would be needed, but that was what she'd heard.

As Laura listened to the woman talk, a feeling came over her that she knew all too well. Something had happened to Harry Wallis that had nothing to do with his argument with Althea Good. As soon as they disconnected, she reached for the phone book and flipped to the yellow pages, trying to find the hospital listings. For some reason, she knew that was where Harry Wallis had gone.

And, in a way, it made sense. Harry Wallis was a doctor. Doctors worked out of hospitals. But he wasn't that kind of doctor. He doctored minds, not bodies. Still, she couldn't get the feeling out of her head. With the phone propped between her ear and her shoulder, she began at the top of the listings and started to dial. Harry Wallis was somewhere within the maze of medical facilities in the Oklahoma City area, and when she found him, she would personally take him to OSBI headquarters herself, if she had to.

The early morning thunderstorm had lingered into midday, leaving the city streets wet and slick. Kirby Summers was of the opinion that his day had peaked around five minutes after nine, which was about the time they'd arrested Gabriel Donner. It had been going downhill ever since. He typed the last of his notes into the computer and hit Save just as the phone began to ring. Moments after he picked up the receiver, he was telling himself he'd been right all along. That downhill roll he was on…it was getting steeper with each passing minute.

Not trusting the weather any more than he trusted his mood to stay even, he grabbed his raincoat on the way out the door. He'd just gotten an order to see a man at Saint Anthony's Hospital. The man's name was Harry Wallis—Dr. Harry Wallis.

All the way out the door, he kept hearing Laura Dane telling him that he'd made a mistake. Kirby yanked his hat down low on his forehead, muttering as he strode to his car, "Damn this day. Damn that woman. Damn this whole miserable mess."

All he knew was, if Gabriel Donner's arrest hadn't been righteous, he would never hear the end of it.

A short while later, he stopped at the nurses' desk to ask directions to Harry Wallis's room when someone touched his elbow. He turned. It was Laura Dane.

"Agent Summers, thanks for coming."

His smile never reached his eyes. "I wasn't given any choice," he said briefly.

"Dr. Wallis's room is this way," she said, and started down the hall. "He got mugged last night on the way to the precinct. He was in surgery all morning, but I understand he's going to be fine."

Kirby looked skeptical, but Laura couldn't blame him. This whole incident was too impossible to be believed. She paused at the door before taking Kirby inside.

"He's still pretty groggy," she explained. "But he's been so insistent on talking to the police that his doctor has allowed this visit in the hopes Dr. Wallis will calm down after he's said his piece."

Kirby didn't respond. He was reserving the right to judgment until after he'd heard what the man had to say. Right now, he was of the opinion that this was nothing more than a crazy alibi that had come a little too late. And then they entered the room, and the array of flowers stunned him. He couldn't help but glance at some of the cards, and when he did, his opinion of this man quickly changed.

"Well I'll be a—"

Laura turned. Her voice was just above a whisper. "Is something wrong?"

Kirby held up the card he'd just plucked from a basket of mums. "These are from the mayor, and those over there are from the governor and his wife."

Laura nodded. "Dr. Wallis has a fine reputation."

As Kirby poked the card back in the arrangement, he could feel that ball rolling him faster and faster downhill.

Laura stood at the side of Harry's bed, hating to disturb his uneasy slumber, but cognizant that Gabriel's well-being depended on what this man knew. Yes, in time, they would have been able to subpoena records from Reed House that would have proven their story, but they didn't have time to waste. Every minute that Garrett Donner was still free on the streets was another minute someone's life was in jeopardy.

"Dr. Wallis...it's Laura. I got the policeman, just as you asked." She motioned for Kirby to come closer and turned to him. "Say something to him," she said. "Let him know you're here."

Kirby leaned forward. "Dr. Wallis, I'm Kirby Summers, OSBI. Miss Dane said you wanted to talk to me."

The police? Why did he need the police? And then Harry remembered and began struggling to pull free of his drug-induced haze. He lifted his hand.

Kirby caught it, surprised by the strength of the man's clasp.

"Nee' tell you," Harry mumbled. "Stop him."

"Stop who, Dr. Wallis? Who do I need to stop?"

"Donner. Dangerous."

Kirby frowned. "But we already have him in custody," he said.

Harry stumbled on words and thoughts. "Found him? You found him already?"

"Yes, sir. We arrested him this morning."

Laura glared at the agent. He was purposefully misinterpreting what Harry Wallis was trying to say.

"Tell him who you arrested," she urged. "Tell Harry who you put in jail."

Kirby rolled his eyes. He was tired of playing games with this woman.

"Gabriel Donner. We arrested Gabriel Donner. The DNA was a perfect match."

Harry's grip suddenly tightened on Kirby's arm. "Wrong one, wrong one," he kept muttering. "Not Gab'rel…Garrett. Garrett…my patient. Stop him…don't let him do it again."

Kirby's last hope died. Short of calling this man a liar, which in his condition he could not, he had to accept what he'd said. At the least, he had to investigate it as fact.

"Are you telling me that you have a patient named Garrett Donner and that he's Gabriel Donner's identical twin?"

Harry closed his eyes and swallowed before whispering, "Yes."

Kirby was fit to be tied. "I suppose you're also going to want me to believe that Gabriel Donner did not know he had a brother?"

Harry nodded.

Laura added. "The housekeeper knew…the one who fainted at your feet this morning. But she'd honored her employers' wishes and kept their secret."

Kirby felt sick. Not only had they arrested the wrong man, but he was going to have all that paperwork to do over again.

"So, do we know where he is?" Kirby asked. "Has he been in contact with the family?"

Laura sighed. Unless Kirby was willing, here was where she would lose him again.

"In a manner of speaking, yes," she said quietly. "But only with Gabriel...and only from a distance."

Kirby frowned. "What do you mean, from a distance?"

"Umm, it's a bit like telepathy."

Kirby threw up his hands. "Now, why didn't I think of that myself? With psychics and visions, of course it would be telepathy. How could I have missed it?"

"Make fun all you like," Laura said. "But Gabriel is the only link that we have to Garrett, and even he can't control it."

Kirby looked at her and then shook his head in disgust. "Why am I not surprised?" he muttered.

Laura refused to be swayed by the agent's undisguised sarcasm. "You remember we told you that Gabriel kept hearing a voice?"

Kirby nodded.

"It's Garrett. Somehow, I believe he's linked

himself to Gabriel…sort of like a homing device…and that he will eventually wind up at the Donner estate." Then she played her last card. "Your best bet of capturing Garrett Donner before he does any more harm is to free his brother. Let Gabriel go home. Garrett will come, I know it."

"Just like you knew Henry Loo would die?"

She lifted her chin and stared him straight in the eye. "Just like that," she said softly.

"How do you live with yourself?" Kirby asked. But her answer shamed the cockiness out of him.

"Carefully, and only one day at a time."

Gabriel hit the ground running and didn't look back at the cab that was driving away. Before it dawned on him that he didn't have his keys, Laura was standing in the doorway. In one leap, she was in his arms, laughing and crying all at once as he pulled her close.

"You're home. You're home," she kept saying.

"And you're still here," he said gruffly.

"Someone had to be here to welcome you back."

He closed his eyes as he pulled her close. His last homecoming had been from the hospital, and except for Matty, he'd come home to a huge empty house. Now there was Laura, and although she was only one more small female, she was everything that mattered. He gave her a quick, hungry kiss.

"How's Matty?"

"I sent her home."

He grinned. "Good."

Laura chuckled. "I know that gleam in your eye."

Gabriel's grin widened. "Well, you know how it is in the Big House. No comforts of home. No women."

Laura laughed aloud. "You were only gone a little over ten hours."

"Ten hours, ten years—from where I was sitting, they seemed about the same."

Laura rolled her eyes. "I can only imagine."

Gabriel led her into the house, shutting the door behind them.

"Did you call Uncle Mike?"

She nodded. "He'll be over tomorrow. Said he has an idea he wants to share."

Gabriel's eyes gleamed darkly as he raked her face with a hungry gaze.

"How late tomorrow?" he asked.

She grinned. "Oh, late enough. Besides, since you've been away for so long, I don't imagine your uh…endurance…is quite up to par."

He laughed and then stood in sudden silence as the dying sound echoed within the great hall.

"What is it?" Laura asked.

He looked at her, and then briefly touched her mouth with the tip of his finger.

"I didn't think I would ever be able to do that again," he said.

"Do what?" Laura asked.

"Laugh." He held out his hand. Laura took it. "Come make love with me, Laura Dane."

Tears quickened in her eyes, but she refused to succumb. "It would be my pleasure."

She led the way upstairs.

Thirteen

He stood on top of a small, grassy knoll, silhouetted against the night sky like a strange, tragic beast. His thick dark hair, in need of a cut, brushed the edge of his collar and almost covered his ears. Even though his clothing was dirty and stained, he still changed his clothes every day, just like he'd been taught. His broad shoulders were thrown back, his arms outstretched, as if he were trying to catch hold of the world.

Only the moon saw the tears streaming down his cheeks. Only God knew the depths of his sorrow. In his mind, his people had thrown him away. The only link he still had was what came from his soul. Somewhere out there was a place he belonged, and he was following his heart to get there.

An owl hooted from a nearby tree. His hands instantly curled into fists as he spun around, his eyes straining and wide with fright. The bird lifted off from the tree, its great wings carrying it silently out of sight. When it was nothing but a memory, he relaxed.

Down below the hill, there were lights as far as the eye could see. He thought of his mother's smiling face, his father's happy laugh. Without making a sound, he dropped to his knees and began rocking himself to and fro.

Sometime later he slid all the way to the ground in exhaustion and pulled his bag up against his chest, cuddling it as if it were a pillow. The grass felt damp against his cheek, the ground rock hard against his bones. Too weary to find somewhere else to hide, he let his eyelids droop to a slow, sleepy close. A whisper slid out into the darkness. The whisper became words, one after the other, spilling out into the silence.

"'Now I lay me down to sleep. I pray the Lord my soul to keep. If I should die...'"

He fell asleep.

One minute Gabriel was asleep, and in the next breath he was awake and wondering why. Laura was right beside him, with her backside curled up against his lap. Her eyelashes fanned the crests of her cheeks; her breathing was slow and even. Even though all seemed well, there was an uneasy feeling he couldn't ignore. The alarm system was on, so the security of the house had not been breached. Still concerned, he tilted his head, listening for sounds that were out of place. He heard nothing.

He glanced back at Laura, and as he watched her, she sighed deeply. He leaned close, eyeing a slight frown that was beginning to indent the middle of her forehead. After that, her lower lip slipped out in a pout.

He grinned. Must be one hell of a dream. He brushed a curl away from the corner of her eye and then pulled the covers up over her shoulders. As he did, the pout and the frown went away.

"Love you, baby," he said softly, then slipped out of bed, careful not to waken her. Until he knew for sure that everything was all right, he wouldn't be able to sleep.

As he stepped out into the hall, the hair on his arms suddenly stood. At that moment, he was struck with a sadness so profound that it was all he could do to keep walking. He moved past room after empty room, compelled by an urge he didn't understand. And then the voice filled his head, and he knew what was happening.

Can't find you...can't find you.

It was Garrett. He was trying to come home.

Blanking out everything but following his heart,

he disarmed the security system and then walked toward the French doors that led to the patio.

The flagstones were cold beneath his feet, the night air slightly damp from the rain that had passed. By the time he walked off the path and into the grass, the cuffs of his pajama bottoms were already wet, but he didn't notice, and if he had, he wouldn't have cared.

The sadness was growing stronger. Every breath he took caused him pain. By the time he'd walked past his mother's rose garden and into the grounds beyond, tears were running down his face.

Suddenly he stopped in the middle of the lawn and looked up at the sky. A few straggly clouds still lingered, drifting across the face of a new moon. Beyond that, a sprinkling of stars could be seen, winking and blinking as if they knew a secret they couldn't tell.

"What is it?" Gabriel whispered, and then spread his arms, reaching for something that just wasn't there. "What do you want from me?"

Another great wave of sadness washed through him, sending him down to his knees.

Find me. Find me.

"Why, God, why is this happening to me...and to Garrett? Haven't we lost enough? Haven't we suffered enough?"

Now I lay me down to sleep...

Gabriel choked on a breath. The words in his head were as clear as if someone were standing beside him reciting the rhyme. He exhaled sharply and then shuddered, waiting...waiting. But nothing happened. Just when he had decided the messenger was gone, something flashed in his mind—the image of two little boys on their knees by their bed. And in that moment, he knew what he was supposed to say. The next line. He was supposed to say the next line.

"'I pray the Lord my soul to keep.'"

If I should die...

By the time the voice answered again, Gabriel was shaking with an odd sort of joy. This was beginning to feel familiar, and he wondered if he and Garrett had communicated like this as children. He took a deep breath. It was his turn next.

"'Before I wake...'"

Gabriel waited, expecting the next line of the verse. But none came. For some reason, Garrett must be unable to finish. Gabriel lowered his head. It was the least he could do.

"'I pray the Lord, my soul to take.'"

As soon as the words left his lips, the sadness disappeared, leaving him drained. Weary in both body and spirit, he stretched out on the ground and closed his eyes. Within minutes, he was asleep.

Laura was dreaming. In her dream she was lost in a house with no doors. There were bars on the windows, and if she stood on tiptoe, she could see Gabriel outside in the rose garden, but he couldn't see her. She couldn't get out—and he couldn't get in.

She heard footsteps behind her. As she turned, frustration turned to fright. Gabriel was standing before her with a rose in his hand. Behind her, someone was beating on the window. She looked over her shoulder. There was Gabriel again, staring at her through the bars. That didn't make sense. He couldn't be in two places at once.

Just as she was about to scream, she awoke, and in the few seconds it took to regain her sense of self, she realized she was alone in the bed.

There were any number of reasons why Gabriel would be up. It could be anything from going to the bathroom or getting a drink of water, to suffering a case of insomnia and simply deciding to read a book. But instinct told her it was none of the above. Without giving herself time to think, she rolled out of bed and reached for her robe, slipping it on as she ran.

Hurry. Hurry.

The urgency of the message left her shaking. That wasn't the same voice Gabriel kept hearing. This voice was soft and definitely feminine and, from what she could tell, hadn't bothered to speak to anyone else but her.

"I am," she whispered, then raced up the hall and down the stairs, led by an inner sense to the man she loved.

When she realized the security system had been turned off again, her hopes plummeted. That meant he'd gone outside. She kept thinking of the other times she'd found him out on the grounds, disheveled and bleeding, sometimes confused, and each time convinced that he'd watched someone die.

Hurry. Hurry.

The same word kept pounding over and over in Laura's head as she searched through the rooms.

"Then help me," she begged, and when she turned, the first thing she saw was that the French doors were ajar! Ah, a place to start looking. "Thank you very much," she said softly, and bolted outside.

As she stepped out on the patio, she said a quick prayer. Someone—and she was calling on God for the job—needed to be looking after Gabriel, because she didn't seem to be doing a very good job.

The grass was damp beneath her feet, and in spite of the heat of the days, the night air was almost cool. Glad for the robe she was wearing, she pulled it close around her neck and kept on walking. Past the rose garden, out beyond the tennis courts, onto the wide expanse of lawn that lay between the rock wall and the road.

It was there that she saw him, asleep on the ground, curled up on his side. One arm was stretched above his head for a pillow, the other tucked under his belly, as if he were cradling something—or someone.

Laura dropped to her knees beside him and then laid her hand on his heart. He shifted in his sleep but didn't seem aware she was there. She took a deep breath and then slowly closed her eyes, opening her mind for whatever was there to come in.

At first there was nothing but darkness and the memory of the last thing she'd seen; a vast, velvet sky with a sprinkling of stars. His heartbeat was strong beneath the palm of her hand, and for a moment all she could feel was his life's blood pumping in, pumping out, pumping all through his veins. Then the feeling began to expand.

She felt his breath.

Felt his skin.

Felt his tears.

Felt his pain.

Cold. So cold.

Laura shivered. That wasn't Gabriel's voice. She listened more closely, but when silence prevailed, she opened her eyes. Gabriel was looking up at her in sleepy confusion.

"Laura?"

She shook her head. "Not now," she said softly. "Let's just get you inside." Then she pressed her hand against his cheek, frowning at what she felt. "Oh! You're so cold!"

"What happened? Did I—"

"Don't worry about it," Laura said, and helped him to his feet. "Just come with me, love. We've got to get you warm."

She was right, Gabriel thought. He was freezing. What in hell had prompted him to lie down outside in the dark? And the moment he asked himself that question, he realized he already knew. He stopped and looked back at where he'd been, and the knot in his belly hitched a little bit tighter.

I'm still mimicking Garrett's moves.

His hands clenched into fists as he stared across the grounds.

"Garrett...where are you?"

Laura paused, her heart aching for all he and his brother were suffering.

"Gabriel, I'm so sorry."

His eyes were dark with pain.

"How can I help him? I don't know how to help him."

Laura took him by the hand. "Come inside. You won't be able to help anyone if you get sick."

He followed her into the house, locking the doors and then resetting the alarm without speaking. By the time he got upstairs, she had a hot shower running and dry clothes on his bed.

When he entered the room, she saw the guilt on his face but refused to let him accept it.

"Don't say it," she said shortly. "This is not your fault. None of this is your fault."

Gabriel was silent as he picked up his dry clothes, but as he got to the bathroom doorway, he stopped and turned.

"Laura, I *am* my brother's keeper. I have no other choice."

Althea Good was in a panic. Harry Wallis was in the hospital and talking his fool head off to anyone who would listen. The CEO had called her twice. It seemed Harry had raised one too many questions about a missing patient. She feared it would be a matter of time before it spread to the others.

Damn them all. If they only knew how desperate her life had become, they would have understood. These people in Reed House were of no use to society. They were nothing but a drain on their families and on humanity. In her opinion, most of them were less than human. They didn't need all this extra care. She was the one who needed help, not them.

She laid her head down on her desk and wanted to cry. If only she could take back that day from her past. It had started as a flight of fancy. A fun but foolish thing to do on her fortieth birthday. After all, she'd thought, if she couldn't make her own decisions by now, it was never going to happen. And it wouldn't have been a big deal, except her old friend had lied.

"One hit won't hurt. Just one little line. You only turn forty once in your life. After that, everything will be going downhill. Try it while you're still young enough to enjoy it."

That in itself had been enough to make Althea give a foolish taunt some serious consideration.

"Come on," he cajoled. "You'll love it. You'll fly high and come down like a feather on the breeze. No fuss. No muss. What do you say?"

She stared down at the neat little lines. White powder on glass to sniff up one's nose. Such a treat! Such a gamble! And he'd promised the sex would be great.

So she sniffed.

And she lost.

And he lied.

Her old friend hadn't turned out to be a friend after all and her habit was pushing a thousand dollars a day. Desperate to fund her growing need for the drug, she'd sold her interest in the co-op in Aspen. She'd sold her Mercedes and was driving a Ford. Her jewelry was gone, and her credit cards were maxed out. It was after she'd realized she had nothing left to sell that she'd come up with the plan. And up until now, it had worked like a charm.

It had been simple. The patients of Reed House were in here for life. None of them was ever going to get better, and there were a goodly number of them getting old. In certain instances, some aging patients hadn't a living relative among them. Their care was then paid for through different avenues that the families had set up in their wills. No one came to visit. No one cared, as long as the checks arrived from the trusts set up in their names.

All Althea had to do was forge a couple of papers for each file. To anyone concerned, it would appear that, at some distant relative's request, the aging patients had been transferred to another facility in another state. But what Althea was doing was packing them up, along with their meager belongings, and dropping them off in various downtown locations. Locations that were filled with vagrants, locations where homelessness was commonplace and mindless people went unnoticed. On one paper, the patient had been transferred. But the executors and law firms knew nothing of the fictitious moves. They kept sending the money to Reed House as they'd been requested to do, and Althea Good put it right up her nose.

And it had been working perfectly, until she'd turned the younger man free. In this instance, age shouldn't have mattered. She still didn't know what had gone wrong. Less than a week after Garrett Donner's parents were killed, she'd gotten a letter from a law firm stating that, until further notice, all the payments for his care would be coming from them. She'd done a quick scan of his records. The only visitors he'd ever had were the parents, and now they were dead. She hadn't known about the brother. Why hadn't someone made mention of the brother? Secrets! That was what was wrong with this world! Too many secrets!

The phone rang just as she was reaching for her coffee cup. It went tumbling to the floor, and in spite of the thickness of the carpeting beneath her desk, shattered into dozens of pieces.

She stared down at the mess in disbelief and then reached for the phone instead.

"Althea Good."

"Miss Good, this is Kirby Summers, from the Oklahoma State Bureau of Investigation. I was wondering when I might come out and talk to you about one of your patients."

Bile rose in the back of her throat. She cleared her throat, then took a deep breath.

"I'm sorry, Mr. Summers, but the records of our patients are confidential. I'm sure you understand."

Kirby was prepared. "What I've been given to understand is that Reed House has somehow loosed a very dangerous man into society. And, the media being what they are, I'm sure you would like to respond to my inquiries before they get wind of this latest development. Trust me. When they discover the news—and they *will* discover it—they will descend upon you like flies on shit. Do I make myself clear?"

Althea didn't miss a beat. "I'll clear my afternoon calendar. Come any time after one."

It was the distinct click in her ear that set her pulse into overdrive. Her hands were shaking when she hung up the phone, and there was a bitter taste in her mouth that no amount of swallowing could relieve.

"Oh God, oh God, what do I do?"

The urge came on her then, stronger than it had this morning, stronger than it ever had before. The police were coming. The OSBI for God's sake— and in less than two hours. If she couldn't get her act together before they got here, they would know something was wrong. Administrators of elite places like Reed House didn't go into withdrawal. She couldn't be shaking; she had to be strong. She needed to score before it all blew up in her face.

"Put your hands up, lady, you're under arrest! Charlie, cuff 'em both."

Clutching the small bag of white powder to her breast, Althea thought about running. But she had on high heels, and the man looked too mean. And there was the gun he had in her face. She had a gun of her own. If she was a little bit braver, she might pull the—

"Well, now, would you look at this?" Charlie said, pulling the gun out of her jacket. "I don't suppose you've got a permit for this?"

She rolled her eyes. *Permit? Don't make me laugh.*

God, she kept thinking, this was such a mistake. In typical Althea fashion, she eyed both cops, judging their faces as well as the street clothes they were wearing. Without taking into consideration the fact that they were dressed this way because they'd been undercover, she opened her big mouth and made another mistake.

"Look, I was buying this for a friend. I've never been in trouble before in my life, so how much?" she asked.

"How much what?" the cop asked.

"How much will it take to let me walk?"

The cop looked at his partner and then grinned. "Ooh boy, Charlie, we got ourselves a real piece of work." He looked back at Althea. "I'd say…ten to twenty…at the least."

Her mind started whirling. Ten thousand? *Twenty* thousand! She had a little bit in the bank, and there was still the Ford. She could still sell the Ford. She glanced at them and then smiled. It was true. Every man did have a price. She lowered her voice.

"Who do I pay?"

"The State of Oklahoma," the cop said, and snapped the handcuffs around her wrists. "We aren't talking thousands of dollars lady, we're talking years. You're carrying a concealed weapon.

You tried to bribe two officers of the law, and you are in possession. You *are* green.''

The blood drained from her face. Minutes later, she was on her way to the precinct. Panic mixed with nausea. She was going to be late for her meeting with the OSBI agent. Then she almost laughed. My God, that stuff had really messed up her brain. Missing a meeting should be the least of her worries. But there was one consolation to this mess she was in. Possession of drugs...embezzling money...they were both crimes, but they couldn't hang her twice.

Ray Bush was just going off duty when both suspects were brought in for booking. He didn't pay much attention to either of them until he heard the woman giving her name. At that point, he stopped.

"Althea Susan Good, 911 Sooner Road, Del City, Oklahoma."

He stood to one side, listening to her responses to the questions.

When they asked for her job, she mumbled, reluctant to tell, but well aware that a lie at this point would not be in her best interests.

"Administrator at Reed House."

Ray couldn't stop staring. He'd talked to Kirby

only a couple of hours earlier and begged off from accompanying him to that very same place.

"'Scuse me, Charlie, but could I ask the lady a question?"

The cop looked up from his desk and then shrugged. "Fine with me."

Althea was past caring who was grilling her next. All she wanted was her phone call.

"Ma'am?" Ray asked.

She leaned back in her chair and looked up.

Now that he had her attention, he paused, sorting through his thoughts.

She rolled her eyes. "Spit it out, boy."

An old anger hit Ray where it hurt. Boy. He should have known she would be one of those.

He leaned closer, giving her the full brunt of his brown skin and black eyes.

"Kirby Summers was coming to see you today, wasn't he?"

She shrugged and then glanced up at the clock. It was thirty minutes past two. He'd been due there at one.

There was a sarcastic smirk on her face as she answered, "Looks like I'm running a little late."

Ray straightened up. "More than you know, lady. More than you know." Then he headed for a phone.

* * *

For a man plagued with gout and a trick knee, Mike Travers was moving at a very brisk pace. He'd just come from a meeting with Brent Donner's law firm, and he was still trying to absorb what he'd learned.

It had all started with something Gabriel had said after learning about Garrett's existence. If his parents had loved Garrett all that much, then why hadn't they thought to take care of him in their will? That was when things had started to bother Mike.

After Gabriel's injuries had proven so serious, Mike had been appointed temporary executor in Gabriel's stead. The will had been straightforward. Gabriel inherited everything. Mike vaguely remembered hearing the lawyers make mention of various endowments the Donners had made, but he'd paid little attention at the time. Nothing had mattered but getting Gabriel well. By the time Gabriel was on the road to recovery, the will had gone through probate and everything was set in stone. Mike had gladly turned the paperwork over to Gabriel a few days after he'd come home, and that was that.

Or so he'd thought.

Only he'd been wrong, and so had Gabriel. Mike

had just spent the better part of an hour with a lawyer who claimed that Brent Donner had established a trust fund meant to take care of Garrett for the rest of his natural life. And, according to that same lawyer, a substantial check was cut and mailed to Reed House every month for Garrett's care. At that point, Mike had found out what he needed to know and had taken his leave.

Gabriel sat in the middle of the library floor, surrounded by photograph albums. Laura lay on her stomach beside him, propped up by her elbows. Comfortable in one of Gabriel's T-shirts and her own jeans, she leaned against his knee, watching as he turned page after page. Every now and then her gaze wandered from the pictures before her to Gabriel. In repose, he seemed calm, but she could sense how unsettled he was, how difficult it was for him to maintain control.

Gabriel stared down at the image before him, trying to remember the day that particular shot had been taken. It was at Grand Lake on the Fourth of July, and he was ten years old. He knew that simply because it was what his mother had written underneath the snapshot.

Ten years old. Five years after Garrett had been put away.

The fish he was holding was large, his smile even larger. He wondered if Garrett had ever gone fishing. He frowned and turned the page.

He was angry. Even the word *brother* made him mad. He was worried. Garrett had been born to a life of suffering. When they caught him, it would advance to a whole new level. And in a way he didn't understand, he was afraid. Afraid of the man his brother had become. He had killed more than once, and if Harry Wallis was to be believed, had no understanding of remorse.

Suddenly ashamed of his own fears, he slammed the book shut, then tossed it aside and thrust his fingers through the curls on Laura's head.

"This was a good idea, sweetheart, but as you can see, there are no pictures of us as twins. Only me."

He gave the curls a gentle tug, and then leaned down and pressed a kiss on the top of her head.

Laura rolled until she was lying on her back and looking up at him. Her gaze slid from his face to the breadth of his shoulders beneath his knit shirt, then to the length of his legs. It took a lot of denim for Levi's jeans to cover up this man.

"I'm sorry," she said softly, and laid a hand on his knee.

He shook his head and then cupped her cheek.

"You have nothing to be sorry for. It's my parents who dropped the damn ball."

Matty walked in on the heels of that remark, and once again, her conscience tugged. But she hoped the manila envelope she was carrying would, in some small way, alleviate part of her guilt in the deception.

"Gabriel…"

Unaware that she'd entered the room, he looked up in surprise.

"Matty! I didn't hear you come in." He gestured at the albums strewn over the floor. "We were just looking for pictures of Garrett."

"Did you find any?" she asked.

"No, although I can't say I'm surprised," he said, unable to disguise his bitterness. "My parents were hell on secrets."

Matty's lower lip trembled, but she kept her control.

"I came to tell you that Dr. Mike called. He's on his way over here with some news."

A sardonic grin broke the somberness of Gabriel's expression. "Don't let him in unless it's all good," he said.

Laura chuckled, which made Gabriel's smile widen.

Matty's mind was on other matters, so she completely missed what he said. "Will he be staying for lunch?" she asked.

Gabriel glanced at the clock. It was a quarter to one.

"I imagine. Go ahead and set another place just in case, okay?"

She nodded, but stood where she was. Last night she'd made a decision, something she should have done years ago. Gabriel was a grown man. He should have had the right to decide on his own whether he wanted a relationship with his brother or not.

"Gabriel…"

He could tell by the way she was standing that something was wrong, and from the way things had been going, he didn't want to be sitting on his ass when he heard it. He got up, pulling Laura to her feet beside him.

"What's wrong?" he asked.

"I have something for you. Something I've been saving for years."

She handed him the envelope.

"What is it?"

"Your past…your future…whatever you choose to make it, it belongs to you," she said, and then gave him a hug before slipping out of the room.

Gabriel stared down at the envelope and then strode to the desk and turned it upside down. Pictures spilled out onto the desktop, one after the other, until the envelope was empty and the desktop was covered with black-and-white images of a life he didn't remember.

"Oh, Gabriel! Look! It's pictures of you and Garrett when you were small." Laura picked one up, frowning at the stunning resemblance the two toddlers had. "How on earth did they ever tell you two apart?"

Gabriel picked up another, staring into the mirror image faces as if he were looking at strangers. And even though the pictures were mute reminders of a time gone by, somehow he knew the answer to Laura's question without hesitation.

"I was the one who never cried."

A startled expression crossed Laura's face. "What?"

Gabriel's gaze never wavered from the picture he was holding.

"I never cried...because it made Garrett hurt."

Tears suddenly spiked in Laura's eyes as a lump came to her throat. She laid her cheek against his chest and wrapped her arms around his waist. The children in the picture were barely more than babies, yet even then, Gabriel had somehow understood and compensated for his brother's weakness.

"Oh, Gabriel."

It was all she could say.

Fourteen

A few minutes later, they heard the familiar sound of Mike Travers' voice as he entered the house. Gabriel's mood shifted almost instantly. Laura watched as he began to wall himself up. Please God, she thought, don't let this be bad. Gabriel had been given more pain in the past few months than most men had to bear in a lifetime. She didn't know how much more he would be able to take without breaking.

They could hear Mike's footsteps nearing the library. Gabriel glanced at Laura. She could feel his uneasiness. She stood.

"Would you rather I left you two alone?"

He grabbed her arm. "No!" Then he frowned and took a deep breath, softening his tone and his touch. "Please. Don't go. Whether you like it or not, you're a part of what happens to me."

Laura shook her head and then smiled. "It's all

right," she said softly. "If you need me, I'm here."

His eyes darkened. *I'll always need you.* But he didn't feel free to say what he felt. There was too much riding on hope and not enough on a sure thing. Until Garrett was found, he couldn't rest easy.

And then his uncle Mike bolted through the doorway. Slightly winded from his sprint down the hall, he waved to compensate for other greetings.

"You won't believe—" He collapsed into the nearest chair and then groaned, holding up his hand as if to retain the floor while trying to catch his breath.

But Laura was worried. The old man's pallor was pronounced.

"Dr. Mike, are you all right? Can I get you anything? A glass of water, maybe a—"

He waved her off and then shook his head. "No, no, I'm fine. Just let me catch my breath."

"Here," Gabriel said, and handed him a straight shot of bourbon.

Mike eyed them as if they'd both lost their minds, but he took the drink anyway, downing it neat. It slid down his throat and into his system like butter over a hot skillet. When he'd emptied the glass, he leaned back in the chair with a sigh.

"Better, Uncle Mike?" Gabriel asked.

He nodded. "Better, boy, much better."

"So, what's the big news?" Gabriel asked.

Mike leaned forward, the fire in his spirit catching hold. He felt like an avenging angel, searching for justice.

"I've been thinking about Garrett's care. Brent Donner was my friend for more than twenty-five years. He was a very kind man—a very thorough man. I couldn't believe that he would have been so thoughtless with his own son's well-being, especially if that son was incapable of caring for himself."

Gabriel stiffened. "What are you saying?"

Mike started to grin. "That your parents *didn't* abandon Garrett. That they *had* prepared for his future as cautiously as they'd prepared for yours. There's a trust fund in Garrett's name that is large enough to keep him in comfort for the rest of his natural life."

"Yes, but unless we find him, that won't be needed."

Mike interrupted. "That's just it, boy! Somebody obviously needs it. The money was—and still is—being paid to Reed House on a regular basis. No one notified the lawyers that Garrett was missing…missing now for almost two months. What's more, the last check sent in his name was cashed less than four days ago. He might be lost, but they're still taking his money."

Gabriel was speechless. He kept thinking of what his brother must have endured, was still enduring, and of all the wasted lives. His lips thinned as his eyes glittered darkly.

"I swear on our mother's name that someone is going to pay and pay dearly."

"I want my lawyer!" Althea screamed. "Don't I get a phone call? I want my phone call now."

The jailer glared at Althea as he opened the cell door and gave her a push inside.

"I told you, lady, all the phone lines are out. A backhoe operator dug up a trunk line by mistake. They'll have it fixed soon. Then you can make your call." The door clanged shut as he pointed behind her. "Do something constructive while you're waiting, like saying hi to your new roommate."

"I don't want a roommate! I want a phone! I know my rights! Bring me my cell phone. I'll call my lawyer with it."

"Shut the hell up, bitch. This ain't the Ritz, and you're giving me a headache."

The voice was female—somewhere between a

growl and a whine—and the order was unmistakable. Althea watched the jailer walking away and felt a great need to call him back. She grabbed hold of the bars, afraid to turn loose, afraid to turn around. The voice might be female, but she didn't sound like anyone Althea would claim as a friend. No one *she* knew ever used the word *ain't*.

When she remained silent, the woman muttered, "That's better. You was gettin' on my last nerve."

Althea finally let go of the bars. When she did, the turn was automatic, an instinctual need to see the enemy's face. She took a deep breath. When she exhaled, it came out as a squeak. All she could think was that if it weren't for the woman's pendulous breasts, she could have passed as a man. Her head was bald, and she was dressed in black—black leather, black boots—and had more tattoos than Althea had seen outside of a circus. When the woman grabbed her own crotch and made kissing noises toward Althea, she panicked.

"Get away from me, you pervert. You leave me the hell alone." Then she backed herself into the farthest corner.

The woman laughed, a loud cackle that sent Althea's heart into a flutter. Within seconds, she slid to the floor in a faint.

* * *

Kirby Summers was in an extremely bad mood. It had taken the better part of two hours to get across town during the noon hour, only to find that he'd been stood up. Not only was Althea Good not at Reed House, but she was also not on the grounds. When it was discovered that her car was missing, it had taken all his patience to remain calm.

"I'm very sorry," the guard said, as he escorted Kirby to the front door.

"Yeah," Kirby muttered. "So am I."

Just as he got in his car, his cell phone rang.

"This is Summers," he said shortly.

"Kirby, it's Ray."

Kirby started the car, angling the air-conditioning vents toward his face and making a mental note to buy himself a new summer suit. This one was too damned hot.

"Be glad you didn't come with me," Kirby said. "The woman didn't show."

"That's because Charlie Slater was booking her for possession."

"What? Are you sure?" Kirby's voice hit a high note as he aimed for the curb and then braked to a stop.

"Oh yeah," Ray said. "One hundred percent."

"Where did they get her?"

"A couple of blocks south of downtown. You know the area."

"Yeah, I know the area too well," Kirby said. "Isn't that where the first Prince Charming victim was found?"

Ray paused as an odd expression crossed his face.

"Now that you mention it, I believe you're right," he said.

Kirby had a pretty good guess as to the kind of people who entrusted their loved ones to Reed House. Rich ones. He'd seen Althea Good's office, as well as the lushness of the patients' surroundings. It might be a crazy house, but it was not a poor one. He tried to picture a woman in charge of a place like that buying a hit from some nickel-and-dime pusher.

"Okay, so where is she now?" Kirby asked.

"Last I heard, a holding cell downtown."

"Don't let her out until I get there," Kirby said.

"I'll pass it along," Ray said, and hung up.

Kirby tossed the phone down on the seat beside him and pulled back into traffic. He hadn't gone far when it rang again.

"Summers," he said briefly, negotiating a sharp turn in the road.

"This is Gabriel Donner. I found out something I think you should know."

Considering their brief history together, Kirby was surprised the man was civil.

"And what would that be?" Kirby asked.

"My uncle just came from seeing the lawyer who probated my parents' will."

"And?" Kirby asked.

"When Dr. Wallis first came to us with Garrett's story, we were told that he had gotten himself lost."

"Yeah, I remember."

"I think they were lying."

Kirby frowned. "How so?"

"Checks are issued regularly from a trust my father set up especially for Garrett. Someone has been cashing the checks all along. The last one was cashed only four days ago, and Garrett supposedly disappeared nearly two months ago."

"Damn," Kirby muttered. How did this fit in? And then a thought occurred as he braked for a red light. "Hey, Donner, how much money are we talking about?"

"A little over five thousand dollars a month."

Kirby whistled through his teeth. "Look, I appreciate the call. I'm looking into some stuff now that this might tie into. I'll get back to you when I know more, okay?"

"Okay," Gabriel said, and started to hang up when he heard Kirby calling his name. "Yes?"

"About your brother..."

Gabriel's eyes narrowed. "What about him?"

"I'm very sorry. No matter how it happened, it's...unfortunate."

Gabriel wanted to scream. Unfortunate? It wasn't unfortunate, it was a sin...a heart-wrenching, pitiful sin.

The silence in Kirby's ear said it all. He blushed, angry and embarrassed with himself for being so thoughtless.

"Look," Kirby said. "I'll be in touch. There's something we need to discuss."

"You have my number," Gabriel said and hung up.

Kirby disconnected. He drove on for several blocks with his own anger building. Unfortunate? What a piss-poor choice of words. Unfortunate that a family had to die? Unfortunate that a dangerous man had been turned out into society? Unfortunate that five innocent people were dead because of it? No wonder Gabriel Donner hadn't bothered to respond.

''If that had been me, I wouldn't have answered myself, either,'' he muttered.

Then he floored the accelerator and headed toward the police precinct. He had an appointment to keep with Althea Good.

The house was silent. But it was the kind of peaceful silence that comes from comfort and safety, not dread. Laura sat before the mirror in her room, absently brushing her hair. She glanced at the clock. It was almost five. Gabriel had been gone more than two hours now. Gone to check on a client who was having problems with the new security system he'd had installed.

Matty was downstairs, putting the finishing touches on the evening meal. She, too, would be gone within the hour. If Gabriel didn't get back, Laura would be all alone. She should have been nervous, but for some reason she wasn't.

She wrapped her arms around herself and let her mind go free. Maybe it was the lingering love that she felt...or maybe it was just her imagination. Maybe she was so much in love with Gabriel that she was blinding herself to the obvious, that she would have been happy with him no matter where they were.

She stood suddenly and left her room without

looking back. There were calls she should make and things she should do. She hadn't been home in more than two weeks. She would call her service and check on the staff. Before long, she would have to go back.

And then her steps slowed, and her spirit dropped. Therein lay her problem. She didn't want to leave Gabriel, but she hadn't been asked to stay. Yes, he said he loved her...even said he needed her desperately. But he had never actually said the words that it would take to keep her here.

By the time she got downstairs, she was feeling thoroughly sorry for herself. As she passed by the library, she glanced toward the patio and the rose garden beyond. In the farthest garden, she could see Matty puttering about. She paused and smiled. If she was a betting woman, she would be betting there would be roses on the table for dinner tonight.

She walked on past, heading for the kitchen to get something to drink before making her calls. Somewhere in another part of the house, she could hear a clock beginning to chime. One after the other, it chimed out the hours.

Five o'clock. It was already five o'clock. Gabriel should be home soon. She hastened her steps, turning the corner leading into the kitchen and almost mowing Matty down.

"*Madre de Dios!*" Matty screeched, and grabbed her chest with both hands.

Laura skidded to a stop. "I'm sorry. I'm so sorry. I thought you were—"

She froze. Her eyes widened, and her heart began to pound, as she turned and stared out the back door. Gauging the distance from the rose garden to the kitchen wasn't hard. At the very least, the length of three football fields. She took a deep breath. When she turned back to Matty, her voice was shaking.

"Weren't you just out in the rose garden?"

Matty rolled her eyes, still shaken by the nearness of their collision.

"No, no, of course not," she said shortly, pointing to the pastries laid out on the counter. "I've been baking all afternoon. I have no time to mess with such things."

Laura walked to the windows, staring intently into the late afternoon shadows spreading across the grounds, trying to find another glimpse of the woman she'd seen in the roses. And yet the harder she tried, the more certain she became that she wouldn't see her again—hadn't really seen her before—that what she'd seen had been nothing more than a lingering memory of the woman to whom the roses belonged.

Matty brushed the flour off her chest and gave a delicate sniff as she returned to her tasks.

But Laura wasn't ready to drop the subject, at least not yet. "Matty, may I ask you something?"

"Sure, sure," Matty said. She handed Laura a soft drink and a smile. "Sit here," she said, pointing to a stool at the end of the work island.

Laura sat, sipping at her Coke and trying to think of the best way to ask what she wanted to know.

Matty dusted a cutting board with flour and then began rolling out dough.

"So, ask," she said.

Laura took a deep breath. "Gabriel's mother…"

Matty paused and looked up. "Angela. She was named right. An angel on earth, that one."

Laura nodded. "What did she look like?"

Matty smiled. "Oh, she was a pretty thing, but the boys…Gabriel and Garrett…didn't look a thing like her. You know how dark Gabriel is…all that olive skin, dark hair and green eyes. He looked more like my people than he did his own."

Completely caught up in the past, Matty giggled and pointed to herself. "People used to think Gabriel was my grandson.'' She sighed. ''Sometimes I pretended that it was so.''

She lifted a pan from the cabinet below and began laying the rolled crust inside. ''We guessed they got their coloring from their daddy's side of the family, although no one could be sure.''

She lowered her voice. ''Mr. Brent was an orphan, you know. He never knew who his people were.'' Then she frowned. ''Sometimes I think he felt guilty about Garrett, believing that the part that crippled one of his sons must have come from him. Angela was a real blue-blood. She could trace her family all the way back to the Revolution. They were convinced that the fault in Garrett lay with some unknown from Brent's background.''

And then she shook off the mood. ''But you asked about Angela, didn't you?''

Laura nodded, then glanced over her shoulder once more, just to make sure. There was no one in sight. Matty smiled and changed mental gears.

''She wasn't much taller than me, but she had the sweetest face and the prettiest smile. Her hair, when she was young and before it began to turn gray, was a golden brown. She called it puppy brown. Brent said it looked like warm honey. They were so in love.''

Blinking back tears, she looked up and then

sighed. "As bad as I hated to lose them, I have to say it gave me some comfort to know that they'd gone on together. I can't imagine one of them living without the other."

Laura pointed over her shoulder. "The rose garden...it was hers, right?"

Matty nodded. "Oh, yes. She spent most of her time there each day, pruning and snipping and babying those things like they were people."

She paused, wiping her hands as she went toward the window near where Laura was sitting and peered out.

"See how the gardens are divided up into sections?"

Laura nodded.

Matty's eyes narrowed. "She loved them all, but one of them was her favorite. Some days she would be out there for hours." She leaned closer to the windows. "Let's see...I think it was—"

"It was the farthest one, wasn't it?" Laura asked. "The one with the wishing well and the wagon wheel used for a trellis."

Matty nodded. "Yes, that's the one." And then a thought occurred. "But how did you know?"

Laura turned. "Matty?"

"Hmm?"

"Have you seen her?"

"Seen who?" Matty asked.

"Angela. Have you seen her here…since she…"

Matty rolled her eyes and made the sign of the cross. "Do not speak of such things! It is bad luck!"

There was something in the tone of Matty's voice that told Laura she was lying.

"Have you?" she asked, and then turned and stared out across the lush grounds. "I did…just a few minutes ago. At first I thought it was you."

Matty grew quiet as her eyes widened in fear. "Well…maybe I thought…" And then she shook off the notion. "But I was mistaken," she said quickly. "Angela Donner was a saint on earth. I know she is with God." Her voice broke. "I have to believe she is with God."

Laura stood and put her arms around Matty's shoulders. "Sometimes I sense a lingering sadness in this house… Other times the place feels full of love. She was a good mother. If her spirit still lingers, maybe she's just waiting for Garrett to come home."

Matty shuddered. Unlike the fears she'd been having on her own, the idea made sense. Both Brent and Angela would have been heartbroken over what had happened to Garrett. Maybe Laura was right.

"Were you afraid of Angela Donner in life?" Laura asked.

Matty shook her head. "Oh, no, never!"

"Then why would you fear her sweet spirit?"

Matty stilled. She'd never thought of it like that. She looked at Laura and began to smile.

"You're right," she said softly, and hugged Laura tight. "You're absolutely right."

A door slammed in the front of the house.

"Gabriel's home," Matty said, and gave her eyes a quick swipe as she hustled back to her dough.

"Are you going to be all right?" Laura asked.

Matty nodded, shooing her away. "Of course I'm all right. Go head off that man before he finds his way into my kitchen and eats up all of my baking."

Laura left, her mood still pensive as she headed toward the front of the house. She could hear Gabriel calling.

"I'm here," she shouted, and impulsively started to run.

When she saw him, she gave a small leap. He caught her in midair, laughing and hugging her and turning her around and around until they were both staggering and dizzy.

Gabriel put her down reluctantly, still pressing kisses all over her face. "A man could get used to a welcome like that," he growled.

"And if you got used to it, then what?" she asked.

Suddenly the laughter stopped. There was too much riding on the answer for either one to crack jokes. Gabriel tugged on a loose curl at the side of her cheek.

"I'm afraid to make promises I won't be able to keep."

Laura started to look away, but he cupped her cheek, forcing her to meet his gaze.

"Don't," he whispered. "It isn't that I don't want to make promises, but right now, I can't count on anything but living in the moment. Until Garrett is safe, no one is safe. Understand?"

"More than you know," she said.

It hit him then what she meant. Just looking at her now and realizing what Garrett could unintentionally do made him sick. His stomach knotted. My God, how could he live, knowing his own brother had killed the woman he loved? He pulled her close.

"I've got to get you out of this house—out of this city. Until Garrett is found, you're not safe."

Laura knew he was right, but there was no way on earth she could leave him. Not now.

"Until Garrett is found, no one is safe," she argued. "Besides, maybe I can help."

Gabriel frowned, resisting the urge to shake her. "Laura, please. Get on the first plane home tomorrow. When this is all over, I will come to you, I swear."

She pulled out of his grasp and walked toward the windows.

"Damn it, Laura, didn't you hear a single thing I said?"

"I heard you."

Gabriel sighed. "What are you doing? Are you expecting someone?"

She turned. "Maybe...maybe not. At any rate, I can't leave, even if I wanted to."

"Why the hell not?" he muttered.

She looked back out the windows. "I have to help Garrett find his way home."

He was so stunned by what she said that for a moment he couldn't think. When he finally reacted, it was out of dismay. "What do you mean, *you* have to help? Why does it have to be you?"

She shook her head. "I don't know, it just does."

Gabriel threw up his hands in disgust. "Who said?"

Matty called from the end of the hall, interrupting their argument and changing the conversation, for which Laura was glad. There was no way she was going to tell Gabriel what she had seen, or, for that matter, what had been happening ever since she arrived.

"Gabriel...Laura...I'm leaving now," Matty called.

Gabriel shoved his hands in the pockets of his slacks, gave Laura a glare, and then strode down to the end of the hall to bid Matty goodbye. Laura took advantage of the situation to bolt for her room. But Gabriel wasn't through. The moment Matty closed the door behind her, he went up after her.

She spun as her door slammed against the wall. It was Gabriel.

"You listen to me," he growled. "I don't want you—"

Laura pretended a calm she didn't feel and glanced at her watch. "We're supposed to meet Kirby Summers at six. That's a little bit less than an hour. Can you make it?"

A little confused as to where the conversation was going, he frowned and thrust out his jaw. "He didn't call me."

Laura's voice was muffled as she pulled a clean shirt over her head.

"I didn't hear you," Gabriel said, as he yanked it the rest of the way down for her.

"I said," Laura repeated, "he didn't call us. I called him."

Gabriel frowned. "Whatever for?"

"I need to see the evidence they have on the murders, and he wanted me to come down and look at some pictures. So it's time."

He blanched. "Whatever for?"

"Maybe it will help us find Garrett."

Gabriel erupted. "Damn you, Laura! Have you lost your mind? You haven't been listening to anything I've been saying. I don't want you more involved in this mess. I want you out of it entirely."

Laura flew back at him, giving as angrily as she'd been forced to take.

"And damn *you*, Gabriel. You haven't been listening to me. I'm not going anywhere. I'm not leaving you, and I'm not leaving Garrett. When your uncle Mike called me to come help you, I thought he was crazy, and I was certain I was nuts for considering the trip. I had no expertise to help you work through your problems. I deal in the intangible, not in ill health. But I knew the moment I talked to him that I had to come. I trusted my instincts that it would eventually be revealed.'' She thought of Angela, of hearing sobs in her dreams, of hearing footsteps in the hall, and of seeing her walking in the garden. ''There was a reason I was meant to come here, and now I know what it is. There will never be peace in this house again until Garrett Donner comes home.''

Fifteen

It was thirty minutes after six when they pulled into the OSBI parking lot. Kirby Summers was leaning against his car, obviously waiting for their arrival.

Laura nodded as they got out of the car. "Sorry we kept you waiting."

Kirby shook his head. "It doesn't matter. After the day I've had, this is a piece of cake." He led the way back inside and then up to his office. "So, what's the big deal?"

"Don't look at me," Gabriel said. "This is her call."

Laura didn't bat an eye. "You wanted me to look at some pictures, remember? I'll do it—if you'll let me see all the evidence. I need to see the evidence on the Prince Charming murders."

Kirby grinned. "That's a good one." But when no one else laughed, he paused. "You're not serious?"

She nodded.

"Aside from the fact that it's highly irregular, why would you want to see pictures of dead bodies and a map full of pins?"

"To find Garrett."

The grin slid off his face. "You can do that?"

Laura shrugged. "Please."

He turned away from the desk and led them into a small room nearby.

There were pictures on the walls, and more pictures on the table. Laura scanned the photos of the crime scenes with a practiced eye. It wasn't the first time she'd seen things like this. It wouldn't be the last.

Tucking a curl behind her ear, she began with victim number one and started looking at photos. Every now and then, she would reach out and touch one. When she did, she would close her eyes rather than focus on the picture. By the time she got to the last victim's photo, she was swaying on her feet.

Gabriel was worried, but even more, he was angry. "Damn it, Laura, this isn't going to—"

It was as if Gabriel hadn't even spoken. She interrupted suddenly, getting Kirby's attention by pointing to victim number one.

"The stereo. It was too loud."

She moved to the second victim's photo.

"It was the dog whistle. They found it lodged down the victim's throat, didn't they?"

Kirby was stunned. "How did you know that?" he muttered. "It wasn't in the papers."

She didn't answer and instead moved to victim number three. "Here it was the dog that died first. He had to stop the sound of the dog barking."

The skin crawled on the back of Gabriel's neck. He remembered that dog—its obnoxious, high-pitched yap. He dropped into a nearby chair. Poor Stevie. He must have gotten in the way.

"What about this one?" Kirby asked, pointing to the homeless woman they'd found in an alley. "She didn't have a dog. She didn't have a stereo. In fact, she didn't own a damn thing that someone else hadn't thrown out first."

Laura shook her head. "You're still missing the point. Garrett isn't trying to kill these people, he just has to stop the pain. Noise hurts him. Not a little, not even somewhat, but in a way that short-circuits his brain. It's not something he can help, and enduring it is impossible."

Kirby slapped the wall beneath the photo of Bella Cruz. "Then what?" he shouted. "What did she do that caused her to die?"

Laura glanced up at the photo, her gaze moving

past the woman's body to the train tracks just visible in the background.

"The woman was just standing in the wrong place. It was a train whistle. It screeched. When Garrett went crazy, she screamed. I think it all gets jumbled up in his mind."

Kirby swore beneath his breath. "And number five?"

She pointed to a smaller shot below the one of Henry Loo's body to his vandalized car.

Gabriel stared at the dents in the car body for less than five seconds before it dawned on him, too.

"Car alarm," he said softly, glancing at Laura for confirmation.

She nodded.

Kirby threw up his hands. "This is crazy. Are you telling me that this man could go off at any moment like a two-dollar bomb?"

"He has...and unless we find him soon, he will again," Laura said, and then moved to the map on an opposite wall. She looked for a few moments and then turned to Kirby.

"These pins represent where the bodies were found, right?"

"Yes, for all the good it does us," Kirby said.

"So far, we haven't found a pattern that would tell us anything."

But Laura saw a pattern, and it was just as she feared.

Gabriel saw her tense. She saw something the rest of them were missing. His hands were firm upon her shoulders as he lowered his head, his voice soft against her ear.

"What is it, baby? What do you see?"

She wanted to throw herself in his arms and not turn loose until all this was over. But she couldn't. She'd come here for a purpose, and she wasn't leaving until they believed her, one hundred percent.

"Look," she said, pointing to a location near a pin flagged, Victim Number One. "Gabriel, isn't that the hospital where you were staying?"

"Yes, Saint Anthony's," Gabriel said.

Laura was talking, but more to herself than to the men. "That's only a few blocks from where the first victim died."

Gabriel stilled, his mind already racing ahead to the point Laura was trying to make to Kirby.

"Victim number two was found in Johnson Park, right?"

Kirby nodded, following the direction in which Laura kept pointing. "Yes, but I don't see—"

"You will," she said. "Victim number three was Mrs. Husser's houseman, right?"

Kirby nodded.

"Did you know that she was one of Gabriel's clients, and that he'd been there that very day before Stevie died?"

Kirby reached for his notes. "Uh...I think we knew that."

Laura continued to point, moving her finger across the map to the place where Bella Cruz had died.

"This alley is in a direct line between Sadie Husser's home and the restaurant where Henry Loo died."

Kirby stared. "Yes, we'd seen that, but there was no connection between—"

"Oh, but I believe there is," Laura said. "Henry Loo was one of Gabriel's clients, too. At least, he would have been, if he hadn't died."

Kirby spun around, staring at Gabriel as if he'd been struck.

"You? He's following you?"

"We think so," Gabriel said. "At least, Laura thinks so, and I'm beginning to believe she's right."

Kirby's mind was racing. "So you're saying that

all we have to do is put a tail on you and stake out the places you've been?''

''No,'' Laura said. ''It's easier than that.'' She picked up a new pin and stuck it in a spot on the map.

Kirby took a step closer and adjusted his glasses, trying to read the small print.

''I'll save you the bother,'' Gabriel said. ''That's my home. Laura thinks Garrett has locked on to me as a means of finding home.''

''That's absurd,'' Kirby muttered. ''There's no such thing as a psychic link to—'' He flushed, too late, remembering what Laura Dane was all about.

She grinned. ''It's not really a psychic link. It's more like a special connection that identical twins often have with each other. I don't know…maybe Garrett's ability is stronger than normal to compensate for his lack of communication skills in other ways. Gabriel didn't have the same ability, or he would have realized years ago that he had a twin, and Garrett never had the need to communicate with Gabriel earlier, because his parents obviously filled the need for whatever love Garrett was capable of accepting.''

Kirby stared at Gabriel, trying to imagine what such a thing would be like.

''But all that ended when my parents died,'' Gabriel said. "Then Garrett was removed from Reed House, probably against his will." He shrugged. "I guess the only thing he had left was instinct. Once I started coming out of the coma, he tuned in on me."

Kirby picked up a file and flipped it open before tossing it on the table.

"That's the administrative head of Reed House. We got her today on possession."

Gabriel stared into the face, trying to see behind the artifice to the woman beneath. He couldn't see anything on her face but fear.

Laura moved past him, then laid her hand on the file. A few seconds later, she looked up, stunned by what she'd *seen*.

"He wasn't the only one," she said.

"What are you saying?" Kirby asked. "Who wasn't the only what?"

"Garrett. He wasn't the first one who left. Only they didn't leave. She threw them away. She threw all of them away."

Kirby frowned when Laura suddenly changed from singular to plural. "All? What do you mean by *all?*"

Laura looked puzzled, not realizing what she'd done. But Kirby was on to something. After the interview he'd had with Althea Good earlier, this news was beginning to make sense. He headed for a phone.

Gabriel stepped in front of him. "What's going on?"

"That woman—the one who told Dr. Wallis that Garrett had been transferred—if I was a betting man, I'd be willing to bet that when we do a little more digging, we're going to find out that more people are missing than anyone knows."

Laura dropped into a nearby chair. The ugliness of what she'd just seen left her weak and shaking.

"I don't get it," Gabriel said.

"It's simple," Kirby said. "She's an addict with a very expensive habit. You said someone was still cashing Garrett's checks, although he was no longer there. How much would you like to bet me that there's more than one patient whose records won't jibe with the truth?"

"Sweet Lord," Gabriel muttered, staring down at the face in the picture and trying to imagine the desperation behind such horrible deceit.

"I know," Kirby said. "It's awful. Unfortunately, in my line of work, I see awful more than I see nice. We can, however, take comfort in the fact that she's already behind bars. And if my suspicions are true, we can start trying to find the people she dumped."

Gabriel looked up. "Now if we can just find Garrett before anyone else has to die..." He glanced at Laura and then back at Kirby. "Can you put a guard on Laura? If not, I'll hire private security."

"Why her specifically?"

"Gabriel, don't," Laura said. "It was only a dream."

Gabriel continued as if she hadn't uttered a word. "Because she saw her own death." Then he looked at her, and his eyes were dark and filled with pain. "She saw herself dying at my brother's hands. I can't make her leave, but I won't let her die, no matter what she *saw*."

"I can get police protection for your property, but I don't know for how long."

Gabriel nodded. He'd figured as much. "Do what you can," he said shortly. "And I'll do what I have to."

"I'll get on it right away," Kirby said, as he walked them outside.

"There is one thing I might ask," Gabriel continued.

Kirby waited.

Gabriel's voice was low and full of pain. "Don't hurt him," he begged. "I think Dr. Wallis would back me up when I say that you could take him by the hand and walk him all the way back to Reed House without a problem if you chose, but if you turn on sirens or fire guns—or if anyone starts screaming and shouting at him to give up—you'll have a bloodbath on your hands."

Kirby paled. The image Gabriel presented wasn't pretty. "I'll do what I can," he said. "But if he presents a danger to others, they will use any means possible to bring him down. Five people are already dead because of him."

"No," Gabriel said shortly. "Five people are dead because of Althea Good, not because of Garrett. He can't help what he does. She knew what he was like, and she still didn't care."

Kirby nodded. "Where are you going?"

Gabriel took Laura by the hand. "To prepare for Garrett's homecoming." His eyes were bright with unshed tears. "It's been a long time coming."

It was just past midnight when Laura woke. Reluctant to open her eyes, she lay without moving, waiting for sleep to reclaim her. Something brushed against her cheek. She nestled deeper into her pillow and felt it again, soft and warm, like a breath. She smiled to herself. Gabriel's breath.

She sighed and then rolled, expecting to feel the

solid strength of Gabriel's body next to her. But there was nothing beside her but cold sheets.

Again something brushed against her cheek, gently but persistently. She opened her eyes and then sat straight up in bed. Gabriel's covers were thrown back. He was gone. His pajamas were lying on the back of a chair, and the jeans and T-shirt he'd been wearing were missing. She touched her cheek. It was wet...wet with tears. This made no sense. She hadn't been crying. Where had the tears come from?

A shudder ripped through her body as understanding dawned.

Angela! She was trying to tell Laura something.

Within moments, Laura was out of bed and reaching for her robe.

Gabriel moved throughout the house at a slow but methodical pace, turning off the security alarms and unlocking all the doors. When he was through, he headed outside. His stride was certain, his shoulders braced. As he walked, he became aware of his body in a way he could never remember being aware of it before—of the friction of his clothes as they rubbed against his arms and legs, of the texture of the night air as it moved against his face, of the sound of his own heartbeat pounding in his ears. In the simplest form of the word, he was conscious of just being alive.

In a way, he was getting ready—ready for the reunion. It was coming soon, he could feel it. He disarmed one gate, then another, then the last one, before standing in the shadows and staring up at the house, trying to see it through Garrett's eyes.

Would Garrett recognize home if he saw it? Would he remember the first five years of his life, or was his mind too scattered?

Gabriel turned slowly, gazing out across the grounds to the high stone wall that surrounded the estate. Even in the darkness, the roses were beautiful. Like miniature worlds where fairies might dwell.

He stared for a very long while, letting himself remember, letting go of the pain of his loss, preparing himself for a new kind of pain. It was just as he'd told Laura before. He *was* his brother's keeper. Only this time the resentment was gone. All that was left was resigned acceptance and a sweet excitement—the kind a child has in knowing that Christmas is coming but he still has to wait. Yes, Garrett was coming. For the past two hours, the feeling had been growing stronger and stronger. The question was when.

He gave the place one long, last look, his shoul-

ders slumping with weariness. He'd done everything possible to ensure Garrett's safe—

Then he froze. The old gate! He hadn't thought
of it in years. It was set in the stone wall at the
back of the estate, covered with a thick growth of
vines. And it was locked. What if that was the door
Garrett remembered? What if that was the only
way he knew to get in?

Gabriel started running.

Laura ran through the rooms calling Gabriel's
name, but all she heard was the echo of her own
voice. When she discovered that the alarm was off
again, she groaned and headed for the door. She
had to find him.

The front door was unlocked, but when she ran
outside, he was nowhere in sight. She dashed back
in the house, calling his name.

He didn't answer.

To her dismay, every door in the house was unlocked. She called his name again. Again there was
no answer. She exited through the kitchen door.
The grounds at the back of the house were far
larger than those at the front. It was going to take
her a while to cover every inch, but she couldn't
rest until she found him. She walked out of the

house, her eyes wide and frightened as she started down the steps.

"Please, Gabriel, please be all right."

Using the security lights to guide her, she started to search, every now and then stopping to call out his name, praying for an answer that never came.

Her heart began to hammer against her rib cage in a hard, uneven rhythm. Her eyes threatened tears, but she kept blinking them furiously, refusing to give in to the fear. Her body was chilled, her hands cold and clammy. She wanted to scream but was afraid to let go of the sound.

Farther and farther she moved toward the back of the grounds, past the place where she'd found Gabriel last time, until she came face-to-face with a vine-covered wall. She thrust her hands into the leaves, feeling the substance of rock beneath. Then she turned and faced the house, peering through the darkness at its great, looming shape.

"Damn it, Gabriel, where are you? This isn't funny."

Something rustled in the bushes off to her right. She jumped and spun around, staring into the pitch-black shadows and searching for something she could recognize. Just when she thought it had been her imagination, the sound came again, only closer. Without waiting to see who—or what—it might be, she bolted toward the house, running as if the hounds of hell were at her heels.

Through the open spaces of the grounds.

Past the wishing well where Angela's roses grew best.

Past the trees surrounding the tennis courts. Afraid to look behind her and afraid to slow down.

Ten feet from the first steps leading up to the patio, he stepped out of the shadows and into the light. Laura was running too fast. In an effort to miss him, she stumbled and fell. Reaching out to brace herself, she instinctively closed her eyes, preparing to give up some of her skin to the gravel beneath her feet.

She never hit ground. First there was a jolt, as if she'd hit something solid in midair. She felt hands clumsily clutching at her neck; then she was jerked to her feet and released, leaving her staggering to regain her own balance.

"You okay?"

She froze. It was Gabriel's voice and Gabriel's face, but the man standing before her wasn't Gabriel. His hair was too long. His clothes were too dirty. And while Gabriel stood with a demeanor that told any onlooker he was very aware of being a man, this one did not. Laura's heart skipped a beat. He'd had his hands around her neck. But not to kill her, just to catch her from falling. She wanted to laugh from the joy.

"Garrett?" she asked.

He smiled, and the smile broke her heart. It was childlike in delight, and yet a little afraid. And, after what he'd been forced to endure, she could understand why.

"My name is Laura."

He nodded and then suddenly clutched his bag to his chest, like a child holds a toy.

"Home?" he asked.

She took a deep breath. "Yes, dear, this is home."

A great sigh ripped through his body, but within moments, he stiffened, his ear cocked toward the darkness out of which Laura had emerged. Someone was coming.

Laura stiffened. There was only one person it could be, and she had to make sure that his arrival didn't frighten Garrett away.

She stepped forward, aware that she was putting herself in harm's way. She took Garrett by the hand and smiled up at him, trying to let him know everything was all right. Then she called out to Gabriel, just loud enough for him to hear.

"Gabriel...we're here, sweetheart. Over here, near the light."

Gabriel burst out of the darkness. "Good grief, baby, why were you running like that in the dark? You could have fallen and broken your—"

And then he saw them, standing beneath the glow of the security light, and the words died on his lips. Fear for Laura alternated with shock at the sight of the man whose hand she was holding. All he could think was, My God, no wonder they thought it was me.

"It's all right," Laura said, patting Garrett's hand. "See, it's only Gabriel."

Garrett sighed as the tension in his body relaxed. He clutched his bag a little closer to his chest. Gabriel was his brother's name. Although he had no concept of what the word actually meant, he remembered a time when he'd never been alone, when he'd always had someone who shared his world. When Gabriel started toward him, he didn't recognize himself in the man. All Garrett knew was that he'd reached his goal.

Gabriel felt as if he were walking on air. He knew he was moving forward, but he never felt his feet hit the ground. Within the space of a heartbeat, he was close enough to touch his brother.

Garrett could see the man clearly now, and he relaxed even more. He knew who this was. He had a picture.

"My brother," he said, and touched the middle of Gabriel's chest with his finger, then yanked it away in sudden fear.

"No, it's okay," Gabriel said softly, and reached out for Garrett's hand. "My brother, too."

The smile on Garrett's face was angelic. Laura couldn't look at him without wanting to cry, and she could tell by the look on Gabriel's face that he was feeling the same way.

"Home?" Garrett asked. "This is home?"

"Yes, Garrett, this is home," Gabriel repeated, and then suddenly shivered. "Want to come inside?"

Garrett frowned as he turned around to look at the big, dark house, and in that moment Gabriel remembered something…something he hadn't thought of in over twenty-five years.

"You can turn on the lights."

Garrett beamed and then nodded. "Okay."

Like a child waiting to be led, he held out his hand. Gabriel swallowed past the knot in his throat, took his brother by the hand and led him inside, pausing at the doorway and then putting Garrett's fingers on the switch.

Light flooded the room, as well as Garrett's heart. There was no danger here. He relaxed even more.

"Mother? Mother's here?" Garrett asked.

Gabriel groaned. How does one tell a child his parent has died? He would have to call Dr. Wallis to find out what to do. For now, all he could do was put him at ease.

"No, Garrett, Mother's not here. But I'm here. I will take care of you now."

Garrett dropped into a kitchen chair and started to cry, huge, quiet tears that made little clean tracks on a very dirty face.

"Let me," Laura said. "You call, I'll do what I can to make things better."

Gabriel frowned. He knew what she meant, but for some strange reason, he was reluctant to make the calls. The moment he did, this precious time with his brother would be lost forever.

Laura sighed. She knew what he was feeling, but right now, Garrett's well-being had to take precedence over everything else.

"I'll call Summers," Gabriel said.

Laura nodded. "Before you do, why don't you help me get him in a bath?"

Gabriel looked at his brother and then back at Laura. "Are you sure?"

She raised an eyebrow. It was her only comment on the way Garrett smelled. Gabriel rolled his eyes, then turned to his brother and took him by the hand.

"Come with me, Garrett. It's time for you to get ready for bed."

Garrett nodded. "Tired."

"I know, buddy," Gabriel said softly. "I know."

"Been lost," Garrett added.

Impulsively, Gabriel hugged him. "I know that, too. But you found us all by yourself, didn't you? Mother would be so proud of you."

Garrett beamed as Gabriel led him away.

This stakeout was worth every minute of Kirby Summers' lost sleep. The phone call he'd gotten from Gabriel Donner had stunned him. While everyone was out running amuck, trying without any success to find the deadly Prince Charming killer, he'd walked past a succession of unmarked police cars surrounding the Donner residence without being seen.

Kirby had been ready to go get Garrett right there and then, but Gabriel had begged that they wait until morning. Kirby had relented, but only to a point. It would be daylight in a couple of hours. He'd given them until morning, but no longer.

And so he sat outside the gates of the Donner

estate, waiting for sunrise and for the weight to be lifted off his shoulders. Getting this man off the streets was the most important move of his career.

Inside the mansion, Laura sat beside Gabriel's bed, watching them sleep. At first they'd been uncertain as to how to make sure Garrett didn't wake up and wander off. Oddly enough, it was Garrett himself who came up with the solution.

Clean and dry and wearing a pair of his brother's pajamas, Garrett was all smiles as he came out of the bathroom. Gabriel was lying on his bed, waiting for his brother to emerge.

"Did that bath make you feel better?" Gabriel asked.

Garrett nodded. "Feel better," he said, and crawled right in beside Gabriel, bending his body to conform to the way Gabriel was lying. He snuggled in beneath the shelter of Gabriel's arm and closed his eyes, hugging his brother as if he were a stuffed toy.

"Say my prayers," Garrett murmured, already more than half asleep.

Gabriel was so stunned by his brother's innocence, and by the flood of his own emotions, it was all he could do to respond.

"Yes, buddy, we'll say your prayers," he said, swallowing back tears.

Garrett started them. "'Now I lay me down to sleep...'"

Gabriel picked up the refrain. "'I pray the Lord my soul to keep.'"

Garrett's words were slurring. "'If I should die before I wake...'"

"'I pray the Lord my soul to take.'"

Garrett sighed as Gabriel ended the prayer. Within moments, he was asleep.

A short while later he turned over, and when he did, Gabriel turned with him, hugging him as tightly as Garrett had held him before.

Laura sat at their bedside, her eyes wide and burning with unshed tears. Garrett was home, but for how long? It broke her heart to see the brothers like this. And then there was the matter of the authorities. Too much tragedy to just ignore. Only God knew where Garrett Donner was going to wind up. But it was for certain he couldn't stay here.

She stood up to pull the covers up over their legs, and then sat down at her vigil again, trying not to think of the dozens of police cars that were even now surrounding the estate. Trying not to think of the look on Garrett's face when they took him away. He wasn't going to understand. He would never understand.

Sixteen

Matty knew when she arrived for work that the day wasn't going to be normal. Two uniformed officers refused to let her pass, and the neighbors across the street were camped out on their porch in lawn chairs, watching the proceedings through binoculars. At that point she panicked.

"What's going on? That's my family in there! I have a right to know."

"Look, lady, I have my orders," the officer said. "All I know is, no one goes in until the killer comes out."

She gasped. That could only mean one thing. Garrett was inside. She dropped down on the curb with a thump, buried her face in her hands and began to pray.

Inside the house, a different kind of morning was taking place. Garrett was sitting in the kitchen with a tablecloth tied around his neck. Laura was giving him a much needed haircut, while Gabriel was poking spoonfuls of Cheerios in his mouth. Between every other bite, Gabriel had to keep promising that, as soon as they were through, they would go out to the garden and pick some roses.

Roses for going away.

"Go see Dr. Wallis?" Garrett asked, talking around a mouthful of cereal.

Gabriel's heart tugged. "I don't know for sure, maybe later," he said cautiously.

Garrett frowned as he chewed. He didn't like maybes. "You come with me," he announced, and then opened his mouth for another bite.

Gabriel smiled while the crack in his heart continued to widen.

"You bet I will. I'll be with you all the way."

Garrett nodded just as Laura snipped. She groaned, holding up the hunk of hair she'd unwittingly cut. Gabriel grinned.

"Looking good, buddy, looking good. Now, sit real still for Laura, will you? She's trying to cut your hair."

A short while later, just as they were cleaning up the haircutting mess, the phone rang. It was just a small sound, but it was enough to make Garrett wince. Gabriel grabbed it on the first ring.

"I'm sorry, Garrett, I'm sorry," he said quickly, nervously eyeing the wild look on his brother's face. "See, I stopped the noise. It's all better now, okay?"

Laura leaned down and kissed the side of Garrett's cheek, unaware that it was something Angela Donner had always done.

Garrett turned. "Mother!"

Laura smiled. "No, sweetheart, it's just me. It's Laura, remember?"

He shook his head. "No, my mother," he repeated, and pointed over her shoulder.

Laura spun, her heart suddenly pounding. There was no one there. There was nothing...nothing but the smile on Garrett's face.

"Okay," Laura said softly. "Okay."

Gabriel hung up the phone. "It's time," he said, and reached for Garrett's hand. "Come on, buddy. It's time to go."

Still smiling, Garrett let himself be led away. With Laura holding one hand and Gabriel the other, he emerged from the house to the bright light of a new day. He didn't seem to notice the array of police cars visible through the gates, or the car coming down the drive. His gaze was locked on the sky and the trees and then on a pair of butterflies flirting with the deep purple hyacinth blooms surrounding a large marble fountain.

He didn't know there were guns trained on them from every corner of the wall, or that the car coming toward them held people who would take him away. His hair was cut, his belly was full, and he had his brother at his side.

Because the scene was so idyllic, Gabriel let his guard fall. And the moment he lifted his hand to wave at the men getting out of the car, Garrett suddenly jerked free. His demeanor quickly changed from quiet to tense. He muttered a phrase beneath his breath that only Laura and Gabriel heard.

"My roses...my roses...my roses for going away."

He spun sharply and started to run. Although his gait was awkward, his long legs quickly carried him out of sight of the people out front.

Gabriel saw it happening and still couldn't make them stop. The SWAT team spilled over the walls like black flies on new carrion, ordering Garrett to halt.

"Call them off!" Gabriel shouted, grabbing Kirby by the collar. "I promised him roses. Roses for going away. He's not trying to escape, he's just going to get his roses."

Kirby turned and began waving his hands, calling out for the attack to cease. But even as he was shouting, he knew he was too late.

"Ah, God," Gabriel groaned, and started to run, leaving Laura quickly behind.

He turned the corner just as Garrett disappeared behind a shed.

"Don't shoot! Don't shoot!" he screamed, waving at the SWAT team, who were descending on them.

But they didn't respond; they just kept coming. Garrett appeared moments later, running as hard as he could toward the back of the garden. Gabriel panicked. The red ones. He was going all the way to the end for the red ones.

He extended his stride, feeling the hard jolt of the ground beneath his feet, of bone against bone, of a teeth-jarring race that was impossible to win.

"Garrett! Come back. Wait for me. Wait for me."

And then, to his relief, Garrett seemed to respond. He was slowing down on his own and had turned to look back when the first shot rang out.

"No, damn you, no!" Gabriel screamed, and ran headlong into the line of fire without thought for his own safety.

Garrett staggered backward from the bullet's impact, looking down at his clean shirt in blank confusion. He grabbed at his chest, trying to stop the spill of blood with both hands. His face crumpled in disbelief as he fell to his knees.

Gabriel caught him as he rocked back on his heels, and laid him down beneath the bushes his mother had nurtured as dearly as the children to whom she'd given birth.

"My shirt. Spilled somethin' on my shirt," Garrett mumbled.

Gabriel was blind with a rage and pain he couldn't define. In that moment between his life and his brother's last breaths, he knew what it felt like to slip over the line of sanity.

"It's okay," he said, choking back tears. "We'll get you another."

"Hurt," Garrett whispered, moving his hand through the puddling blood.

Gabriel lowered his head, his chin dropping to his chest. "I know, buddy, and I'm sorry, so sorry."

Garrett's eyes slowly closed, and Gabriel's tears began to fall. Moments later Garrett suddenly looked up, his eyes two orbs of clear green, slightly out of focus and staring at the bush near his head and the blooms just out of his reach.

"Roses," he whispered, pointing at the flowers between him and the sky. "Roses for going away."

Gabriel reached out blindly, breaking one stem after another in random haste, desperate to give Garrett his flowers before it was too late. Thorns ripped his palms and then stuck in the pads of his thumbs. Soon blood was dripping from Gabriel's hands and onto the stems, but he kept on picking.

Laura's heart was in her throat as she reached Gabriel's side. She dropped to her knees. One look was all it took to know that this time Cheerios and kisses wouldn't be enough.

"Oh, Gabriel, oh no." She started to cry.

"Hurt," Garrett mumbled. He reached for Laura's hand and placed it in the center of his chest. "Feel my hurt?"

She could barely feel a heartbeat. She looked up, her eyes wild with fright, and focused on some of the officers who were standing nearby. It was obvious to Laura that they, too, realized a great wrong had been done.

"Call an ambulance," she cried. "Somebody call an ambulance."

"One's already on the way, miss."

She looked back at Garrett. It would get there too late.

Gabriel's hands were full of blooms as he rocked back on his heels, laying the flowers down between them. His hands were shaking, his cheeks covered with tears, as he began stripping the stems of their thorns. But the task was too slow, and Garrett was running out of time.

In a blind, choking rage, Gabriel grabbed the top of one stem, then closed his fist and yanked downward, instantly stripping it of both leaves and thorns, and shredding his hand as well. Immune to the pain, he opened Garrett's hand and placed the first flower in it.

"Here you go, buddy. Roses for going away."

A faint smile broke across Garrett's face as his fingers closed around the stem.

One after the other, Gabriel stripped off the thorns until Garrett's hands were full to overflowing and the aroma of roses was almost enough to mask the coppery smell of the brothers' blood.

Kirby Summers stood with the others, watching from a distance because privacy was all he had left to give.

In the background of noise surrounding them, an ambulance siren could now be heard, and even though Garrett was barely conscious, there was enough of him left to react. His eyes began to widen, his muscles tensing, as he unconsciously prepared for the onset of pain.

But Gabriel wasn't having it. Still down on his knees, he leaned forward. Pressing his raw and shredded palms over Garrett's ears, he took Garrett's pain for his own.

A minute or so later, the siren stopped. Gabriel straightened. Either someone had finally had the sense to tell them to turn the damned thing off, or they had arrived at the gate. He shuddered on a sigh and looked down.

Although Garrett's eyes were still open, he was lying so still. Too still. Gabriel's heart jerked painfully.

Their reunion had ended too soon.

Silent tears began to spill from the corners of Garrett's eyes as he looked up toward the sky.

"Goin' to sleep now."

Gabriel winced. There was only one more thing to do. He leaned forward until he could feel Garrett's breath on his cheek. Then he took a deep breath and started to speak.

"'Now I lay me down to sleep...'"

Garrett's pupils dilated momentarily. It was

proof enough to Gabriel that his brother still heard.

"'I pray the Lord my soul to keep.'"

Garrett's fingers tightened around the roses, as if he were afraid they would all fly away. His eyes closed, but his head was turned toward the sound of his brother's voice.

"'If I should die before I wake...'"

Garrett inhaled, slow and deep.

"'I pray the Lord my soul to take.'"

Garrett exhaled slowly.

Gabriel waited for the next breath. It never came.

He was gone.

Gabriel leaned back, focusing on a button on Garrett's shirt instead of his face. He was vaguely aware of Laura sobbing beside him. He leaned into her strength, but there were no more tears left in him to cry.

He looked up at the sky. It was the same soft blue it had been when they'd walked out the door. It didn't make sense. How dare life go on when his kept crashing down around him? And then he felt Laura's hand on his brow, heard her voice against his ear, smelled the scent of her shampoo, and knew one day this, too, would pass.

He pulled her into his arms and closed his eyes, focusing on nothing but the life pulsing beneath his touch. Her life...his life...they were both intertwined. He shuddered and then sighed, letting go of the pain and accepting the grief.

Laura's heart was breaking, and she didn't know how to stop it. Garrett was dead, and Gabriel was coming apart. It was all such a waste.

"The ambulance is here," Kirby said.

"Too late. Everything is too late," Gabriel mumbled without looking up.

Kirby looked down at the man on the ground, then cursed beneath his breath and walked away.

A short while later, after the body had been removed, Laura felt the brush of air against her face, as if someone had just passed by. She turned to look, but there was no one close. Gabriel had moved a short distance away and was talking to Kirby Summers. Laura stood. Again she felt movement against her cheek.

Something made her look up, past the uniformed officers clumped together in quiet groups to the lushness of the grounds beyond. That was when she saw them in the distance...walking hand in hand and laughing as if they'd just shared a wonderful joke.

Her breath caught. All she could think was, Thank God!

It was Angela, and she was wearing something long, something light, something that drifted about her feet like a bride's fragile veil. What was even more wonderful was Garrett beside her, walking tall and proud, with a lift to his step and a smile on his face that was pure and strong. And in Angela's arms, cradled as if she were carrying a child, was a large bouquet of fresh roses.

Garrett's roses.

Roses for going away.

Epilogue

Gabriel leaned inside the doorway. "Hey, Mrs. Donner, aren't you ready yet?"

Laura turned and then grimaced as she turned back around. "You try looking beautiful with a belly the size of Manhattan."

Gabriel caught her up in his arms, kissing at the frown lines on her face until she broke into giggles.

"No fair," she muttered, wallowing in the love he so freely offered, while still feeling sorry for herself.

"You don't have to try," Gabriel said. "You are always beautiful. Besides, I like women with big bellies. You know what they say. The bigger they are…"

Laura rolled her eyes. "Yeah, the bigger their clothes have to be."

He laughed. "That's not what I was going to say, but I won't argue. Not today."

Laura sighed and then wrapped her arms around Gabriel's neck. "You're right," she said softly, and planted a kiss near the edge of his mouth. "Especially not today."

She reached for her purse on the way out the door. "What time are we supposed to be there?"

"Uncle Mike said two o'clock."

"Is he coming for dinner tonight?" Laura asked.

Gabriel shrugged. "Probably, it's Saturday."

She grinned. Mike Travers was definitely a man of habit. But they loved him dearly, and Matty would have been insulted if he hadn't shown up.

Gabriel took her arm as they started down the stairs. "Easy does it, sweetheart. The only thing I want broken around here is the ground at the ground-breaking ceremony for the new wing at Reed House. And, since it's going to be the Garrett Donner wing, they won't start till we get there."

Thankful for Gabriel's firm grip on her elbow, Laura nodded and slowed to a more normal pace. After they were in the car and on their way, she gave him a nervous glance. He looked so solemn, his expression so drawn. The past few months had been difficult, but he'd seemed to take great heart in anticipation of this day, as well as the imminent arrival of their first child. It hurt her soul to think of this man suffering any more pain.

"Gabriel?"

"Hmmm?"

"Are you sad?"

He maneuvered through an intersection and then gave her a sweet, sidelong glance.

"Why? Are you offering me comfort? Would it benefit me sexually in any way if I said yes?"

Her eyebrows arched dramatically. "You know, there's something I can't decide. Either you're awfully sweet...or awfully hard up."

He wiggled his eyebrows and then blew her a kiss. "Put your hand in my lap and then *you* tell *me*."

She laughed.

They rode in comfortable silence for a few blocks more, each thinking of the past few months with thanksgiving. Maybe Garrett had never gotten to go home, but every one of the people Althea Good had turned out of Reed House had been found and brought back. That was something. Something to be thankful for.

When they stopped for a red light, Gabriel began digging through the CDs. Laura glanced out to her right, staring absently at a man and woman walking hand in hand across the crosswalk. She looked back at Gabriel, watching his tan, supple fingers as he laid a disc on the player.

Touch. It was all about touch. Touching hands, touching minds, touching lives, touching hearts.

She laid her hand on her burgeoning stomach, touching as best she could the child they'd made from their love. She closed her eyes as the car began to move. Letting her thoughts go free, she soared above the traffic, above the trees, above the clouds.

''Laura, baby…are you all right?''

Gabriel's voice intruded, yanking her back into the present. She nodded, letting the gentle motion of the car rock her baby in a way she could not while she searched in her mind for the place that she'd been.

There it was. Just as she remembered. She listened, waiting for a sign, for something or someone to tell her what came next, just as she'd done since the day she was four.

Love well.

The words came without thought, without strain or confusion. Just two clear, simple words, but for Laura, they were all that she needed.

''I do,'' she said softly, unaware that she'd spoken aloud.

"You do what?" Gabriel asked.

She reached out and took him by the hand. "Oh, nothing, sweetheart. I was just talking to myself."

He smiled. As long as Laura was fine, he was right with the world.

Love deeply.

Gabriel's image slid into focus, and she sighed. "Oh, I do," she said, again unaware she'd spoken aloud.

This time Gabriel only gave her a quick glance, but had she looked, she would have seen a twinkle in his eyes.

Love me.

She opened her eyes with a jerk. Gabriel was sitting at another red light, wearing a satisfied smirk. She hit him on the arm.

"Gabriel Donner, what were you doing in there?"

He raised an eyebrow. "In where, baby?"

"You know what I mean," she muttered, and thumped him on the shoulder.

He turned and looked her square in the face. "All I did was knock. You're the one who let me come in."

A car honked. Gabriel looked up. The light had turned green. He accelerated through the intersection, leaving Laura to ponder his words. At first it bothered her that he'd been able to get inside her mind as easily as that, but the longer she lived with the fact, the more sensible it became.

Of course she had let him in. She splayed her fingers across the surface of her stomach. He was in her heart and would be forever, and right now there was a part of him growing inside her. It only stood to reason that he would see—*should* see—the rest of her, as well.

A short while later, Gabriel began slowing down to make the turn to Reed House. The baby kicked, and Laura sighed. Soon. She would be here soon. *She?* The moment she thought it, her heart skipped a beat. Before she'd only guessed, but now she was certain.

"Gabriel?"

Aware that he'd trespassed on a very private part of her world, he was glad to hear happiness in her voice. He grabbed her hand and gave it a squeeze.

"Am I forgiven?"

She squeezed his fingers back. "There's nothing to forgive."

"Good, so what's up?"

"We're going to have a baby, and it needs a name."

He laughed aloud. "Honey, that's real sweet of you to tell me, but I figured that fact out for myself some time back."

"No," she sputtered. "I said that all wrong."

His grin widened.

"I've picked out a name for the baby," she said.

"Don't you think you should wait until after it's born?"

She shook her head.

The smile slid off his face. "Do you know something I don't?"

She nodded.

He arched an eyebrow but never broke a sweat. "So, this is one of those things you just know? Is that what you're trying to say?"

She nodded.

"Well then, okay," he said, his grin a little off center.

"Do you want to know?" Laura asked.

Before he could answer, Mike Travers was opening her door and helping her out.

"It's about time you got here," he said, fussing with the sleeve of her dress and holding on to her arm as if she might fly away if he dared to let go.

"They can't start without us," Gabriel said. "And give me back my wife." Then he winked at Laura and laughed at Mike, who was starting to grin.

"Was I hovering again?" Mike asked.

Laura smiled. "Only a little, but I like it. I always like it when you fuss."

The old man gave her a kiss and then grinned. "Good, that means you're going to name him after me."

Laura glanced up at Gabriel. "She already has a name," Laura said.

Gabriel's heart skipped a beat as his uncle Mike crowed with delight.

She?

Laura pulled his hand across the swell of her belly and heard his intake of breath as the baby gave a swift kick.

When Gabriel felt the tiny reverberation against the palm of his hand, he couldn't speak. His thoughts slid to the past, to the brother he'd known only briefly, and all he could think was, Please, God, let her be all right.

Then Laura leaned close and whispered in his ear, "Don't worry, my love. Angela Rose is going to be just fine."

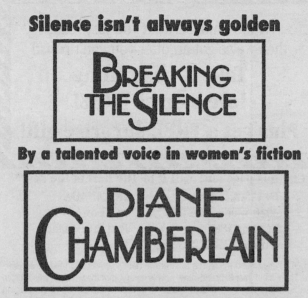

If you enjoyed what you just read,
then we've got an offer you can't resist!

Take 2 bestselling love stories FREE!

Plus get a FREE surprise gift!

Clip this page and mail it to The Best of the Best™

IN U.S.A.	IN CANADA
3010 Walden Ave.	P.O. Box 609
P.O. Box 1867	Fort Erie, Ontario
Buffalo, N.Y. 14240-1867	L2A 5X3

YES! Please send me 2 free Best of the Best™ novels and my free surprise gift. Then send me 3 brand-new novels every month, which I will receive months before they're available in stores. In the U.S.A., bill me at the bargain price of $4.24 plus 25¢ delivery per book and applicable sales tax, if any*. In Canada, bill me at the bargain price of $4.74 plus 25¢ delivery per book and applicable taxes**. That's the complete price and a savings of over 10% off the cover prices—what a great deal! I understand that accepting the 2 free books and gift places me under no obligation ever to buy any books. I can always return a shipment and cancel at any time. Even if I never buy another book from The Best of the Best™, the 2 free books and gift are mine to keep forever. So why not take us up on our invitation. You'll be glad you did!

183 MEN CNFK
383 MEN CNFL

Name	(PLEASE PRINT)	
Address	Apt.#	
City	State/Prov.	Zip/Postal Code

* Terms and prices subject to change without notice. Sales tax applicable in N.Y.
** Canadian residents will be charged applicable provincial taxes and GST.
   All orders subject to approval. Offer limited to one per household.
® are registered trademarks of Harlequin Enterprises Limited.

BOB99   ©1998 Harlequin Enterprises Limited

From the bestselling author of
Shocking Pink and *Fortune*

ERICA SPINDLER

THEY OPENED THEIR DOOR TO A STRANGER...AND THEIR DREAM BECAME A NIGHTMARE

Julianna Starr has chosen Kate and Richard Ryan to be *more* than the parents of her child. Obsessed with Richard, Julianna molds herself in Kate's image and insinuates herself into the couple's life, determined to tear their perfect marriage apart. But the nightmare has only begun. Because Julianna is not alone. From her dark past comes a man of unspeakable evil.... Now no one is safe—not even the innocent child Kate and Richard call their own.

CAUSE FOR ALARM

SPINDLER DELIVERS "A HIGH ADVENTURE OF LOVE'S TRIUMPH OVER TWISTED OBSESSION." —*Publishers Weekly*

On sale mid-February 1999 wherever paperbacks are sold!

MIRA®

Look us up on-line at: http://www.mirabooks.com   MES497